C000127282

Matilda's Magic Circle and the Book of Secrets

Copyright © Jeffrey Brett 2020

Front cover design: Kathleen Harryman

kathleenharryman.com

For more information, please contact: magic79.jb@outlook.com

First Published January 2021

Matilda's Magic Circle and the Book of Secrets

Emily

With Love Always

Matilda's Magic Circle and the Book of Secrets

The art of the clairvoyant medium is a special calling, not something that has been read in a book or through the tarot cards and I am a believer in both magic and what lies beyond our world after we pass from this lifetime.

My views are my own and what licence I have as a fiction writer permits me to include certain characters and events that could possibly take place. It is up to you to decide what is real and what is not, only I would like to take this opportunity to advice any sceptics out there that somebody might be watching you and when you least expect!

Matilda's Magic Circle and the Book of Secrets

Chapter One

Matilda Barron sat pensively in her parlour drumming the ends of her fingers on the polished surface of the circular dining room table playing back and forth along an imaginary piano as she surveyed the décor.

'You know, this place it looking tired and could really do with a lick of paint.' She checked the time once again with the clock sat on the mantelpiece. Alongside the clock sat a metallic framed photograph of her late husband Albert. He was always smiling back at her.

'It's okay for you standing there Cyril with your favourite pipe in your right hand, but you forget that it is me who has to keep this place maintained.' She sighed.

Looking at his smiling face Matilda hesitantly allowed her thoughts to take her back in time to the distressing moment when she had arrived home to find that Cyril had been involved in a very unfortunate accident.

Having climbed up the eighteen rungs of the wooden ladder to cut back the wisteria on the rear wall of the house she could only surmise that Cyril, pleased with his afternoon in the garden had stepped back to

4

admire his handiwork and thus fallen to the patio below breaking his neck. How exactly a ceramic pot of daisies, Matilda's favourite flower had come to be positioned between his legs still remained a mystery. What was also a mystery was why as a clairvoyant she had not received a vision of the accident. Having died as a result of his injuries Albert would have liked to have known why as well.

In the silence of the room the echo of the clock was calming although somewhat deafening. Matilda glanced around again deciding that the décor wasn't that bad and that it gave the room a certain atmosphere adding to the ambience of the house. Dotted about were half melted candles the burnt wicks resembling agonised arms that could not escape the fire. Here and there the bright sunshine had faded the pattern in the pattern of the wallpaper and the potted flowers cast strange shadows on the wall behind. Best of all Matilda thought were the sunburst red curtains with gold stars, occasional crescent moon with flying bats that had been skilfully stitched into the fabric. Albert had never liked the curtains saying that they introduced bad vibes although Matilda would argue back that he was just letting his imagination run riot and that instead he should open up his inner aura and allow the light to flood in.

She sighed once again. 'I could have understood had it been dark and you fell Cyril, but during the day and with the sun on your back, you must have been very distracted.'

Matilda stopped her drumming, 'I should get around to washing the lampshade over the table, the cover has cobwebs hanging down from the lace.' Stretched out comfortably on the window cill the black cat was contentedly purring in its sleep.

Matilda was trying hard to banish the thoughts racing around inside her head and clear her mind for the coming session when the doorbell was rung flooding the hallway with a brief extract of Tchaikovsky's Nutcracker Suite. Looking at the clock she nodded approvingly. Dead on the dot and she did like punctuality. She rubbed the palms of her hands together as the cat opened one eye.

'As a special treat I'll open a tin of tuna for you later.'

Wiping the soles of her shoes on the doormat Sylvia Burtonshaw appeared to be panting as the ample bosom inside her flowery blouse went up and down like the bellows of an old watermill pump. 'Am I late Matilda?' she asked.

Matilda smiled as she took Sylvia's coat hanging it on the hook. 'Not at all my dear... perfect timing in fact, but of course I sensed your approach as you came through the front garden gate.'

Sylvia placed both hands across her chest in admiration. 'You really are so gifted Matilda. I ran from the corner thinking that I was late and that the spirits would be getting impatient.'

Matilda patted the back of Sylvia's wrist. 'Time is irrelevant where they dwell my dear. Don't fret, they'll come through knowing that you had an appointment.'

Sylvia's eyes opened wider, *'really...?'*

Matilda gestured that Sylvia should follow her. 'They see who needs help the most and prioritise their workload accordingly.' Like an obedient dog Sylvia followed Matilda into the back room where she did her readings. Casting its eye over the visitor the cat raised then lowered its head just the once thinking to itself *'here we go again!'*

Not her first visit paying for Matilda's spiritual help Sylvia did like the small, although very quaint house set at the end of the cul-de-sac with its all-round lilac coloured wisteria. Sitting herself down one side of the circular table she apologised when her stomach lurched loudly.

'I've had trouble keeping anything down today because I have been so excited.' Matilda cracked the window open a fraction to help inject some fresh air into the room much to the cat's annoyance.

'The birds have been singing for the past hour, perhaps a little birdsong will help calm your stomach. It's good that you feel like you do, it demonstrates to the other side that your inner juices are flowing through the right channels. Now settle yourself Sylvia as I feel that they are getting ready to come through.' Sylvia wriggled on the chair until her posterior was proportionately positioned agreeably.

'I'm ready...' she announced, 'and all weekend I have had this buzzing in my head, like static. Do you think that they knew I was coming?'

Matilda settled herself. 'Yes undoubtedly. The spirits have to flit here and there, passing through snow storms, leaping aside for thunder and lightning, but they still manage to pick up on your positive vibes.' Reaching across Matilda took hold of Sylvia's hands. 'Now clear your mind and think of me as a beacon between two worlds, a spiritual telephone

7

line crossing the void.' Sylvia responded with a convincing smile, she was putty in Matilda's hands.

Glancing quickly at the mantelpiece and the framed photograph of Albert, Matilda had hoped that Albert would have picked up the receiver by now and answered her call telling her where the key to wall safe was hidden. For months the safe behind the oil painting of their late pet Labrador had remained locked and Matilda was desperate to look inside. She had even considered going to visit another clairvoyant to see if their powers of persuasion were more significant than her own.

Taking one last look at the man who had spent his entire working life in the civil service, Albert had surprisingly been a technical wizard on the laptop and there was nothing that seemed to faze him. Swaying gently from side to side she and Sylvia waited patiently for the *other-side* to come through.

Using the last few moments of silence to make the connection Matilda wondered what was hidden in the wall safe. She had known that Albert kept quite a bit of cash in the house, telling her that he had a particular propensity for keeping his money close to him rather than in the vaults of the bank. Some time back she had also mislaid precious stones that her mother had given her, they were of great sentimental value, she wondered if they also were behind the metal door along with the share certificates that Albert had purchased dabbling in the stock market. Lastly were the deeds to the house.

She squeezed Sylva's hands. 'You're doing great, keep the thoughts strong I can hear them they're coming through.' Sylvia lay her hands palm down on the table in readiness. She closed her eyes and silently prayed that they would. Ermintrude opened an eye once again, she'd seen things that neither of them had seen.

Matilda looked at the thoughtful lines etched across Sylvia's brow, it was a good sign and that she was concentrating hard. 'Do you remember the last time that you were here Sylvia, we had that dark shadow standing somewhere in the background which we thought it was a man. Tell me, has a man come into your life since the last visit?'

'Only in my dreams.' She replied.

'Ah I see, never mind that's close enough.' Matilda reached across the table stroking the back of Sylvia's hand. 'Let us see if this time he will step away from the shadows. Let us make the magic happen.' Sylvia took a deep breath and held it, moments later the tips of her fingers began to tingle with anticipation and she felt her heart fluttering.

'I see him,' she cried, 'he's tall, very handsome and has a kind face.'

Matilda closed her eyes as well. 'Yes, he's coming closer. He is rather handsome at that!' She opened one eye to peek at Sylvia who was convinced the man was almost in front of her. Matilda continued while she had Sylvia in the grip of her belief. 'He has a full head of hair as well, not dyed, but natural.'

Sylvia felt the pins and needles pass through her fingertips not quite sure if it was the man reaching out and touching her or whether she had a touch of arthritis. With her eye still open Matilda nodded. She had Sylvia mesmerised, caught nicely in her spiritual web.

'He tells me that he is lonely… that he is looking for love!'

'So am I…' Sylvia responded eagerly, *'oh please, let him know that I'm free…'*

'Can you feel his heart beating Sylvia, he heard you?'

There was a sudden change in her expression, a look of shock and concern. *'He's not dead, is he?'* There was panic in Sylvia's voice.

'No… no, his connection is far too strong. He is amongst the living, but he is desperate for love.' Matilda saw Sylvia's shoulders sag with relief. 'His soul has just taken a leap of faith and stepped forward so that he can touch you. Do you feel him Sylvia?'

Sylvia shook as she felt the tingle move from her hands to her shoulders and down onto her chest. *'Oooh yes, I like a man with strong hands and who is not afraid to express himself.'* Ermintrude wanted to shake her head in disbelief. She was used to the deception, the spiritual act performed by her mistress, but this was pushing the boat out.

Suddenly gripping both of Sylvia's hands Matilda went tense. 'Wait… he's trying to give me a name… be patient and keep the vibes strong Sylvia because it will come.' Matilda paused letting the tension infuse the air in the room, it was all good theatrics. After a few moments of tense waiting, she sighed. 'There's a woman coming alongside. A short lady with grey hair and wearing spectacles halfway down the bridge of her nose. She has a gold chain attached to the side arms of the spectacles so they don't fall and break.'

Sylvia cried out. *'It's mother... oh no, what a time to come through. Does she know who this man is...?'*

Matilda allowed the tension to ebb from her body letting Sylvia down gently. 'Yes, she is smiling at me, so she knows of him.'

The blood pumping quickly through Sylvia's eardrums was like a torrid sea. *'And does she approve?'*

Ermintrude stretched out and yawned emitting a strange noise, it made both Matilda and Sylvia look her way, but Matilda wasn't fazed by the interruption.

'Even the cat senses that he is a good man.'

There was a sudden breeze which surrounded them both much to Matilda's surprise. Before the reading she had checked around making sure that all doors and windows were shut tight. She felt a strange energy take hold of her body and mind. Looking at Ermintrude she wondered why the cat had not detected the breeze as well. The second surprise came from between Sylvia's lips. *'Mother has a message.'*

'What...?' said Matilda, **'that's not possible.'** The surprise that she had heard something made Sylvia open both eyes.

'Mother tells me that she's with Albert.'

'Well get her to ask him where the damn key is...'

'Don't you know?' asked Sylvia.

'No.' Matilda replied.

'Well perhaps the fall from the ladder gave him a bad case of amnesia.'

Matilda sat with her mouth open as she scanned the room. This was just not possible, her sessions were meant to be fun not real. She focused on Sylvia, was her friend dreaming or did she really hear her mother's voice. She looked at Ermintrude who appeared to be grinning like a Cheshire cat.

'Is this usual,' asked Sylvia, 'only I thought you should be getting the messages.'

Matilda tried to remain calm. 'It can happen sometimes and especially if you have a strong force field. You act as a magnet and attract an energy from the other side. You were close to your mother so there will always exist a strong bond between you both.' Matilda was thinking quickly on her feet. She had also checked to see if there were any shadows cast by the sun.

Dejectedly Sylvia looked worried. 'Has he gone, did mother talking to me frighten him away?' the frown was now deep and pensive.

'Let's see, let's try the tarot and maybe turning over the right card will give us some answers.' Matilda wanted to break the connection as fast as possible. It had never happened before and it was rather disconcerting. She handed over the deck and asked Sylvia to shuffle the pack.

Having split the pack into two Matilda then arranged the cards into a nine figured pattern on the table top. 'Destiny is at your fingertips Sylvia, I can feel it.'

Matilda turned over the first card making Sylvia gasp as she put her clenched fists to her mouth.

'Oooh my goodness,' she exclaimed, 'the lover's it must be a sign.' It's a bloody miracle thought Matilda relieved that it had been the lover's card. Perhaps the voice had been a blip of their imagination. She was about to go to the next card when Sylvia grabbed her wrist. 'Is mother still around?'

Matilda looked. 'No, she's gone.'

'That's good. We were close, but there are some secrets that I don't want her knowing.' She still had hold of Matilda's wrist. 'I can still feel his energy inside of me. Is that good?'

Matilda smiled sensing that she had regained control of the session.

'Everything that is happening here is because of you Sylvia. Keep that energy going and your thoughts positive, and keep open the lines of communication. The other side work on principal and needs. I assure you that they don't do anything half-cocked or wily-nily up there in the heavens above.'

Sylvia released her grip on Matilda's wrist as the clairvoyant swept her right hand over the cards chanting an ancient incantation *Se sui li, aiutami* which meant 'if you're there help me.'

Dropping her hand down swiftly like that of a hawk chasing a field mouse Matilda took a card from the opposite corner flipping it over. In feigned admiration of her choice she had Sylvia's attention.

'The spirits... they favour us and you coming here today...' she pointed at the card. 'The Wheel of Fortune, another major arcana from the tarot pack and it means that you have reached a crossroads, where dreams can become reality. Take the right path Sylvia and destiny is yours for the taking.'

Having jumped down from the window cill without either of them noticing Ermintrude brushed against Sylvia's ankle. She screamed kicking out wildly making the table shake. Her reaction made another card lap up and flip over. Sylvia reached out to put it back as it was, but she was stopped by Matilda.

'*Noooo, leave it,*' cried Matilda, '*it was meant to be.*' Using the tip of her fingertip she turned the card around. This she thought was turning out to be a very eventful session.

'The Nine of Cups thus representing creativity, an important card and also signifying achievement of a dream. Everything is in your favour Sylvia, but you must go with your instinct and hence do not dither.'

'The man that I saw in my dream?' Sylvia asked. Matilda responded with an affirmative nod. Having munched her way through the biscuits in her bowl Ermintrude came back, only this time Sylvia saw the cat return. She lent down and stroked the back of Ermintrude's head for luck. 'A black cat,' she explained, 'it's supposed to be lucky.'

'She is a lucky cat, she was rescued from an animal sanctuary.' One by one Matilda turned and explained the rest of the cards spread out on the table bolstering Sylvia's belief that romance was about to blossom on the horizon. When the tarot turning ended Sylvia asked to be excused as she needed to use the bathroom.

'I'm sorry, the excitement of reaching out to the spirits always affects my bladder.' She rushed from the room and down the hallway.

Matilda turned to stroke Ermintrude. 'It's funny your daddy always used to say the same thing when he would come back up from the garden shed, only I don't think he meant that he had been communicating with the spirit world. His spirits consisted of whiskey or brandy.' Ermintrude purred back.

When Sylvia returned she sat herself back down. 'Oooh I do like what comes next and it always makes me go all tingly, it positively gives me goose bumps.'

Taking hold of Sylvia left hand Matilda turned it face up so the palm was available. She began tracing the heart line. 'It's long and strong,' she drooled, but 'wait... they're coming through again, they have another message.'

'From Roger...?' Sylvia blurted.

Matilda smiled, at last she thought knowing that eventually Sylvia would let it out of the bag as to who the man was in her dreams. 'Roger, yes that's his name.'

'You must be telepathic Matilda. I was sitting on the loo thinking about Roger.'

'The spirits, they're smiling… they're happy with the union Sylvia.' She paused. 'There's a lady standing behind them as well and she has her thumbs raised.'

Sylvia sagged. *'Mother… she never did like missing out on anything!'* Bringing her knees together she felt the urge once again before leaping from her chair. Letting out a couple of *oooh ooohs* then rushing to the bathroom Matilda heard the door in the hallway close.

Matilda turned to Ermintrude who had once again perched herself back on the window cill. 'That took some coaxing, I thought that she would never give up the name.'

Matilda sat back in her chair and was massaging her temples when the breeze swept through the room again. *'Albert…'* she said sitting bolt upright. She looked around like she had before, but there was nothing there. From the hallway she heard the cistern flush then the taps in the sink being run. A minute later Sylvia returned balling her hands together. She sat back down and held out her left hand.

'I am sorry about that, I'm empty now. It must have been the carrot juice I had before I came to see you.'

'Highly nutritious,' Matilda added as took hold of the outstretched palm. 'The universe is aligning and Jupiter is going into shadow which means the moon can shine even brighter. That's a positive move amongst the planets Sylvia and it means that your natural shyness will follow Jupiter and when you meet Roger, you will be much more confident. You will shine as you never have before.'

Sylvia beamed as she smiled. 'I will wear my special dress for him, the one with roses and cut low at the front.'

'Don't show too much all in one go and remember that planetary alignment can change without warning, displaying too much flesh can send out the wrong signals and you don't want to overshadow the moon.'

'Okay, the blue dress then with the high neck.' Matilda agreed with a nod of her head. She continued until she had read the line of fate, the marriage line and all the little criss-cross line on Sylvia wrinkled palm.

'When you leave here be bold, stride purposefully ahead. Find Roger only don't let him out of your sight.' With that Matilda scooped up the pack and straightened the lace table cloth. 'And that my dear friend concludes the session for today.' Wherever the breeze originated it blew out the candle flame sending a thin veil of smoke rising up to the ceiling above.

'Have they gone?' Sylvia asked the disappointment evident in her voice.

'Yes, they too can grow tired quickly with so much energy spent.'

'And my mother, she's no longer around?'

Matilda gently patted the back of Sylvia's hand. 'She was the first to leave.'

'Thank goodness for that. When she's around I'm always edgy.'

'Well what say you we have a slice of cake and a cup of tea and you can tell me more about Roger and the dreams you've been having.'

Sylvia clapped her hands together. 'That sounds wonderful. Goodness Matilda, I am so pleased that I came here today. For the past few days I've had a funny feeling in my water works that things were about to change, that's why I've been drinking the carrot juice and hoping.'

Matilda didn't quite see the connection although as long as Sylvia was happy and full of hope then the session had been a success. Sylvia knew the drill dropping the cash in the old tea caddy on the kitchen shelf and as long as Roger had featured in her reading she would have happily paid double the amount if needs be.

Following them both through to the kitchen Ermintrude was hopeful of an extra helping of biscuits. It had been an interesting session despite the woman screaming when she had circled her ankles and yet she couldn't understand why neither had seen the man in the room like she had.

Ermintrude also knew nothing about planetary alignment, celestial stars or indeed fortune telling, but she could tell a living spirit from that of a dead one. Maybe later when she was alone she would have her own conversation with one, maybe two.

Chapter Two

The remainder of the afternoon had been spent discussing Sylvia's romantic intentions and of course her desires with Roger of which Matilda kept a mental note as Sylvia was bound to return for another reading before the month was out. Having watched her walk back up the road Matilda was glad of the time alone to reflect. It had been a surprising session in many ways none more so than when Sylvia had heard her mother's voice. Sitting in her favourite chair in the conservatory she stroked the underside of Ermintrude's neck.

'That was a rum do for sure,' she muttered, wondering as to where the breeze had originated. 'And I'd rather not have too many sessions like that. I like to keep them nice and easy, have the customers believe the spirits are there, but where I take control. Did you notice anything odd?'

Ermintrude continued to lick her paws not that she would let on if she did. Matilda was still uneasy about the events that had taken place.

'Somebody on the other side must have tuned into our wavelength or was passing through.' She stopped stroking to let her thoughts clear. 'And do you believe that your daddy doesn't know where he's put the key, I don't. I think he has a bad case of selective hearing as opposed to forgetful amnesia.' Ermintrude began purring loudly like a car engine idling having stopped at a red light.

'Looking at it logically, I think it was Sylvia's fault and her persistent urge to find love. She blocks the lines of communication with her romantic notions and desires.' Matilda opened the lid of the old tea caddy and withdrew four ten pound notes and a single five. 'Still, who am I to quibble and we have enough to keep us both in food for the coming week.' Ermintrude stretched out to spike the five pound note but Matilda beat her to it.

Matilda closed the lid and stuffed the money instead inside her brassiere. 'Keeping secrets, money and things close to your chest seems to be the safest way.' She resumed stroking the cat's chin. 'If only you could talk, wouldn't that be a profitable money-spinner.'

Together they watched the birds outside flitting back and forth from the bird feeder. Matilda liked secrets, liked hearing other people's confidences and it was one of the main reasons for her becoming a clairvoyant. In her beside cabinet she had books on the subject, each read twice until she was sure that she could perform as good as other fortune-tellers.

'I thought Sylvia would never mention Roger's name.' She crossed her arms supporting her chest. 'And look at me a young widow and in the prime of my life. I've still so much more to offer a man. I definitely need to get out more Ermintrude.' She scratched an itch to the side of her left breast. 'Sylvia Burtonshaw takes one trip down the Nile and hey presto she meets dashing Roger, or least I imagine him to be dashing and the next thing you know she's head over heels in love again. She gives under garments a really bad name.'

Matilda was suddenly aware that Ermintrude had stopped purring and become focused on the corner of the room. What was more disconcerting was that the cats head was moving slightly left and right as though following something jigging this way then the other. Matilda looked expecting to see a moth. She joked although unconvincingly. 'Is daddy standing there?'

Without warning Ermintrude suddenly leapt from her lap digging her claws into the fleshly upper parts of her legs. Matilda screamed and cursed the cat as it bolted out of the room. *'Albert is that you...'* Matilda called out angrily, *'show yourself this instance you stupid buffoon and don't go scaring poor Ermintrude and me!'*

When the doorbell echoed down the hallway Matilda felt her heart leap and her chest go up and then down.

'Lucifer and Gabriele...' Matilda muttered as she cradled her beating heart. *'I said show yourself Albert not scare me half to death.'*

Checking the time with the clock on the conservatory window cill Matilda noticed that the hour was getting late and nobody, not even friends came visiting this late. It was eight fifty four and almost time for hot chocolate. Approaching the front door she made the silhouette the other side of the glass to be that of a man and wearing a large hat. Coming from the kitchen Ermintrude was also curious.

21

Despite the late hour Matilda gave herself a cursory check in the hall mirror making sure that her hair was tied properly and there was still sufficient lipstick left after talking so much with Sylvia. She bent down and scooped Ermintrude up into her arms. Whispering she told the cat. *'He looks like the man from that film the exorcist. If he makes any sudden moves you extend your claws sweetie. You show him that us girls are not so easily intimidated.'* Dropping the security chain into place Matilda put her foot behind the door as she pulled it open.

'We don't give to charity, support any donkeys, dolphins, lions or elephants and the Rottweiler is out back taking a leak!' Matilda didn't recognise his face, but it smiled back at her.

The man graciously raised his hat then put it back down on top of his head. His eyes, dark brown in colour were soft and nothing like the menacing image that she had conjured up, and the nearest lamppost was outside the gate of next door.

'Am I addressing Mrs Barron... Matilda Barron?'

Matilda wondered how he knew her name. 'Yes, that's right, but who may I inquire are you?'

He checked the time with his wrist watch. It looked an expensive model. 'I am sorry that it is so late to be calling, but it's been a very busy day and I had to see you.' He did not say why.

'Do you have a spiritual calling?' Matilda asked. She didn't feel any of the normal vibes although things were still a bit jumbled from earlier in the afternoon. He managed to keep his focus on her eyes rather than the

22

show of cleavage that was inappropriately on show. Matilda covered herself using Ermintrude as a shawl.

'Are you religious?' the man asked.

Matilda was slightly taken aback by the question and it was indeed late for a member of Jehovah's faith to be calling. She didn't see any magazine's neither.

'Let's just say that my faith has been somewhat dented of recent.' She had no idea why, but the words just spilled from her lips. 'You didn't know my late husband did you?'

'I meet many people over the course of time Matilda, but sadly I cannot remember all their names. You do seem rather young to be a widow.'

'It was the Wisteria,' Matilda replied, 'Albert took a step back too far and it cost him his life.' She studied the man standing in the porch. There was no ethereal body, he looked solid although taller than her, but wasn't everybody. His one outstanding feature that she couldn't help notice was that he had big feet and she had heard the rumours about men with big feet.

'Ah, I see,' the man said, 'at one with nature. I hope he finds peace in his sleep. I know of you because of a recommendation and you have a psychic ability that I need.'

'It's too late this evening to be calling the spirits now, but you can come in and we could check the diary. I have available spaces I know.' She stood aside having released the security chain. Once inside she quickly shut the door. 'There's a lot of curtain twitchers in the cul-de-sac and they're a nosey load of buggers who live up and down the street.'

The man wiped his feet on the coconut mat and removed his hat, it demonstrated breeding and Matilda liked that in a man. She thought to herself that it was lucky he had not arrived when Sylvia Burtonshaw had been around. The man hungry vixen would have snapped him up and cast poor Roger aside in the blink of an eye.

'May I ask who recommended me to you?'

'Indeed, a friend of mine Elizabeth Marlow. Regrettably also a widow.'

'Elizabeth,' Matilda repeated, 'a very dear school friend. We attended most of the lessons together except she did pottery whereas I went to embroidery. Rather a timid little thing is Elizabeth.' The man nodded. 'Odd though because I've not seen her lately.' Matilda bit her lip only it didn't do to give away so much information and to a complete stranger and yet she felt quite at ease in his presence.

'About a month I believe.' Matilda smiled, he was right and it had been four weeks. She thought the man had a look about him like Gregory Peck. Elizabeth told me that you had a profound talent and that you had recently helped her with a troubling problem.'

Since Albert's demise Matilda had had problems remembering what she had told friends or clients. All she could remember the last time that they had met Elizabeth had seemed very tense. She showed him through to the room where she conducted her readings. Flicking through the

24

pages she looked for a free day. She placed the tip of her finger on the first available.

'What name should I put you under?'

'Smith… my name is Reginald Augustus Symion Smith although most of my friends call me Reg.' He offered his hand in a formal greeting. Matilda felt the energy flowing through her body as she connected hers with his.

'Goodness Reg, you do have a great deal of the force about you!' Matilda let go of his hand, felt the air expel from her lungs before recharging instantly inflating her chest.

'Spiritual connections are often strong around me Matilda. It is alright to call you Matilda?' She smiled back.

'I feel that the spirits would be lining up for you Reg.'

Matilda was slightly embarrassed. Reg Smith was the first man that she'd had for a sitting since Albert's death. She resisted the temptation to fan her cheeks.

'I know it's getting late, but could I offer you some refreshment, a tea, coffee or a hot chocolate?' Going to the mantelpiece she began lighting candles, it added a certain soft glow to the room. Taking her place on the window cill Ermintrude had a good view of everything.

'That is extremely gracious of you, thank you but no on this occasion. I really should be mindful of your evening and get to the real reason for my visit.' Ermintrude pricked up her ears.

'I said that I had a calling, perhaps a summons might be the best way to describe the message. A voice in the middle of the night told me that I should make arrangements to come visit you Matilda.' Her eyes opened wider with interest as Reg continued. 'I woke Elizabeth from her sleep and she told me to make an appointment. Naturally I will pay for your time this evening and the cost is of no consequence.'

Matilda wanted to ask if waking Elizabeth had been by calling her on the telephone or shaking her shoulder.

'My fee is forty five pounds for the hour, rising by ten every thirty minutes past the hour.' She felt the energy was still very strong in the room, stronger than when Sylvia had been present. 'I have to charge the extra as it is so draining on the energy reserves you see.'

'I understand and that all sounds perfectly in order.' Reg stood by the mantelpiece where he had a commanding view of the room. 'What a delightful place you have here. A couple of years back I lost my wife. Since that time I have been wandering through a fog.'

Matilda placed her hand gently on his forearm offering comfort.

'Death can be an incomprehensible event Reg and although time will heal the wounds of love, we often feel the need to seek divine intervention. Fate brought you here tonight and destiny will be your salvation.'

Reg quickly shook his head. 'My apologies, I should have explained better. Abby isn't dead, she's just missing. I went to work one morning and later when I came home I found the place empty. Along with Abby and half of the bank account she had simply vanished into thin air taking twenty years of marriage with her.

Matilda however wasn't fazed. 'Ooh that's awful, tragically sad Reg,' her hand remained on his forearm. 'Together we will find Abby only somebody on the other side has to know of her whereabouts.'

'No,' exclaimed Reg. 'I have not come here to find my no wife. I have grown rather accustomed to living in the house on my own and I like my freedom without Abby breathing down my neck.' Reg paused momentarily. 'I believe she lives on a Greek island with the new man in her life. The voice that came to me in the night was from her aunt, dear Aunt Maud, a lovely old soul who is in the afterlife. It was her insistence that I come and find you. I need your help to know what is buried under the patio in the back garden of her bungalow.'

Matilda felt her hand slip away.

'A body.' she exclaimed.

'I doubt a body, but something else. Something much more important.'

'Wasn't Aunt Maud there when whoever or whatever was buried?'

'No, she was on some Asian river cruise. Abby was though and she was looking after the place. Whatever is there, she buried.'

Matilda was putting together various scenarios in her mind although her ideas were clouded by smoothing and why she pondered was there always an aunt in the background either living or dead. 'Buried treasure, money.' She prompted.

'Quite possibly, although my gut instinct tells me that Abby would be more astute than to bury money. She would have an offshore account and use an alias. No… I feel that it has to be something more valuable.'

'Did she have a lot of money?'

'Who Abby or Aunt Maud?' Reg relied.

'The aunt.'

'I guess so, she went travelling a lot.'

Matilda thought it strange that he didn't know. 'Was Abby the sole beneficiary to the estate?'

'Yes, she was the sole survivor in the family line. With half of our bank account and her aunt's money, she could live out the rest of her life in luxury. Is this relevant?'

'I am just trying to build a picture in my mind as to what could be buried under the patio and that way we can channel our combined energy on resolving this problem.'

Reg smiled. 'I'm sorry, I see what you mean.'

Matilda peered at the wall painting behind which was hidden the safe. Why she wondered did people want to hide things away where others couldn't get to them.

'Do you by chance have a photograph of Abby?'

Reg took a small black and white passport type photograph of himself and Abby from his wallet. 'It was taken at Southend in a photo booth next to the pier during our courting days.'

Matilda studied the photo. 'You've not changed much.' She thought that Abby looked happy at the time that the photograph had been taken. Looking again Matilda thought that Abby's face appeared with a shadow down one side. 'Was there somebody else in the booth with you?'

Reg took back the photo to look. 'No, although I have always wondered what caused the shadow.'

Sitting on the window cill and watching Ermintrude was wondering about her supper.

'When Aunt Maud was insistent upon you coming to see me, did you feel another presence in the room?' Matilda wasn't quite sure why she had asked the question, but the thought had suddenly come into her mind, that and together with the aura of intense energy surrounding Reg.

'I know the message was from Aunt Maud although I had this strong mental image of Abby smiling at me. It wasn't a happy smile, more a contemptuous leer. Afterwards all I could think about was Elizabeth and that she wasn't safe.'

'And you have spoken to Elizabeth?'

'Yes, she told me that I was worrying unnecessarily.'

Matilda was happy to that Reg had made contact, she needed to do the same. 'Souls have a way of latching on in times of stress.' Matilda had told many of her clients the same thing.

'How exactly?' Reg asked.

'The inner light. We each possess a white beacon, a flame of passion where love evolves. It never ceases to illuminate the soul even after death. I feel a strong aura around you Reg and you need to listen to Elizabeth. She is somehow connected.'

'She is just a friend and we play cards together once a month at the local bridge card club. There is nothing romantic in our friendship.'

Matilda however thought different. 'When you have your reading you might see different.'

'Elizabeth was right and you are extraordinary.' He smiled. 'Beacons in the night, I like that.' It was close enough and Matilda wasn't going to correct him. She could do that at his reading.

'Perhaps we do have a spiritual bond as you would put it. Maybe I'll call round and see her later and ask.' Matilda nodded. She thought that he would. Matilda suddenly took in a sharp intake of breath.

'There is a woman coming through Reg, an elderly woman. She walks forward although never coming close. She keeps pointing down to the ground.' Ermintrude rolled her eyes.

'It has to be Aunt Maud, she is even invading my dreams.'

'What you seek needs to be found soon otherwise the spirits will not rest. That is why they are here already.'

'Tell me Matilda, do the spirits watch everything?'

Matilda laughed. 'I hope not. They pick up on negative energy and try to help. Positive energy they do not need to be involved with.' Reg exhaled. Matilda could only think of Elizabeth and Reg together. 'Where a void has to be filled, they will help the soul fill it.'

Reg considered it a strange philosophy, but there were things about him that Matilda did not know. Things she didn't know about her friend Elizabeth. He looked around the room for a crystal ball, but didn't see one.

'Do you have a crystal ball?'

Matilda opened the lid of a square wooden box sat on the side of a large leather travelling chest. 'For special occasions.' She said. Reg appeared satisfied that she had one. Again there was that breeze as it swept through the room. Ermintrude looked up and stared at the corner of the room where Matilda kept her different boxes of tarot cards.

'Did you feel that Reg?' she shivered.

'Feel what exactly?' he replied.

'That cold sensation, like a spirit passing through!'

'No.' He checked his watch. 'Maybe you are tired. I should really think about leaving you to your hot chocolate.' Matilda noticed that her arms prickled with goose bumps.

31

'No, I'm fine. Please tell me Reg, where did you and your wife meet?' she asked.

'We were walking towards one another on the Embankment in London. I was throwing the remainder of my lunch to the ducks on the Thames when Abby walked into me distracted by the frantic furore caused by the fight over the bread. We met up after work for a drink and took it from there. 'She was the most beautiful woman that I had ever cast my eyes upon, much like yourself Matilda.'

Matilda felt her cheeks flush with embarrassment and the heat rising through the thin fabric of her dress. 'My goodness, it's been a long time since I have been paid such a nice compliment.' She fanned the front of her face.

'Would you mind others being present when you come again only there's so much energy in numbers?'

Reg frowned. 'You mean like other spirits?'

'No... living souls, others wanting a message. The spirits vie for attention, but in numbers we can almost control their enthusiasm. I believe that it would ensure Aunt Maud turned up.'

'It would be like a séance?' Reg grinned. He seemed amused. 'Yes, I see the logic in numbers. A gathering of minds, bodies and souls. The greater the number the stronger the energy. Why not.'

Matilda rubbed her hands together thinking of the money that she could amass by having just one sitting.

'When?'

Matilda picked up her diary. 'Let me ring around and I'll see who's available. We need an even mix of men and women to keep the blend even. Are you available any evening this week?'

'Yes.'

'Good. And if Aunt Maud does comes through we can always arrange a private reading a day later. It'll give her chance to re-energise and perhaps she'll have more to say.'

'That sounds perfect.' Reg reached for his wallet.

'Oh there's no need and besides we were only checking the diary.'

Reg Smith however was insistent upon paying and several moments later he was heading for the front door where he shook Matilda's hand before bidding her a good night. He gave her his card so that she could contact him with when and what time the séance would take place. Shutting the garden gate he doffed the peak of his hat then disappeared making for the corner where Matilda expected him to turn right walking in the general direction of Elizabeth Marlow at ninety five Sheringham Drive.

'Well... well,' said Matilda turning to Ermintrude, 'what did you make of that girl. What an unusual man despite his dashing good looks.' The cat purred going around and between her legs. 'And did you notice that he had on his jumper on inside out. My guess is that he had just come from

Elizabeth's flat.' Matilda laughed. 'And his insistence that they just play card's, no wonder Aunt Maud is constantly around.'

Chapter Three

Sitting at the end of the oval table Matilda scanned the faces of her guests beginning with Harold Harrison, Margaret Buckworthy and Arnold Peabody who were sat on her left, where to her right and looking eager to begin were Penny Pringle and Emma Scott-Jackson with Reg Smith nestled snuggly between the two women. There was an empty chair at the far end of the table. Some of the invited participants looked apprehensive.

'I feel that the evening will be very fulfilling,' Matilda said inviting smiles and nods of agreement. To her right Penny Pringle let out a squeal of delight clapping her hands together.

'Does this mean that we can each invite a spirit here from the other side Matilda?'

Rubbing the underside of her nose the clairvoyant medium watched Ermintrude take her normal place on the window cill.

'Last time dear Penny we finished five minutes too early, just as your Cyril was starting to come through. We'll see if we can keep the energy strong this time around and perhaps Cyril will have a message for you.'

Penny Pringle looked down the disappointment evident. 'That night I hardly slept a wink wondering why he had not made the connection in time.'

Matilda stroked the back of Penny's hand. 'Even the spirits on the other side can get delayed. We have to remember that they travel a great distance to be with us and often they cannot be in two places at once.'

Penny looked at Matilda her brow forming a frown. 'Do you know my Cyril would tell me that when he was alive and that he couldn't be in the hospital mortuary and elsewhere at the same time. Sometimes I think the dead came first and before me.' Leaning forward to peer beyond Reg Smith, Emma Scott-Jackson grinned as she replied to Penny. 'Maybe they had more to offer.' There was a gasp from Penny, but Matilda was quick to intervene.

'Cyril had a very responsible job Penny and his delicate appreciation would have sent many a soul on their way with dignity.' The response seemed to please Penny who lent back on her chair ignoring the obnoxious woman at the other end.

'That's if he wasn't raising a few other spirits,' Emma whispered to Reg who smiled, but didn't reply feeling Penny sitting on his other side. Once again Matilda kept the peace. 'What say we let the spirits answer for themselves ladies.'

Having purposefully planned the seating arrangement with the animosity between Penny and Emma sparking like an electrical element about to fuse the evening was already charged with anticipation and emotion.

'I notice that there's an extra chair, are we expecting another person?' asked Reg.

On cue the bell chimes in the hall answered his question. Matilda left the room returning with a tall elegant looking lady with long blonde, intriguing ice blue eyes and a friendly smile. Smiling at everybody around the table she took her place at the vacant chair.

'I am sorry that I'm late ladies and gentlemen, the traffic was heavier than expected.' She looked at Reg and smiled.

'Good now we can begin,' said Matilda, 'although firstly I would like to introduce you to a very good friend, Kathleen Lee. Her grandmother had the gift however it skipped a generation bypassing her daughter, but settled inside with Kathleen's gentle soul. I thought it would be prudent to ask Kathleen along this evening because she would add to the energy needed to invite so many spirits through from the other side.'

Occupying the seat next to Kathleen, Emma Scott-Jackson introduced herself. 'That's if whoever you get come through can get a word in only Cyril tends to elbow the others aside so that he can talk to droopy drawers at the end.' Emma shrugged her shoulders. 'Still having worked in a mortuary, you would think that he had have a good link and know which buttons to push.'

To Matilda's relief Penny huffed, but didn't respond. Instead Matilda made eye contact with Kathleen, her presence would help set the flames of interest going through the roof.

'Just so you know, a gentle soul, my friend is by day a private detective.' All eyes turned to look at Kathleen.

'Eight is a good number,' Harold acknowledged, 'or at least the Chinese believe so...'

Using a foot peddle connected to the light over the table Matilda depressed the lever three times until the illumination dimmed sufficient in the bulb to add atmosphere to the coming session. In each corner of the room the shadows grew larger. Sitting on the window cill Ermintrude decided to groom herself. She liked it when it wasn't so bright.

'Ohhh isn't this exciting,' exclaimed Margaret Buckworthy, *'it was like this when my Derrick proposed to me.'*

'Dark you mean?' asked Arnold Peabody.

'Yes, dark and very romantic although the country lane filled with bats when I accepted.'

'He was probably a vampire on the quiet.' Somebody uttered *Sccchh* at Emma as Matilda suggested that they join hands.

Suddenly the light over the table started to flicker. Matilda checked that her foot was nowhere near the pedal.

'They seem eager to make contact,' said Margaret.

'Is it my Cyril?' asked Penny.

'I'm not sure yet,' replied Matilda, 'the shapes are still forming, I need them to come forward and identify themselves.'

'It's probably my Ernest, he was always a dark horse.' For once Penny Pringle agreed with Emma Scott-Jackson.

'Perhaps if we close our eyes and we try to clear our minds of all thoughts the shapes will form that much sooner, too much expectation can create a telepathic barrier.' They all did as asked with the exception of Kathleen and Matilda who winked at her friend. 'That's better and the force is growing stronger.'

Penny Pringle squeezed Matilda's hand. 'I can feel it.'

Matilda waited until the room was silent again. 'I have a man appearing. He is wearing purple coloured spectacles and he has a single earring in his right ear.'

'It's Malcolm,' cried Arnold Peabody.

'Yes... it is Malcolm. He is waving.' agreed Matilda. The thing was that Matilda could truly see Malcolm. Things were happening with her spiritual connection and her own faith was becoming that much stronger. She wondered why now though and why it had not been as strong before to have prevented Albert's tragic accident.

'Please Matilda, can you tell Malcolm that I have remained faithful to his memory.'

Reg Smith opened an eye to look across at Arnold Peabody. The session had only just started, but already Reg had the impression that the people around the table were a peculiar bunch of individuals. He saw Kathleen looking at him. Reg nodded then closed his eyes once again.

'Malcolm tells me he knows.' She paused receiving more. 'Malcolm says, it's time to end the grieving and that you should be out there again. Life without love is such a waste.'

Reg opened an eye again and made immediate eye contact with Arnold. Kathleen noticed that Reg didn't look at all happy. They were an odd bunch that Matilda had invited and she wondered why. She also got the impression that there was more to Reg Smith than his friendship with Elizabeth. Casting his interest her way Reg wondered about Kathleen too.

Kathleen felt the apprehension grow in Arnold's hands having heard that he should contemplate finding a new companion. 'I would only go looking again if Malcolm was sure. I don't want to upset anyone.'

Emma Scott-Jackson looked at the man sitting opposite her. *'No, Malcolm says its fine, now can we move along.'*

Kathleen wanted to smile, but the tension around the table was super-charged so she bit her lip instead. Matilda also sensed the tension. 'Malcolm has stepped back in the shadows to allow others to communicate Arnold. He looked very happy before he faded. I would take that as a positive sign that he is in agreement with you finding somebody new.' Kathleen nodded and Reg kept an eye on the man sat opposite him. There was another inaudible muttering from the end of the table and everybody guessed that it was from Emma Scott-Jackson, but nobody was brave enough to utter a reply.

Matilda continued. 'I have another man coming close only this time he has something in his hand...' the excitement in the room went up a level, 'he's holding what appears to be a tin of wax.'

The enthusiasm was just too much making Penny Pringle shake as squeezed the hands belonging to Reg and Matilda. *'That's my Cyril... he uses morticians wax to hide any facial blemishes.'*

Emma Scott-Jackson couldn't resist leaning forward. 'Did Cyril keep a stock at home?'

'Why of course not,' replied Penny, 'my Cyril was a professional and left his work at work.' Matilda was a little mystified when Cyril began smearing his face with the wax changing the expression on his face. She asked Penny why he might be doing that.

Letting go of Matilda's hand she snapped her fingers together. 'Make up, Cyril did amateur dramatics, maybe they have a show on the other side later.'

'Oh heaven preserve us,' came the muttering from beyond Reg.

Matilda raised an eyebrow. 'Cyril had an accident when he fell from the rigging on the stage, didn't he?'

Penny joined hands again. 'Yes the troupe were rehearsing *The Pirate Ghost* and my Cyril was playing the second mate. He was climbing the rigging when the mast overhead mysteriously spun on its axis. The wooden beam hit my Cyril sending him flying into the air. It was doubly unfortunate that a stage hand had left the trap door open. Cyril was found dead lying on top of an effigy of Dracula who was asleep in his coffin.'

Matilda looked down the table at Kathleen who she knew was mentally making notes regarding the unusual demise of Cyril.

'Cyril is shaking his head at me. He is not in any spiritual show, but the spreading the wax over his face signifies that he is unhappy, somewhat dissatisfied. Does that mean anything to you Penny?'

Penny thought hard. 'That perhaps his death wasn't an accident. Maybe the facial wax signifies that somebody still living is hiding the truth.' Kathleen Lee nodded, she agreed with Penny's sentiments. Even Emma Scott-Jackson agreed giving a concurring nod much to Matilda's surprise.

'Cyril wants me to tell you that he is sorry.'

Penny looked slightly perplexed. 'It wasn't his fault, at least I don't think so.'

Matilda told Penny that Cyril sent his love and that he had stepped aside to let a lady come through. 'The lady is elderly and she has a bow tied on one side of her white straggly hair.'

Harold Harrison sighed. 'That would be my mother.'

Matilda agreed, 'she's wagging her index finger quite enthusiastically your way Harold.'

There was another sigh only longer and exaggerated. 'If she's come through to tell me about the state of the back garden, tell her that I have been rather preoccupied of late.'

Matilda smiled. 'She is shaking her head. It has nothing to do with the garden, but...' Matilda stopped mid-sentence to understand the communication, 'it's about a woman, somebody that your mother tells me that is bad for you. She describes her as a con artist, a trickster.'

Harold however had not come along to have his love life discussed around the table. *'No, you're wrong mother, Elizabeth is a good woman, kind and very attentive to my needs.'* Kathleen and Matilda both looked at Reg who returned their stares with an impartial shrug implying that there were thousands of Elizabeth's around. Matilda returned to Harold.

'She says that you'll get your finger burnt if you don't call a halt to the relationship. She sends her love.' Sat next to Harold he felt Margaret Buckworthy squeeze his hand offering moral support. He lent her way. *'Mother was always telling me what to do. To be honest I was glad when they carted her off to a nursing home although she made the other residents lives a misery. The families of two had them transferred elsewhere and three others regrettably met their maker long before their time. I don't think their fragile hearts could take my mother's continuous onslaught.'*

Clearing her throat the room fell into silence once again as the force returned to Matilda's end of the table. 'I have Derrick coming through for you Margaret. He tells me that the three ladies are happy once again.'

'Ohhh, I am so relieved to hear that. It was a terribly distressing time having to endure the hateful looks of their poor relatives when they came to collect the personal effects. It made me feel like I had been associated with a murderer.' Kathleen raised an eyebrow.

43

'Derrick tells me that he is also with Charlie.' There was an inaudible cooing as she remembered their pet white Yorkshire terrier. 'Are they happy?' Margaret asked.

'There's another little dog running around Derrick's ankles, so I would say that they're all extremely happy. Derrick hopes that the insurance paid up in full for the car.'

Margaret nodded as she replied. 'It was a write off and I have a nice new Citroen now.' Matilda told Margaret that Derrick was giving her the thumbs up. She suddenly felt the tension flow through her body as the next message arrived.

'Derrick tells me that evil is all around and that you should be careful Margaret. He said that you should not be involved.' Matilda felt the hairs on the back of her neck prickle her skin as they stood up.

Margaret gave a shrug of her shoulders. 'That's an unusual message to send me. Everybody I know has been so kind since his accident.' Matilda told Margaret that Derrick's time was up and that he was fading fast as others were vying for centre stage.

Matilda suddenly unclasped her hands from those sitting wither side of her bringing the session to a close. 'The channel is blocked. I'm not sure how as there was another coming through, but something very powerful shut the door in my face.'

Emma looked disappointed and alongside Reg Smith didn't look at all amused. 'What about me,' he asked, 'didn't anybody come through for me?'

Matilda tapped the foot peddle under the table adding more light to the room. 'I am sorry Reg, unfortunately the spirits don't always feel that the force is strong enough to come through any longer and there was a more powerful entity this evening, one that wanted the channel of communication closed. Maybe next time.' Matilda noticed Kathleen frowning at her.

Reg suddenly pushed his chair back standing up. 'Next time... I am not sure that there will be a next time. I will bid you all goodnight as I have another appointment soon.'

Matilda quickly excused herself from the room to see Reg to the door.

'I am truly sorry Reg, but it happens like that sometimes. Something did close the lines of communication, something strong and that I have not experienced before. Maybe later they'll be open again. If I get any message for you, I'll call you!'

Reg Smith pulled out his wallet, but Matilda prevented him from opening it. 'No, please there's no charge for this evening. I think we should arrange a private reading, one where others thoughts cannot interfere. Maybe a group meeting wasn't right.'

Reg dropped the wallet back into the jacket pocket.

'I don't know, quite a lot happened and it was interesting. I have some free time next week perhaps you can call me with a convenient time?'

Matilda held open the front door. 'Yes, next week would be good. I will have a look in the diary after they've all gone.' He thanked her then left.

Returning to the others who were waiting back in the room Matilda took her seat at the head of the table again as the general chatter died away. 'Well, what an evening this has turned out to be.'

'Teel me... is Reg a free agent?' asked Emma.

'Not exactly,' replied Matilda as she looked the length of the table at her friend sat the opposite end.

'Typical, the handsome ones never are,' Emma replied, getting a supportive nod from Margaret.

'Right who is tea, coffee and cake?' Matilda asked.

Chapter Four

'Well what do you think?' asked Matilda once they were alone.

'Very interesting,' replied Kathleen, 'and there is definitely a common denominator running through the vibes which came from the people sat around the table, except perhaps Reg Smith. With him I detect something else.'

'Like what?'

Kathleen Lee picked up her glass of wine considering carefully her reply. 'He knows our friend Elizabeth and whether or not they're lovers isn't necessarily our concern. Reg is reserved and won't ever give much away, but I felt that he hides a secret and that's why he seeks your help.'

'Like what? Matilda asked picking up her glass.

'He was expecting this Aunt Maud to come through and yet she didn't. If she is that insistent then she should have been first in queue.'

Matilda licked her lips the wine was good that Kathleen had brought with her.

'Aunties dead or alive can be fussy individuals. They know the family secrets and yet some they keep close to their chests.'

'Where's his wife now?' asked Kathleen.

'On a Greek island and according to Reg, she is with another man.'

Kathleen was pensive. 'So why the interest in the aunt I wonder?'

Matilda topped up Kathleen's glass. 'As I told you over the phone. When the aunt was on some cruise the wife stayed to house sit the place. The aunt believes that her niece buried something under the patio. Something valuable according to Reg.'

'But he doesn't know what?'

'No.'

Kathleen stopped drinking. 'My gut tells me that it could be a body.'

'That was my initial thought although Reg doesn't think so. Why do you think that I invited you along this evening, you've a keen nose for these things.'

Kathleen smiled. 'Thanks. What hit me most was the number of accidents that resulted in the unexpected demise of spouses.'

'Not forgetting my Albert.' Added Matilda.

'Including Albert,' Kathleen agreed. 'I noticed that Emma Scott-Jackson didn't have anybody come through for her and yet although she seemed disappointed, she was keen to ask about Reg and his availability.'

Matilda was quick to respond. 'Emma can be a real dark horse at times and surprisingly she is conservative about her life.'

'And the jibes that she unleashed at Penny Pringle?'

'The two of them were the best of friends for many years, but something happened that cut the relationship dead. I can only suspect that it had something to do with Cyril Pringle dying, but neither woman is prepared to say exactly what drove a wedge between their friendship.'

Making the tip of her finger moist Kathleen ran it around the rim of the glass until it produced a high pitched squeal. 'What happened to Emma Scott-Jackson's husband?'

'He dabbled big time in horticulture and Ernest belonged to a well-known local society. One Sunday summer's afternoon he was found wandering the village in just his underwear. Ernest was delirious and had no idea who he was when questioned by the police. An ambulance was called and they too found Ernest babbling away to himself. Alcohol or drugs was suspected, along with that he had been over working and suffered some sort of nervous mental breakdown. On his way to hospital Ernest suffered a heart attack in the back of the ambulance. He was pronounced dead by the casualty doctor at the hospital.'

Kathleen nodded making an assumption. '*Atropa Belladonna*, more commonly referred to as deadly nightshade here. It's one of the most toxic plants this side of the Eastern Hemisphere. Producing a variety of symptoms, not least an increased heart rate, other side-effects are hallucinations, disorientation and convulsions. It is not always easy to detect nor treat on initial examination which is why the ambulance crew might have thought Ernest drunk or having a quick fix. I would like to get my hands on a copy of the coroner's report to determine the level of toxins found in Ernest's body.'

Matilda swallowed the wine in her mouth. 'You think the circumstances are suspicious?'

'Let's just say that this evening threw up a lot of unanswered questions. People die through illness and tragic circumstances every die, but being hit by a stage prop mast and falling through a trap door to land on Dracula is certainly unheard of, plus Cyril being a mortician. I cannot explain it, but a little voice inside my head tells me that Reg Smith is connected somehow.'

'The murderer who came to seek his victims' relatives?'

'Something like that.'

Matilda looked puzzled. 'A walking, talking handsome specimen on the outside, but perhaps with a hidden demon on the interior.'

Kathleen laughed. 'You've been reading too many detective novels of late.'

Matilda grinned admitting that she liked the thrill of the chase. 'We should remember that it was Elizabeth who recommended Reg come and see me.'

'So he tells you, but neither of us have heard anything from Elizabeth in weeks.'

Matilda nodded. 'That's right. She was supposed to call us and arrange a supper for the three of us. Did you know that she was going to sell up and move from the flat?'

'No.'

'She came to see me last month. She wanted me to conduct a spiritual session because she said she had issues. She didn't say what issues, but I knew that they were worrying her. There was nothing out of the ordinary about her reading except when I pulled the death card from the tarot, she said it was a sign.'

'That's right,' Kathleen agreed, 'not always death, but new beginnings.'

Matilda continued. 'Like moving to a new house, letting go of the past. Maybe starting a new relationship, only she told me that there was nobody special in her life.'

'That rules Reg out then,' said Kathleen. Matilda agreed.

'Was there anything else about Elizabeth when she came to see you, anything that struck you as odd or out of place?'

Matilda thought as she took another sip.

'She seemed preoccupied, deep was how I would describe her mood. Whatever was troubling her she wasn't prepared to open up, not even to me.'

'Watching Reg Smith this evening I got the same feeling. What's your intuition tell you about the patio?'

Matilda rubbed the top of her brow with her free hand. 'If I'm honest, Reg isn't telling me much and whatever is buried in aunties back garden is a secret that somebody needs to keep secret. I'm worried about Elizabeth.'

Kathleen nodded as she thought.

'Yes, me too.'

Matilda put down her wine. 'Oh no, please tell me that's not what you're thinking and that is why we haven't heard from her in weeks.'

'Being murdered then buried under some old biddy's back garden patio is hardly new beginnings.'

'It is if you're on the other side,' replied Matilda.

Kathleen took her notepad from her shoulder bag and began writing down salient points from the evening. 'When Harold happened to mention the state of his back garden as the reason for his mother coming through I noticed the look of surprise in Reg Smith's eyes. I need to follow our mysterious new member to the spiritual club and see what secrets he is hiding under that hat of his. Consider it a fact finding mission.' Kathleen was aware that Matilda's thoughts were momentarily elsewhere. 'Is something troubling you?'

'Albert was good up ladders, always so careful. Do you feel that somebody had a hand in his death?'

'Well...' Kathleen commenced, 'at school he was good at gym work, scaling the highest climbing frame, he went orienteering with the scouts and in his late twenties was a part-time fireman. Falling off a ladder was not Albert's style. Did you know of any visitors that he was due the day of his accident?' she was careful to suggest that it still might have been an accident rather than deliberate.

'He didn't mention anybody calling,' before I left the house. 'I have tried going over and over that day in my mind as I feel that something is missing, only I keep walking down a blind alley.'

'That's because you are too close and connected. You know that those on the other side can feel your anguish. You're thoughts are also jumbled because of what might be hidden in the wall safe.'

Matilda sat with her mouth open. *'How did you know about that?'*

'Because you look at that damn painting so much. You never did like it, but you put up with it being there for Albert's sake and because he liked it. Besides when you was making coffee I took the liberty of having a look behind to see what was there.'

Chapter Five

Kathleen put down the receiver having recorded the address for Arnold Peabody that Matilda had given her. Having sat next to Arnold at the table and heard Malcolm come through with his message, she had decided that Arnold should be the first person on her list to visit.

Pushing aside the freshly painted gate she instantly surprised to see the splash of colour that the many flower petals gave the front garden. Matilda had said nothing to her about his passion for horticulture and she wondered if Arnold had been a friend of Ernest Scott-Jackson. She had her nose buried in the head of a deep red scented rose when the front door opened. Arnold was startled to see that it was Kathleen Lee admiring his roses.

'It is aptly named *Eternal*. I planted the bush out front for all to see after that lot upstairs took my Malcolm from me.'

'The scent is heavenly.' Replied Kathleen. 'I do so admire roses and especially sweet scented varieties. She hoped introducing a common interest would help the coming conversation.

'I had a feeling in my water works that you would be calling at some time. Would you like a coffee, I was going to partake of a mug on the back veranda?'

'Coffee would be very welcome, thank you!'

The interior of the house was decorated much like the garden and very colourful, with framed photographs dotted about the walls of Arnold and a man she took to be Malcolm. The furniture looked expensive as did the ornaments and paintings. Arnold took the coffee out on a tray accompanied by a plate of assorted Belgian chocolate biscuits.

'My early morning luxury as I skip breakfast these days.' He promptly patted his stomach. 'Keeping a waistline trim is such an effort though.'

'Looking good, makes you feel good.' Kathleen replied and necessary she thought in case another man did come into his life.

There was a wry smile from Arnold as he passed across her coffee. 'You remembered Malcolm's advice and that I should get out more often!'

'I've a memory for detail,' Kathleen responded 'it's what I do.'

Arnold looked at her over the rim of his mug the steam from the coffee instantly vanishing in the air around. 'I'm not ready for another relationship, not yet and not while the memory of Malcolm is still raw. His death was such a shock.' Arnold gazed at the top of coffee. 'Time is they is a healer, yet in my case it seems to drag on by. I spend so much time out here on the veranda, it's the one place where I can escape and relive the good times. Some bad.'

'The bad times...' Kathleen repeated, seizing the opportunity to draw upon an inference from his experiences.

'Bad being the day that the police came to tell me that Malcolm had been tragically killed.'

'Killed... not died?'

Arnold looked pained to say it. 'I would say that having a pterodactyl fall on your head as being killed rather than the heart stop beating.'

'I take your point. And where exactly was this pterodactyl?'

'It was a paper mache and clay replica which hung from the ceiling of the local museum. It was only there on loan from the Natural History Museum so that local schools doing classroom projects on the Jurassic era could see extinct creatures up close. The newspaper was so cruel in describing the incident as *the winged monster that struck again*. I can only assume that poor Malcolm never knew what hit him as he fell to the floor dead.'

'Did the police conduct an investigation into how the pterodactyl came to fall from its secure mounting?'

'Oh yes, they even had a health and safety official there too, but they could only conclude that the bracket holding the guy wire tensioner had somehow worked itself loose. The official verdict recorded by the coroner was *accidental death*.'

'Why was Malcolm at the museum that morning... afternoon?'

'He was a freelance roving reporter. Overnight the museum had suffered a burglary. Probably local youths high on drugs and the only thing stolen was an insignificant earthenware pot. In my opinion they needed something to help melt down their narcotics.'

Kathleen unwrapped her chocolate biscuit flattening out the wrapper. 'Did Malcolm cover stories just locally or go further afield?'

'He would chase a big story if the incentive was right, otherwise Malcolm liked to stay close to home. He never ventured far. We were close.'

Kathleen felt the chocolate melt in her mouth. 'The day that Malcolm died, was there anything unusual in his routine?'

Arnold nibbled away at his chocolate ring like a chipmunk having trouble with a tough hazelnut. He appeared to be deep on thought.

'No, the day started as usual. A contact that he had at the museum called him on his mobile and told him about the break-in. The only thing unusual that day was that Malcolm didn't come home that evening.' Arnold stopped nibbling, raising an index finger as he remembered something significant. 'There was something. Malcolm's notepad, his book of contacts and his digital camera was missing from his shoulder bag. The police said that it could have been picked up by mistake when other museum visitors rushed to help.'

'My guess is that you would have liked those effects back?'

Arnold shrugged wiping the corner of his eye which had become moist. 'I am not overly fussed as it was his work and we didn't connect professionally, only at home.'

'You're not a reporter or work for a newspaper.'

He rippled all ten fingers across the veranda table top. 'Goodness no, I'm a concert pianist. Music flows through my veins and my life.'

Kathleen noticed that his fingers were long and slender good for playing the ivory keys of a piano. 'Did he like music?'

'Malcolm never missed a concert, he loved to hear me caress the ivories.'

'I know you didn't get involved in his work, but was there any particular cases that he felt compelled to tell you about?'

Arnold polished off the rest of his biscuit as Kathleen sat waiting for an answer. 'Not really. I know that he was working on a theory, just a theory although he wouldn't say what exactly except that some nights it kept him awake all night. He told me that the times he did sleep, in his dreams he was always running down a dark alley that had no escape.'

Kathleen stopped folding her biscuit wrapper. 'That sounded like it was a nightmare...' She left the reply hanging hoping that it would get Arnold to offer more.

'My theory is...' he took in a deep gulp of fresh oxygen, 'that it was his theory, his investigation into whatever that killed poor Malcolm.'

'Not the pterodactyl?'

'The bird was merely the weapon and I don't believe for one second that the tensioner failed. Somebody released the tension on the belt drive and made the pterodactyl drop onto on my Malcolm who happened to be standing underneath. I doubt that he saw it coming.'

'The same person that took his shoulder bag, notepad, book of contacts and camera.' Arnold nodded.

'The other evening, Matilda introduced you as a friend, private detective and that you also had the sight into the other side.' There was a look of desperation in Arnold's eyes. 'Maybe you could communicate with Malcolm and have him tell you who it was who killed him!'

Kathleen sensed the sadness in Arnold, but she wanted to keep the thread of her visit going for a little while longer. 'Souls who have passed over will at times latch onto a thought made by a living person, but the connection has to be strong. I didn't know Malcolm so perhaps he would see me as a stranger and not come through. I think that if he came through for anybody, it would be you Arnold.'

He let go an exaggerated sigh. 'Thank you.'

'And the shoulder bag,' she pursued, 'it was never found, discarded without the contents?'

'No. But then there are anomalies, irregularities with the other deaths as well. I did know that Malcolm had been chasing down those.'

'You mean Ernest Scott-Jackson, Cyril Pringle and Derrick Buckworthy?'

'Yes and together with Albert Barron, although Malcolm never not got around to visiting Matilda to investigate his unfortunate demise.'

Kathleen was intrigued. Arnold continued.

'I was hoping that Malcolm would mention something the other evening, something tangible that I could take back to the police.'

'Have you discussed your theory with them, about his death I mean?'

Arnold nodded. 'With a Detective Sergeant Jenks. He was nice and he listened, only like some of the others at the station he had nothing to go on. As soon as you mention hearing voices from the other side the police tend to switch off. I can't blame him really because he is young and in time Jenks will appreciate everything, even if it comes from an old queen like me.'

'How young?' Kathleen asked.

'Too young for me, I like my male friends older.' Kathleen had considered Malcolm older in the photographs than Arnold.

'And you think that Albert, Cyril, Ernest and Derrick were killed like Malcolm.'

'Yes, and all taken in the prime of their life. And I think you would agree looking at the circumstances that each was very odd. A runaway tractor, another trimming back the wisteria, the poisoning of a skilled horticulturalist, the loose rigging of a stage prop and lastly a museum exhibit that killed my Malcolm. What do you think Miss Lee?'

'I'm inclined to agree with you Arnold and that they all need further investigation.'

Chapter Six

'Where was you when Albert had his accident?' Kathleen asked.

'Buying meat and groceries in town. Would ham with pickle be okay in your sandwich?'

Kathleen nodded as she made notes. 'Yes, that's fine, thank you.'

'I was only gone about an hour.' Matilda added, spooning the pickle evenly over the cooked ham.

'You pre-empted my next question.'

'I know I can read your thoughts.' Matilda cut the sandwich into quarters. 'You've known me a long time Kathleen and you've always had the stronger connection and yet here I am now with a greater appreciation of the spiritual connection. How is that possible?' She pushed the plate across the worktop.

'Maybe the other side decided that you needed help.'

Matilda consciously put the lid on the pickle jar in an effort to keep to her diet. She noticed Kathleen watching. 'I hate diets. My body fights every time with my willpower and I end up somewhere in between. I quickly lose heart. Albert used to say that he liked me just as I was and that he had something to hold onto at night when the winter months were long, dark and Jack Frost was nipping at his toes. He did not want a skeleton renting a skin.'

Chewing on a bite that she had just taken Kathleen replied through the side of her mouth. 'You miss him terribly don't you?'

'Yes, although I don't miss his annoying habits. His tripping over his slippers that he would leave around in the bathroom after taking a shower, the used toilet roll hanging on the pole and the sound of his hammering down in the garden shed, although I never ever saw any of his creations. He would spend hours alone down there some days.'

Kathleen stopped chewing. 'Did you go look in the shed. After he died, I mean?'

'No, I didn't think about it and besides it was Albert's trouble-free haven, or so he would describe it. I thought it was best to leave it that way. In an odd way the garden shed reminds me of him and his odd quirky ways. Late at night I would sit on the patio and look down the garden wondering I will see his shadow pass across the window on the inside of the wooden shed.'

Kathleen was concerned about Matilda. 'It doesn't always work like that.'

Matilda sighed. 'I know, but looking all the same makes me feel better.'

'About what, you feeling guilty?'

Matilda responded with a shrug of her shoulders. 'About not being here. The coroners verdict didn't say conclusively if Albert had died immediately after falling from the ladder or whether he had lay injured hoping that I would come to his rescue.'

Kathleen washed down her mouthful with a sip of her coffee. 'You shouldn't dwell on such things Matilda. Instead use your new found spiritual magic to send messages to the other side and ask your guide for help. I am sure that wherever he is Albert will get the message and that he has already forgiven you your sins.'

Matilda nodded as she looked through the kitchen window at the garden shed. 'I hope so.' She continued eating her sandwich wishing that she had added pickle. 'Did you get anywhere with Arnold this morning?'

'Interestingly enough yes, I did. He is convinced that Malcolm's accident at the museum was the result of foul play.'

'I know...' replied Matilda, 'shortly after it happened Arnold came to me for a reading, but disappointingly nothing happened. I told him that it was too soon and that the souls of dearly departed loved ones took time to leave this life and travel onto the next. He told me about the pterodactyl.'

'Why didn't you forewarn me?' Kathleen asked.

'Because it was best that you went visiting with an open mind and without any preconceived ideas. If I had told you that Malcolm had been killed by a dinosaur, you would have laughed and I'm not ready to be carted off to any funny farm just yet.'

Kathleen nodded agreeing that it was best she had not been told.

'Mental Institutions try to steer clear of having clairvoyants amongst their guests. They see too much into the future. Can you imagine the chaos you could cause with the other patients. It would be like looking in the mirror after a good night out at the pub only seeing another face looking back at you.'

Matilda had finished her sandwich, but the growl in her stomach told her that she was still hungry. 'At times I see a different face when I look.'

'And so do I...' Kathleen admitted. 'That's the penance we pay for seeing into the beyond.'

'So what did Arnold tell you about the accident?'

'That Malcolm had been given a tip-off about a burglary at the museum. My assumption is that somebody knew he would be there. I think the crime was staged to get Malcolm at the museum.'

'But to kill him he had to be standing directly under the pterodactyl before anybody released the tensioner holding the model aloft.'

Kathleen was impressed. 'Yes, that's right. Maybe I should take you along on some of my more difficult cases.'

'I might like that.' Matilda looked down wondering if Kathleen was going to finish the last quarter of her sandwich.

'Here, you have it...' Kathleen said pushing the plate over 'anything to stop your stomach rumbling!'

The pickle tasted divine making Matilda appreciate that Albert had been right. To hell with the diet and from now on she was going to add anything that took her fancy stocked on the shelves of the larder. Licking her lips she remembered something she thought might help. 'That night after Arnold's reading earlier in the evening I had the strangest of dreams. In the dream I was being chased by a shadow. It was the form of a man only every time I turned left or right it merged into a dead end. When I woke I was covered in perspiration and my legs ached where I had been running hard.'

'Dreams have a way of sending us a message. Have you experienced the same dream since?'

'Thankfully no. I use an alley to cut through to the shops, but now I prefer to take the long way round to the bakers.'

Kathleen was thoughtful perched which her elbow on the island worktop. 'My guess it that somehow latched onto the soul of the person responsible for Malcolm's death.'

Matilda shivered. 'That was my interpretation, but should I not have been chasing him, not the other way around?'

'You didn't need to chase the murderer, instead subconsciously you were leading him down many blind alleys. You were the one setting the trap.'

Matilda felt that her stomach was nicely full and that her appetite was at last satiated. 'There is just one problem Kathleen, I had the same dream after Albert died.'

'Then there is a connection, we just need to establish where and with whom.'

Chapter Seven

The constable on desk duty looked ever so young as though he had just stepped from the sixth form of an education college and dressed himself in a police uniform. Approaching the enquiry desk Kathleen returned his smile.

'Good afternoon madam and how can I help you?' he asked.

Up very close his complexion looked almost ivory. 'Do you have a Detective Sergeant Jenks working here in the station?'

'William Jenks, yes we do. Is he expecting your visit?'

'Not exactly although I did consider that what I have to discuss with him might justify five minutes of his time.'

'May I ask what the enquiry is in connection with before I interrupt DS Jenks?'

Fresh faced he might be thought Kathleen, but he had the sense to ask before barging in on a senior detective. 'My name is Kathleen Lee and I am a Private Investigator. I'm looking into the unusual circumstances surrounding a deceased man's death. I thought that with a joint effort we might be able to help one another.'

The constable politely asked Kathleen to take a seat whilst he went to find Jenks. Several minutes later he returned with a tall smartly dressed man older by ten perhaps fifteen years than himself.

Jenks held out his right hand in appreciation of her visit thinking to himself that Kathleen was very attractive. 'Good afternoon, I'm William Jenks and you I understand are Kathleen Lee, a Private Investigator.'

Kathleen gave him one of her best smiles. 'This is very good of you to see me at such short notice. I've not come to waste your time.'

Jenks was intrigued as their hands fell apart. 'I'm intrigued only young Bobby here told me that my visitor was pretty, blonde and here to help solve a mystery regarding a man's demise.'

Kathleen launched straight into her reason for coming to the station. 'I believe that we could combine forces and help one another. I think you investigated a recent death regarding a Malcolm Swift, a freelance reporter.'

Jenks nodded. 'Yes, I remember that. The case of the falling pterodactyl. Would you like a coffee, it'd be the instant variety, but I am sure that we can find two clean mugs upstairs in CID?'

'Coffee black, no sugar would be great, and thanks.'

They walked the single flight of stair to the first floor of the station where Jenks showed Kathleen to his office before disappearing, returning several minutes later with the coffee. He found his visitor looking out of the window at the back yard.

'The view never changes unfortunately except the patrol cars move daily, the tanker fills the fuel pump and wooden shed in the corner where the patrols keep their spare vehicle equipment occasionally gets swept out on a Sunday morning.'

Kathleen shifted from the window taking her seat opposite Jenks. 'This the first time that I have been in a police station.'

He pulled some sachets of sugar from his desk drawer. 'I'm afraid I can't offer you a biscuit, snacks of any kind doesn't last long around here.'

Kathleen chuckled. 'Don't worry, Felix my cat normally gets the last one from the packet although I don't mind because the manufacturer loads them with sugar and additives.'

'So how can our combining forces help?' Jenks asked as he stirred his mug.

She made herself comfortable in the chair. Jenks was rather handsome. 'I suppose that I should begin by saying that I am not just a private investigator, but that I have a spiritual connection.' She thought Jenks might be instantly sceptical, but his expression never changed.

'You mean clairvoyant medium.'

Kathleen nodded. 'Have you heard of Matilda Barron?' she asked.

'No, but I've a feeling that she is connected too.'

'She is and a very good friend of mine. Matilda lost her husband recently.'

William Jenks looked across the desk and directly at Kathleen. 'I am really sorry to hear that. I hope he didn't suffer too much!'

'Probably, he fell from a builder's ladder whilst cutting back the wisteria.'

'Many accidents in and around the home result in death.'

'I'm not entirely sure that it was an accident.' Kathleen replied.

Jenks looked surprised. 'I thought you were here for Malcolm Swift.'

'I am, but there could be others too.'

William Jenks adjusted his sitting position on the chair. Kathleen continued. 'Go on...'

'Matilda performed a spiritual evening inviting six guests, all clients know to her, but to cut a long story short the evening went well although I for one was left with mixed feelings.'

Jenks put his mug down on the desk top. 'Because of who came through,' he asked, 'I've a distant aunt who tells neighbours where she lives that she is a Romany gypsy. I think she wears the hooped earrings and headscarf when she goes to the shops as though marketing her spiritual connection.'

'Has she told you your fortune?'

Jenks laughed. 'No and I'd prefer to let destiny deem what comes next rather than have Aunt Jessie tell me. Anyway, back to the meeting with Matilda?'

Kathleen was still sipping her coffee. 'The messages were mixed that evening, but what I learnt after the meeting was what really set my juices flowing, if you'll excuse the idiom. You see one of the attendees that evening was Arnold Peabody.'

William Jenks pushed the end of the spoon around the desk top with the tip of his finger. 'Ah, the inevitable and relentless Mr Peabody. Tell me is he still banging the drum about his reporter partner meeting with a sticky end?'

'He believes that guy wire tensioner was tampered with which is why the pterodactyl fell killing Malcolm who happened to be standing underneath.'

'We had a health and safety representative check both the tensioner and the strength of the wire. The report stated that they could find no fault in wire or mechanism.'

'Which would make it possibly a case of murder and that the pterodactyl was intentionally released from its mounting point. What was recorded as the cause of death?'

'The victim died as a result of internal haemorrhaging from a fractured skull sustained when the dinosaur fell on his head. Did Arnold Peabody omit to tell you that his partner had the onset of kidney failure and that the coroner at the post-mortem said that heavy drinking and smoking had taken finally its toll on the late Malcolm Swift. The coroner gave him three to six months to live had the pterodactyl not intervened.'

Kathleen held the rim of the mug an inch from her lips. 'Surely you're not suggesting that it was suicide?'

Jenks laughed. 'No... of course not and being killed by a dummy dinosaur is the stuff normally of fictional fantasy. What I am saying is that Arnold Peabody might have known about the kidney failure. Reality and shocking news can materialise in different forms. He might have seen his partner's death as murder rather than a blessing in disguise.'

'Did you know that Malcolm Swift's shoulder bag with his personal effects was missing?'

'Yes... his reporter's notepad, book of contacts and a digital camera. My team reviewed the museum CCTV immediately after the incident took place and it was reported to us, but there was so many people trying to help, members of the public, emergency service personnel and museum officials that it was impossible to say who picked up the bag. You said you could possibly help me Miss Lee... how exactly?'

'According to Arnold Peabody, Malcolm's last project was looking into the unusual and possibly suspicious deaths of several local men.'

William Jenks nodded. 'Yes, he told me that.'

Kathleen was unperturbed. 'Well sat around that spiritual table that evening were five people, each with a spouse or partner who had died suddenly, unexpectedly and almost certainly from unusual circumstances.'

73

Jenks lent slightly forward. 'Can you enlighten me as to how you reach that theory?'

'You already know about Malcolm Swift. Next comes Ernest Scott-Jackson who...'

Jenks interrupted.

'Died digesting Atropa Belladonna. Yes, we found the cracked bottle where Ernest kept the fruit. Did you know that he suffered from severe muscle spasms and that the berries when crushed can help relax the muscles.' This time he waited for a reaction, but there was none so he went on. 'And Ernest Scott-Jackson was a committee member of the local horticultural society plus a leading authority on herbology. In days gone by such people were regarded as...' he hesitated, but Kathleen took up where he had left off.

'Wizards or witches. Spell-binders or mystics plus a few other names. I know because I have been called similar in my time.'

Jenks raised his hands in submission. 'Actually I was going to say a skilled nature biologist.'

Kathleen relaxed her guard. 'So you think the Atropa Belladonna was self-induced to help with his body cramps?'

William Jenks lowered his hands. 'The jury is still out on that one.'

Kathleen pushed harder. 'Alright, but what's your personal opinion?'

Jenks obliged. 'Ernest Scott-Jackson was no fool and he was considered a clever man according to his peers in the horticultural society. His wife also told us that he would dabble with chemicals looking to find the perfect nutriment that would assist the soil and grow their vegetables.'

Kathleen slapped her leg assertively. 'And that's just what I am saying sergeant. Two deaths, both suspicious and not just a case of wrong place, wrong time... and next we have Cyril Pringle.'

William Jenks couldn't resist the grin on his face. 'The pirate who fell from the rigging of a stage prop while performing at a rehearsal. It does happens you know.'

'I don't deny that, but being a mortuary attendant you would have thought Cyril Pringle would be more sure footed than most.'

Jenks nodded. 'You missed out on your vocation. You should have been a police officer.'

'What and join the thankless rank and file on the never-ending, unappreciated trail to satisfy the nervous hormones of the men in the ivory white towers. No thanks, I like to run at my pace, not theirs.'

William Jenks finished his coffee. He liked Kathleen Lee. She was straight talking, didn't flower things up or beat about the bush.

'I can see why your interests have been aroused. A fake dinosaur, a dose of deadly nightshade and an unexpected fall through the stage door, they are all unusual to say the least.'

Kathleen wanted to fist the air, but she didn't as she wasn't finished. 'And then we come to Derrick Buckworthy, crushed by a tractor driven by a mystery farmer who has never been identified...'

'His car was parked in an unmade road lane normally only used by farm vehicles.'

'Yes, and why was that sergeant?'

'Because he was involved in a clandestine relationship and they chose an obscure, out of the way leafy venue to satisfy their carnal desires.'

Kathleen wondered if Jenks had ever been down such a lane. *'And your evidence is...?'*

'There was a roll of lipstick found on the back seat.'

Undeterred Kathleen came straight back. 'But Derrick Buckworthy was devoted to his wife Margaret.'

'That as might have been, but she doesn't use lipstick and certainly not that particular colour.

'Rimmel?' asked Kathleen.

Jenks nodded to confirm. 'And before you ask we had the casing fingerprinted. The dabs that came back are not in our system.'

Kathleen sensed that her persistence to find the truth was fast losing stamina. 'Don't tell me, they didn't match those taken from Margaret Buckworthy.'

William Jenks grinned raising his eyebrows. Kathleen liked it when he did. 'You know you really did miss your calling.'

'I'm quite happy with the one that I have got thanks and with the odd communication from the other side I've enough calling already.' She suddenly laughed as the tension left the room. 'And beside which I like the pay check after each job, but like you the hours can be murder sometimes.'

'The hours don't help with personal commitments.' Kathleen wondered what exactly, but Jenks was hooked and keen to know more. 'From the look in your eyes, they tell me that you're not finished yet. Discounting you, you said that there were seven others around the spiritual table that evening.'

Kathleen acknowledged with a nod. 'You don't miss a trick sergeant.'

'So who's next on your list?' he asked.

'Albert Barron, the late husband of my friend Matilda.'

'I thought the name sounded familiar when you asked if I had known Matilda Barron earlier. I was in Madeira on a complex case when Mr Barron met with his unfortunate accident. One of my colleagues conducted the investigation.'

Kathleen took her notepad from her jacket pocket, flicked it open and struck through a name with her fingernail. 'As you were out of the country that rules you off my list of suspects.'

Jenks laughed. 'I'm pleased to hear it. What makes you think that his accident was anything except an accident, only people are always falling off ladders?'

'Albert was a part-time fireman and good at orienteering.'

'Now why am I not surprised to hear that.' William Jenks rubbed the underside of his chin. 'Before I surrender completely to your theories is there anything else?'

'Have you ever come across or heard of Reginald Smith?'

William Jenks shook his head from side to side. 'No, is he dead too?'

'Not yes, although he was at the spiritual meeting the other night. No, it's just there is something about him that I find intriguing. He's dark and a deep thinker. He's handsome if you like that kind of man, like a Robert Redford rolled between the fag paper with the Sundance Kid and Johnny Hooker.'

'Who's Johnny Hooker?'

Kathleen was surprised that Jenks didn't know. 'Yes you do, the movie *The Sting* and in the film he played a con man called Johnny Hooker.'

'Oh, I see. No, I have not seen the film nor have I heard of Reginald Smith. What makes him suspicious in your book?'

'There's something cagey about him that makes the hairs on my neck stand up on end. That and we think… that's Matilda and I, that he is involved with Elizabeth Marlow. She's an old school friend. We think he might have kidnapped her or perhaps worse.'

'Based on what evidence?'

'Neither of us have heard from her in weeks and that isn't Elizabeth.'

William Jenks sat back in his chair to study the woman sat opposite. 'You do realise Miss Lee that if I undertake to investigate any of this and at this moment in time it is merely speculation, that I would have to go further along the corridor to one of the other offices and tell my detective inspector why.'

Kathleen gave a shrug of her shoulders. 'Well there a basis of suspicion to begin with each victim. That would be a good starting point.'

Jenks exhaled between his pursed lips as he thought. 'Have you discussed this with anybody else?'

'Only Matilda and she's completely on my side.'

William Jenks stood up and went across to the office window where a patrol were driving back into the yard.

'Do you know in all the time that I have served here, I have never noticed that we have a dog kennel in the station yard.' He turned around to look back at Kathleen. 'If overnight there should be a blood hound suddenly appear in the kennel, you'll be the first person I call.'

Kathleen went to join him by the window to look at the kennel. 'Does that mean that you'll reopen the case on each of the men I have mentioned?'

'I'll give it serious consideration, on one condition.'

'What?'

'That we have dinner together one evening?'

'Agreed.'

'Good. There's Just one other thing. This Reginald Smith is he married?'

'His estranged wife is allegedly on a Greek Island and living with somebody else. Smith came to see Matilda because he needed to contact the wives aunt who is in spirit.'

'To get a spiritual message about his wife?'

'No, but to find out what is buried under the aunt's patio.'

William Jenks couldn't help the laugh coming from his chest.

'You don't just bring suspicion to my office door, now you throw in a mystery as well. What exactly do you think is buried in auntie's garden?'

'I have really no idea, but I intend finding out.'

Jenks pulled open his office door and stood to one side.

'I've changed my mind and decided that you would have made a fine lawyer for either defence or prosecution.'

'I'd prefer prosecution.'

They laughed.

'Somehow I thought you would. I'll take you down to the entrance lobby.'

Chapter Eight

'That was unexpected...' Matilda observed as she poured the wine, 'and for you to accept!'

Kathleen stroked Ermintrude's head. 'Call it a moment of weakness.'

'I take that the detective sergeant is good looking?'

'I thought so and intelligent. Not your normal tape-inserted flatfoot.'

'So what was the outcome of your visit?'

'William Jenks is reopening the file and reviewing each set of circumstances again.'

'Did you tell him about my Albert?'

'I did, only I left out the bit about the missing key and safe, it was bad enough when I mentioned Reg Smith and what could be buried in Aunt Maud's back garden.'

Matilda looked at Ermintrude who was happy to be pampered.

'Do you know I've a feeling that she knows where it is, but she wouldn't tell me even if she did, she was always loyal to Albert.'

Kathleen stared at the black cat who looked up and stared back. They focused upon one another until at last Kathleen conceded and looked away.

'She's a typical cat, mysterious and elusive when you need them most. I wish I could read her thoughts.'

Disinterested in their conversation Ermintrude raised a paw, rubbed the end of her nose then settled down closing her eyes.

Matilda returned to Kathleen's visit. 'At least he agrees then that the deaths are suspicious?'

'He's curious, but come to that aren't all police officers. It's what makes them tick. I know he likes biscuits.'

Matilda swilled the wine around inside her mouth, 'While you was making eyes at William Jenks I took the opportunity to catch up on the sleep that I lost last night. I had the oddest of dreams which turned into a kaleidoscope of subconscious meetings with faces and places that I didn't know.'

'You didn't recognise Reg Smith amongst them did you?' asked Kathleen.

'No, although there was a dark shadow that seemed menacing. I thought it belonged to a man. I wanted Albert to come and rescue me, but he never materialised.'

'Why would Albert hide from you, he was devoted to you?'

Matilda seemed somewhat bewildered. 'I'm not entirely sure why. I can't explain how, but I feel that whatever is in the safe might answer some unanswered questions. At least stop the bad dreams.'

'I believe that you're right and that what could be buried under Aunt Maud's patio is perhaps a link to this all.'

Matilda sighed. 'I've been trying hard to make the connection myself, but for some reason I can't. Up until last week I had never come across Reg Smith, his estranged wife or Aunt Maud and yet now I sense a strong connection with me, with Albert.'

'That's interesting.' Kathleen licked the taste of the wine from her lips. 'Maybe Reg is the innocent party and I've judged him wrongly, if only he wasn't so secretive.'

'Maybe he has good reason for keeping things close to his chest. We arranged another reading only this time in private.'

'Perfect. Did you know that the police found a pink lipstick on the back seat of Derrick Buckworthy's car and that Margaret never wears lipstick?'

Matilda felt the wine slip down the back of her throat. 'I was at the hairdressers a month back and overheard two women talking about Derrick. From what I heard things weren't all roses at home.'

Kathleen was pensive before she expressed her thoughts. 'Watching her the other night I got the distinct impression that Margaret could be a little prickly.'

'She can be moody at times, even a tad dark. I didn't know Derrick that well, but he and Albert got on well.'

'Well whatever their relationship Derrick met with a tragic end when the tractor ran over his car with him inside it.'

'I don't suppose that the police know who was driving the tractor at the time of the accident?'

Kathleen gave a shake of her head. 'No, William Jenks didn't say.'

'He was on holiday when Albert had his fall.'

'I know, he told me.'

Matilda offered more wine, but Kathleen politely refused. 'Do you think that Albert had another woman?' Matilda suddenly asked.

Kathleen stood with her mouth agape. 'Whatever made you think that... no, most definitely not. Albert adored you and he was never that adventurous.'

Matilda shook herself to clear the thought from my mind.

'It was just a thought and one that I had the other night. I was always conscientious of my lumps and bumps, and that they were still appealing.'

Kathleen let a sigh issue forth. 'Men go weak at the knees when you walk by and believe me your bits wobble just right. I wish I had more like you.'

Matilda looked at herself in the reflection of the darkening glass window where the evening sun had passed beyond. 'Thanks. Maybe I was thinking of how Margaret Buckworthy felt having lost Derrick and why he should be found down a desolate leafy lane.'

'You're getting your foliage mixed up. Derrick was probably all hawthorn and wild, whereas Albert liked to keep his wisteria looking nice.' Kathleen saw Matilda turning and looking at herself in the window. 'And you my girl have changed since we were in the sixth form together. You had an ample bust back then and the envy of the other girls.'

'If only I wasn't so damn short. Five, seven and three quarters is hardly what I call looking directly into eyes of the man who is standing before me. I got a crick in my neck the other evening just looking up at Reg Smith.'

'Men should be an inch or so taller. It makes them feel superior and leaves an air of mystique hanging as we walk away. Why do you think that men have bigger tongues.'

'I've never thought about it, but why?'

'So that they can drool over goddesses like you.' Kathleen changed the subject back to Derrick. 'Have you ever seen Margaret wearing any makeup?'

Matilda stopped checking her figure in the reflection. 'It's not something that I've conscientiously given any thought too. She always seems to wear black to me.'

'You say that Derrick and Albert were good friends?'

'Yes. They belonged to the same snooker club and they went to football on a Saturday afternoon meeting up with some of the others.'

'The others who are now dead?' Kathleen asked.

'Yes.'

Kathleen rubbed her brow. 'I'm sensing the same as you and that there's a connection. Maybe William Jenks will find a link.'

'Maybe...' invited Matilda, 'when I get to meet him we can have him round here for afternoon tea and especially as you say his aunt is a descendant of a Romany gypsy.'

Kathleen smiled. 'In some ways William Jenks is as dark and mysterious as Reg Smith. I saw it in his eyes and that he thinks through a problem before offering a solution.'

'You took a chance going to the police with this. They could have laughed you out of the station and in doing so it could have ruined your reputation.'

Kathleen scoffed. 'It would be the first time that my reputation has taken a knock, but this case is worth a few extra dents.' She looked down at Ermintrude who was stretching. 'I too had a dream the other night only in it I was getting married.'

'That's a nice dream and that event is long overdue.'

Kathleen raised an eyebrow. 'In my line of work marriage is not an option, but more a hindrance. Can you imagine me telling a husband *'I'm just popping out for the night to watch another man at work!'*

Matilda topped up Kathleen's glass before she could refuse.

'If fate deems that it should happen, then you know it will. I've salmon for supper, will you stay and share it with Ermintrude and myself?'

'Yes please, but on one condition and that is you let me take a look in Albert's garden shed afterwards?'

'Okay, but what do you think you'll find amongst his tools and scraps of wood.'

'Answers...' Kathleen replied confidently, 'answers to riddles going around and around inside both our heads.'

Chapter Nine

The shed was as Matilda had said it would be both messy and full of meaningless odds and ends. Cobwebs had become entangled with others where garden spiders had taken up residence having the inside space all to themselves.

'I can't go inside,' Matilda declared peering in through the open door at the gloomy inside, 'spiders and webs are one of my big phobia's'

'I did tell you bring Ermintrude along, she would have cleared the way in no time.'

'Eating spiders isn't good for her, the vet says it will make her thin.'

'Well judging by the size of her after she had devoured the rest of the salmon I'd say that she's not been very successful in catching any lately.'

Matilda stepped forward once again before retreating. 'It's no good you will have to go in by yourself. I'm sorry, but it's not just the spiders. I feel awkward as though I'm trespassing on Albert's inner sanctum, his privacy.'

'Here's not here remember.'

'I know, but we had some strict ground rules. Albert never went into my walk-in wardrobe and I vowed to stay clear of his shed. I feel it is only right that I observe the same even in his death.'

Kathleen nodded as she stepped inside. She picked up the odour of old paint, thinners and oil. Neatly arranged on boards either side of the shed were Albert's carpentry tools, a clip or peg for every size and shape.

'You kept things neat, I'll give you that Albert,' she muttered as she started to rummage. *'There's something here I can feel it,'* she scratched the top of her neck, *'and its close by.'* She continued to look moving Albert's effects to one side then the other being drawn by a strong force, sensing that she was being invited to look by a strong external influence. One she felt was from Albert, but it was the other that worried her. *'You're evil...'* she mumbled so that Matilda didn't hear. Taking her mobile phone from her pocket she used the screen illumination to search below the worktop. 'Come on Albert be a sport and help me only I cannot go back outside with nothing and disappoint Matilda.' She stood up to see that Matilda had sat herself on the garden bench under the large oak.

Tugging at an old wooden box beneath the workbench it was heavy and she only managed to move it an inch before she decided that whatever was contained within didn't want to be moved. Pulling up the lid she wasn't surprised to find a selection of large tools, plumber's wrenches, metal clamps and jaw lock mole grips along with hammers and cold chisels. Removing them one by one she lay each on the shed floor.

'You sly old bugger...' she said as she ran her fingertips over a secret floor in the box. The inner compartment was secured by a combination lock.

'Now what would you have used Albert to open the lid, something not to elaborate I'm guessing.' Her fingertips danced on the lid as she considered the possibilities. 'You were a man with simple, laid back tastes.'

Kathleen tried Albert's date of birth and then Matilda's, but both failed to release the lock. With a flick of her thumb and middle finger she had an idea trying the date of their wedding.

'Only a close friend would have known that,' she said the catch sprung open. Lifting the lid she was confronted by a narrow gauge box containing an assortment of screws, small nuts and bolts. Lifting it clear from the inner compartment she grinned in triumph. 'Just as I thought...' lying beneath were an assortment of papers. She carefully withdrew everything and lay them on the worktop spreading across the surface.

'Now why...' she questioned, 'would you have a load of old papers hidden away in a nondescript box. Most of the documents were written in Latin. Using the late evening sunshine she held up one or two to the light. The parchment papers were old, very old. She continued searching and sifting until she came across an old photograph which was of a Boy Scout troop. Flicking it over to the reverse side she found an inscription pencilled *The Order of Tintagel Knights.* Kathleen looked at Matilda who was enjoying the peace. 'Schoolboys and their dreams.' She muttered.

Suddenly the lid of the box slammed shut although the evening was still and without the faintest hint of a breeze. It made Kathleen jump.

'Okay,' she said, 'I can take a hint Albert. I promise that I'll put everything back, but with one exception... this photograph I need to show to Matilda.' Replacing the papers she closed the lid, spun the combination lock before putting back the heavy building tools.

'How's your memory?' Kathleen asked approaching the bench under the oak.

'Not bad, why do you ask?' Kathleen handed the photograph over to Matilda who studied the faces in the three rows of uniformed boys and the older officers in the troupe.

'My goodness,' she said pointing at a young boy in the front row, 'that's Albert, he didn't change much as he got older.'

'Do you recognise anybody else?' asked Kathleen.

Matilda took another look tracing the faces with her fingertip as she went along the three lines. Kathleen saw the colour drain from her cheeks.

'Did you find this in the garden shed?'

'I found it hidden in a secret compartment in Albert's old tool box, under an assortment of screws, nuts and bolts.'

Matilda checked again along the rows, pointing out five other boys. 'There and there,' she said, 'sitting in the middle row is Ernest Scott-

Jackson and Cyril Pringle, and on either side of Albert is Arnold Peabody and Derrick Buckworthy.'

'I thought that's who they might be, but I needed you to confirm it.'

Matilda turned the photograph over looking for a date that it had been taken. 'What's 'The Order of Tintagel Knights'…?' she asked.

'I have no idea other. A young boy's secret organisation perhaps only if you remember we had similar when we were their age?'

'We did didn't we, Matilda grinned, 'and we were known as the 'MK Virgins'.

Kathleen laughed. 'I always thought it stood for the *minus knickers club.*'

Matilda looked up the falling rays of sunshine catching the top of her forehead. 'You talk for yourself Kathleen Lee and I always thought that it was Olivia Trunt who started the club. Do you think it's real?'

'What the photograph or Olivia Trunt having a reputation?'

Matilda sighed. 'The photograph. King Arthur and Tintagel are mere legends, story books stuff that they made into films.' She paused looking down at the end of the garden. 'And why did Albert have this in the garden shed I wonder?'

Kathleen pointed at another face in the line-up. 'Take another look Matilda… isn't that boy Malcolm Swift?'

Matilda looked. 'I'm not sure. I've only ever seen when he's come through for Arnold. What made you think that it could be?'

'I saw photograph's of them together when I went to visit Arnold.'

Matilda looked again at the boy. 'They're all here Kathleen, the boys and now they're dead, except Arnold.'

'I was wondering about that too.'

'Do you think that the killer is in the photograph?'

Kathleen sucked air in through her teeth. 'Possibly, psychopaths lead normal lives until a switch flicks something in their brain and turns them into deranged serial killers.'

'I think we should warn him.' Said Matilda.

'And how do you propose we do that. We can't very well go knocking on his door and scare the living daylights out of the poor man just because Malcolm is dead and he might be one of the boys in the photograph.'

Matilda watched as the sun dropped below the tops of the hedges on adjacent gardens.

'No, I guess you're right. What do you think we should do?'

'I suggest that we hold another spiritual meeting and see who comes through or what the spirits have to divulge.'

'Inviting the same people?' asked Matilda.

'The same people,' Kathleen confirmed.

'Okay, I'll begin ringing around the morning. I am sure that they'll all be eager for another evening session. I will have to bake another cake.'

'Can you make it a Victoria sponge this time only it's a long time since I've had a slice and it is one of my favourites.'

Matilda said he said a recipe for a really good sponge. Kathleen noticed that Matilda was once again studying the faces along the three rows.

'Recognise anybody else?' she asked.

'I can't be entirely sure, but look at the boy on the back row, far right and standing next to the man with the grey beard.'

Kathleen looked. 'Surely not... that's Reg Smith.'

Chapter Ten

As arranged Reg Smith returned for his private spiritual reading with Matilda a couple of days after Kathleen had found the photograph in the garden shed. Putting his mug of coffee down on the coaster he took his seat at the table. Reg was being watched by Ermintrude.

'Is the cat always present at every reading?' he asked.

'More or less. I have always considered that Ermintrude influences the channel of communication.'

Reg wasn't convinced. 'How exactly?'

'The Ancient Egyptians regarded cats as sacred, magical creatures with links to the afterlife. Many households even now believe that a cat in the house is a good omen, a bringer of good luck to whoever lives under that roof.'

Reg stared at the black cat with the small white tuft under her chin. 'Your late husband might disagree with that sentiment.'

Matilda continued to shuffle the tarot cards. 'Albert was a man who believed in making his own luck. He was a religious man and he would say that God sat in judgement of his life and when his day of reckoning arrived, Albert would go forth without any argument.'

'Even when it came to pruning the wisteria.'

Matilda looked up from the cards that she had placed before her visitor. 'And how would you know that Mr Smith?'

'I read the article in the evening newspaper.'

'Ah yes, of course and Malcolm Swift did write a nice piece about Albert. It was very emotional.' She kept her hand over own at the centre of the table. 'We'll leave the cards there until the times comes to use them. That will give any of my energy time to ebb away.'

'Can that happen, can you influence things to make them happen?'

'It depends, although I would like to think only good things Reg, nothing bad.'

Reg Smith nodded although his expression was non-committal.

'Was you there when your late husband had his unfortunate accident?'

'No, I was in town.' Matilda was a little puzzled as to why Reg was taking such an interest in Albert and his demise. Matilda felt compelled to quell his curiosity. 'I doubt that God keeps a diary for such moments, they just happen. Tell me, was you ever in the boy scouts?'

Reg saw the cat lift its head.

'I was although we're going back quite a few years now, two perhaps three decades.'

'Happy years?' Matilda asked. She had cleverly turned the questions around to focus on Reg.

'Some, but growing up has its own set of challenges. I liked the summer camps more if the girl guides were in the next field.'

'Is that where you met your wife?'

'No, not there.' Reg didn't offer where.

'I was in the girl's brigade, I liked the uniform better.'

Surprisingly Reg admitted something about him that Matilda wasn't expecting. 'I was something of a loner back then.'

'That's sad,' said Matilda, 'let us begin and let's see if some of those lonely days can be filled with good memories.'

'It's the present that I am interested in most.'

Matilda smiled. 'Sometimes it helps introducing a little of the past to come forward. The spirits appreciate everything and they draw upon your energy as time is irrelevant on the other side. I find that an aunt or uncle who has passed over has many memories that they wish to share.'

Reg settled himself back on his seat as Matilda closed her eyes momentarily before opening them again to begin.

'Your first girlfriend Reg... her name was Betty.'

Reg sat open mouthed opposite Matilda. 'Yes, but... how did you know that. Not even my wife knew about Betty.'

The revelation surprised Matilda, but she knew that she had to carry on with what she was being told. 'I have a lady here in spirit who tells me that her name is Betty and that you went to the youth club on a Saturday night where the organisers held a weekly disco. She said that you plucked up the courage to ask her to dance. Afterwards you walked her home stealing a kiss under the arched gateway in St Mary's churchyard.'

Reg nodded remembering the moment. 'It was spontaneous. I couldn't help myself. Is Betty on the other side?'

'Yes.' She's smiling and is telling me that she remembers that kiss. It didn't last though and you dumped her in favour of another girl.'

Reg dropped his head forward so that Matilda couldn't see his eyes.

'I was young and love was confused. I thought that I was in love with Betty and although I shouldn't have had feelings for somebody else, I did. Can you tell Betty that I was sorry.'

'She heard you Reg and she accepts your apology. If you hadn't dumped her she would never have met Michael.'

'Michael Boland?'

She's nodding.

'How and when did she die?'

'She was on holiday with her family, she caught a tropical disease. The end came quickly.'

'I didn't know, I am sorry and I hope she didn't suffer.'

'Betty has moved aside for another, an older female.'

Reg was left wondering why Betty had wanted to appear in his reading. 'Don't tell me, this other woman does she have a tweed cloche hat with a couple of cherries sewn into the side?' It was said in jest, but when Matilda closed her eyes she smiled.

'Yes and she has a skirt to match.'

Reg Smith clenched his fists together in a triumphant gesture. 'That's Aunt Maud. Does she have a message for me?'

'She wants to know why you've not gone to Greece to fetch her niece and bring her back home.'

Reg seemed confused. 'Can you tell her that it's not as simple as that. I was hoping for something more positive and about the patio, not Abby.'

Matilda leant closer to Reg to whisper. *'Aunt Maud is wagging her index finger at you Reg.'* He mumbled an apology as Matilda continued. 'She wants you to know that Uncle Dick had a good spade in the garage and that to discover what lies beneath you should dig up the patio.'

Reg didn't look at all pleased with the advice.

'That's risky and the neighbours could call the police if I'm seen. I have no idea what Abby buried under the stonework. It could be a body and I would be the first to be arrested. My estranged wife would like that. Not bloody likely.' He apologised again. 'Doesn't she know, can't Aunt Maud tell me?'

Matilda gave a shake of her head. 'She wants me to tell you that everything is turning dark again. She says that you'll understand and that finding Abby can bring about the light.'

Reg saw Ermintrude move as he focused on Matilda. She could see that he was deep in thought. Reg leant over to whisper. 'She's not mentioned Elizabeth so I can only assume that she doesn't know. I can't go to Greece, I'm needed here.'

Matilda straightened up. 'Aunt Maud is insistent that connections will be made when you find Uncle Dick's garden spade.'

Reg let out an exaggerated sigh. 'Okay Aunt Maud, I'll try to make contact and see what she has to say, but I can't promise anything.' There was no response until Reg asked. 'Has she gone?'

Matilda nodded.

'The spirits, the other side do they ever give straight answers?' he asked.

'At times what they have to say is like a riddle and sent for you to work through. Their involvement has to be impartial. I think that is why Betty came through for you today as well. My senses tell me that both ladies are telling you to tread carefully Reg.'

'And Abby, does she need protecting?'

'I'm afraid I don't know the answer to that.'

Reg started to raise his hands in frustration before placing them back down on the table top. 'I'm sorry Matilda I am just slightly frustrated. I seem to be no further forward than I was a week ago.'

'You are in as much that Aunt Maud is convinced that there is something under the patio worth digging up.'

'Or somebody.' Reg replied. 'I guess I'll find out when I start digging.'

'Before we do the tarot cards please let me see your left hand, palm up.'

Matilda studied the lines and patterns of his left palm.

'You've an interesting hand Reg. I see responsibility, decisions and yet I see a hesitancy as well.' She continued to trace the lines. 'Your head line is intuitive with an abundance of intelligent thought. Although recent events are clouding your judgement. You need to remain calm and let events unfold naturally. Jupiter is sitting on your heart line. A strong indication of confidence, but beware of the shadows.'

Reg looked at her bemused. 'The shadows, what does that mean precisely?'

Matilda was as confused not understanding why she had added the warning.

'That you should remain focused and not become distracted in your quest.'

'Abby or Elizabeth?' he asked.

Matilda found it interesting that he had put Abby first. She ran fingertip along on his heart line running it back and forth.

'My spiritual energy tells me Elizabeth. I don't know why but I see Abby in shadow. Does that makes sense to you because it doesn't to me?'

Reg nodded. 'Yes.'

Matilda moved to his line of fate. 'Can you see the way that it curves left, then right and is crossed by a number of other lines?'

Reg looked. 'Yes, it's always been that way like a snake heading for home.'

'The curves indicate an imbalance in your plans Reg.'

He spoke out aloud. 'The parallel is about to cross.' Matilda looked back at Reg although she wasn't sure quite what he meant.

'Perhaps.'

'And what about the big wiggle at the end that looks like a fishhook?' he asked.

'You are turning a corner in your life.'

'And the dissecting line that makes it look like a busy junction?'

'That is where you've reached a crossroads which brings me back to Abby and Elizabeth. You have a decision to make, left or right, go back or forge ahead.'

Reg pointed to a line that he knew. 'Isn't that my wealth line?'

'Yes, again though it is crossed by small lines.'

'Meaning what?' he asked.

'You gain wealth, you lose wealth.'

Reg laughed much to Matilda's surprise. 'That big line that crosses near to the little finger that must have been when Abby cleaned out half of our joint bank account.'

Matilda went on.

'Your life line shows signs of wear and tear Reg. You need to slow down the pace and look after yourself both physically and mentally.'

'I had a medical only last month and the doctor said I was in perfect health for my age.'

'Doctors always say that.' Matilda replied. 'I was referring to your physical well-being and your spiritual psyche. Keeping the balance right between body and mind makes the karma sit right with our Chakra.'

Reg sat himself up straight.

'Have I got spots, floaters...?' he asked.

Matilda grinned. I was studying your aura not your eyes. If you want to know it's a blueish grey.'

'Is that good?'

'White is purity, grey to blue means you're in an in-between state. A place of indecision. You need to meditate at least once a day and let the energy cells replenish.'

Reg nodded accepting that blue grey was good enough. He looked at the cards in the middle of the table.

'Do you mind if we leave the tarot for another time only I've an idea that my karma will reveal events to come. I've a good idea now where I'm heading.'

With that Reg suddenly pushed himself up before laying his forty five pounds down on the table.

'I'm sorry Matilda, but have just realised that there is somewhere where I need to be right now. I'll be in touch and thank you, you been inspirational. I'll see myself out.' Reg collected his hat from the stand in the hall and gently pulled the front door shut.

Watching from behind the lace curtain in the front bedroom Kathleen saw him close the garden gate. 'Well did he fall for it?' she asked.

'I think so. He seem very determined that he needed to be elsewhere. Matilda stuffed the folded bank notes inside her brassiere. 'He didn't let me get to the lines of travel on his hands.'

Kathleen grinned. 'Don't tell me an island in Greece.'

Matilda smiled back. 'No, I've a feeling it'll be Aunt Maud's back garden.'

Kathleen nodded as she stroked Matilda's arm. 'You done well.'

'I done wrong you mean. Aunt Maud did come through and so did an ex-girlfriend. I've a feeling that Reg is heading for trouble. What do you propose doing now?'

'I turn up for my dinner date with William Jenks, then I follow Reg Smith. I have a sneaky feeling that he'll soon be on the move. I want to see where exactly he's heading.'

'I feel guilty adding in the extra little bits to suit our curiosity. Readings are supposed to be private and give enlightenment, not send you on a false trail. I hope the spirits don't come down to chastise me.'

'Don't worry. Tell them it was all my idea.'

This time Matilda held Kathleen's arm. 'There was something else that I didn't add.'

'And what was that?'

Matilda's eyes conveyed a concern.

'I had to warn Reg about a dark shadow. I had a premonition that what would emerge from within would spell danger.'

Kathleen was quick to reply. 'Some people, even men are frightened of the dark and their own shadow.'

'I know, although my inner energy sees the shadow belonging to either Abby or Elizabeth.'

Chapter Eleven

'So what's been keeping you busy for the past week?'

Kathleen had been waiting for William to ask as they sat opposite one another in the restaurant. 'Is that a friend asking or the police?'

'A friend with the police coming in second.'

'At least you're honest. I like that.' She placed the menu down on the table. 'Tying up some loose ends on cases that I had been working on. Nothing really exciting and mainly missing persons, fraud and following wandering husbands.'

'Wandering husbands?' Jenks grinned.

'You know the ones, the type that stray from the straight and narrow. Temptation must be hard to resist when you men have a younger woman revealing herself.' She watched for a reaction, but William Jenks was as cool as a cucumber. 'I never did ask... are you divorced, living with anybody or you invited me out because you find my work interesting?'

William lay his menu down. 'To answer all three the answer would be no and I asked you out because you're an attractive, intelligent and fascinating woman. You have a mind that ticks over similar to my own and I felt a connection.'

'I don't get many compliments in my line of work, so thank you! And in case you're wondering I've never followed you or taken your photograph with somebody that you shouldn't be with.'

William grinned. 'That's a relief although I warn you, I'm rather camera shy.'

'Funny, that's what the victims usually say when the wife takes them to court!'

They laughed sensing that the evening was going to be a casual, relaxed affair where they enjoyed a meal together and that they could take the opportunity getting to know one another.

Reviewing the wine list Kathleen peered over the top. 'So how about you, what's your week been like?'

'Much the same as yourself. Chasing down leads, tying up loose end and recording crimes. We have a burglar in the area after cash and credit cards. Thursday night was busy with assaults when a fight erupted inside a nightclub and a local missing man who we thought had been dead for the past five years, turned up robbing a jewellers in Newcastle yesterday morning. We could have used Matilda's help with the last case, or yours.'

'I have never been called upon by the police for my psychic abilities. I thought you only called in spiritualists as a last resort?'

'There are too many sceptics in the job. Me personally, I believe in leaving all avenue's open in an inquiry including the paranormal.'

Kathleen put down the wine list. 'Extrasensory perception or in the force you call it a gut reaction.'

He acknowledged picking up the wine list. 'What would you prefer, red or white?'

'White please. Less heady and I've an important assignment coming up soon.' She watched as he signalled for the waiter to come to the table. 'Was you ever in the boy scouts William?'

'You mean Baden Powell's teenage army. No, I much prefer water so I joined his brother's organisation and became a Sea Scout instead. I like sailing and have my own boat.'

'I didn't know that he had a brother.'

'Henry Warrington Smyth Baden-Powell, a knight of the realm.'

Kathleen smiled. 'And that is why I accepted your invitation because I knew you'd be full of interesting facts.'

William was amused. 'Is that all... just interesting facts?'

She noticed that his eye were a shade of hazel, amber tinged with green. 'I'll let you know you more after the meal?'

They chose steak with sautéed potatoes, sea salt and pepper accompanied by mushrooms and peas. William chose a light white wine as he too had an early start the next morning.

'So what was the fascination with the scouts about?'

'I found an old photograph of a boy scouts troupe along with the leaders in Albert Barron's garden shed. What I found really interesting was that the five dead men who we talked about the other day including the mysterious Reg Smith all appear in the photograph.'

William held his wine glass away from his mouth. 'Now that I do find relevant. Perhaps I could see the photograph at some time.'

Kathleen reached down plucking an envelope from her handbag. 'I came prepared knowing that you would want to see it.' She gave him the copy. 'You can keep that as I run off several on the printer.'

One by one William studied the face of each of the dead men. 'So which one is Reg Smith?' Kathleen pointed to the tall young man at the back.

'He was a good looking young man.'

'He still is, although he's not my type.'

The waiter arrived with their food whereupon the conversation ceased until he turned away from the table returning to the kitchen. Kathleen looked down at the food.

'This looks good, I'm absolutely famished.'

William agreed stating that he had not eaten since early that morning. Cutting through his steak he took another look at the faces in the photograph.

Kathleen turned the photograph over to show the name on the back. 'Have you ever heard of The Order of Tintagel Knights?'

Adding a fork of sautéed potato he shook his head. 'No, although it has an ancient ring to it, something from King Arthur's era.'

'I googled it earlier and found nothing, it's like it doesn't exist.'

William grinned. 'And you would like me to delve into the non-public archives as see what I can find out about the order?'

'Please... You have more resources at your disposal than I have ten fingers.'

'I'll see what our system throws up. How's your steak?'

'Excellent, thank you.'

Having produced the scout photograph William's curiosity was heightened. 'In Albert Barron's garden shed, did you find anything else?'

'Only old papers, documents and letters, but most had been written or produced in Latin. I did French at school and found that was hard enough. I was never destined to be an academic and my desires yearned for the wide open spaces rather than being stuck in an office all day. '

William sipped at his wine. 'I am glad that you elected to come and see me with this...' he tapped the photograph. 'I pulled the files on the case and began putting together a mood board the other day. It does read like a Sherlock Holmes plot, thick and intriguing.'

'Have you involved Robert Shawhead, he had that keen look in his eye when I visited the station?'

William laughed. 'That's because you walked through the door. Front desk enquiries tend to be rather boring most of the times and involves a lot of form filling. I'd assume that you was like a breath of fresh air.'

Kathleen smiled, she liked William Jenks and considered that it wasn't only the young Robert Shawhead who found her attractive. She wanted to tell him about her plans to follow Reg Smith, but a little voice somewhere inside her head told her to keep it secret until she had more concrete evidence.

'Who did you start with on the mood board?' she asked.

'Ernest Scott-Jackson. Did you know that prior to his marriage to Emma Scott he was simply Jackson and that by all accounts he was a proficient gardener besides being academically gifted at chemistry?'

'No, I didn't know that.' She turned the photograph around to look at Ernest as a young boy. 'Curiously he would have known about the dangers associated with Belladonna.'

William agree. 'Along with the other chemicals used in gardening practice. When we investigated the circumstances surrounding his death we found a spray called beta-cyfluthrin. Commonly used as a pesticide it can cause headaches, muscle weakness, salivation, a shortage of breath and seizures.'

'Did you check out Emma Scott?' Kathleen was looking for a suspect.

'Yes, an odd woman. Like a starchy ghost that didn't exist, she was evasive with her responses. The daughter of a village green grocer and her mother a school secretary, she never got her hands dirty in the garden and had other hobbies. She doesn't appear in our system.'

Kathleen grinned. 'A starchy ghost, I like that description and it suits her.'

'She left me feeling cold as though there was no warmth inside.'

'Was she remorseful that Ernest had died?'

William perceived where she was going with her question. 'Not exactly.'

Kathleen scooped up the last of her potato. 'I wonder what she hopes to achieve by coming along to the spiritual evenings.'

'I would like to know that too. You say that Emma Scott-Jackson and Penny Pringle were the best of friends before they had a big falling out. During our investigation we heard a rumour that it might have been over Cyril.' He topped up her wine glass without asking.

'The eternal love triangle... so many of my private investigations involve three people.'

'Do you think that Emma and Penny are the jealous type?'

'I have never really thought about it, but they could be. Both are still attractive and solvent. A man could muddy the waters.'

'And with your powers of deduction and sight you've no idea what could be buried under the patio at Aunt Maud's bungalow?'

'No…' she squared off the cutlery on her empty plate. 'That was really good, thank you William. My gut reaction is that it has a connection with the five dead men.'

'And what's your take on Harold Harrison?'

'He's another dark horse. It was his mother who came through. She obviously unsettled Harold telling him that he was treading on dangerous waters and becoming involved with a woman named Elizabeth.'

'Elizabeth Marlow, your friend?'

Kathleen sucked in through her teeth. 'I can't really answer that either way because neither of us has seen Elizabeth recently.'

'You mean you and Matilda?'

'Yes.'

William picked up the menu politely passing it across. 'Would like a dessert?'

'Not for me thank you, the tank is nicely full, but I could squeeze in a coffee.'

He ordered two coffees returning the menus to the waiter.

'Now that you're involved, would you like to come along again to the station and go through our files on the case, you might spot something that I have overlooked.'

Kathleen response was a look of surprise. 'Won't you get into trouble, involving an outsider?'

'Not necessarily and if anybody come snooping about I'll tell them that you're using physic abilities to help open up possible channels of further investigation.'

'That sounds exciting. You think it would fool the senior management.'

William appeared confident. 'Using lots of nouns normally confuses the brass hats.'

After coffee and paying the bill William saw Kathleen back to her car which was parked outside. 'Can I give you a lift home?' she asked.

'No, my ride is parked just around the corner.'

Without warning Kathleen stepped forward and planted a kiss on William's mouth. 'Thank you, it was a great evening. I would like to do it again soon, only next time I pay.'

'Fair enough,' he replied, 'and I'll make it my mission to get some chocolate biscuits in for when you visit.'

Kathleen watched until William turned the corner before she turned the ignition key. She had been in two minds and had wanted to invite him back to her flat for a coffee, but maybe next time. Tonight she had another mission.

Chapter Twelve

Sometime around midnight Reg Smith appeared alongside the darkened path that ran adjacent to his garage dressed from head to foot in black clothing. Kathleen surmised that when unfolded his black woollen winter commando hat would hide his face leaving just the eyeholes visible. Scanning either end of the street for any unusual vehicles or movement Reg was confident that he had not been observed. Using the programmed transponder on his key fob he unlocked the driver's door and climbed in.

'Right, here we go,' mumbled Kathleen who was sat behind the steering wheel of her own car. She turned the key of the ignition letting the engine idle as Reg fired the engine of his car into life. Once again he looked left and right. Did another car start up, he wasn't sure, but strange things had been happening lately, odd noises, lights flashing on the bedroom ceiling at night and shadows that he thought moved. He dismissed the idea that he had heard another engine believing that it was probably only his nerves which were stretched tight.

Selecting reverse gear he cursed the sound that his tyres made on the gravel drive. 'Bloody car will wake the dead,' he said as he watched for the car parked in the street opposite.

Kathleen left it until Reg was at the junction before she pulled away from where she had been parked on the drive of an empty house that had been sold subject to contract. She kept a safe distance and used a covert mode of driving to follow. Normally she followed suspects around on foot, jumping onto buses, sitting several seats back on trains or dressed as a jogger she would run past with a wrist camera disguised as a heart monitor receiving an acknowledging nod from the two people that she had been filming.

Sitting at the end of the road with her lights extinguished Kathleen watched Reg park his vehicle on the front drive of a bungalow. *'That has to be Aunt Maud's,'* she whispered as she bit down on a fingernail, concentrating although not chewing, just biting. *'This is a really nice area, expensive.'* She continued to watch as he opened the garage door and disappeared inside.

Reg emerged a minute later clutching hold of a shiny new spade. Pulling the up and over door down he quietly engaged the lock. The properties opposite and on either side of the bungalow were all in darkness. Reg took on last look before vanishing down the side of the property. A month or so back she had removed the interior light so that it didn't give her away as she slipped surreptitiously from the car.

Keeping to the hedgerows Kathleen made her way down to Aunt Maud's where she found the side gate propped open. She looked, saw nothing knowing that it would leave her vulnerable if she used the same way in so instead she reached over and pulled back the keep of the bolt securing a neighbours gate hoping that there wouldn't be a sleeping dog out back of the property extension with a view of the rear garden.

Weaving her way carefully between abandoned pedal cars, bikes and other garden toys the bungalow she assumed belonged to a young family. Adjusting her vision she looked in through the extension window where more toys were lying about. A games room she thought as her eyes surveyed the layout.

Kathleen chose a gap between the petals and thorny stems of a dog rose which overhung both properties to watch Reg Smith as he knelt down on his knees seemingly marking out where he needed to dig. In his free hand he had hold of a garden hose from which a trickle of water was running. Kathleen nodded to herself agreeing with Reg's approach to the problem. *'He's looking for a soakaway where the earth had been disturbed,'* she thought noting that the flagstones were damp, but no puddle was building which was a promising sign.

Moving about on his knees Reg ignored the fact that he was getting wet in the process and when he saw the water disappear he introduced more. Confident that he had found the right spot he set aside the hose letting it snake onto the nearby grass and righted himself. Inserting the blade of the spade between the flagstones he used his weight to lever up the first slab. He had managed to raise and stack five slabs when all of a sudden the earth began to rise.

Reg jumped back with the spade raised shoulder height not quite sure what to expect as Kathleen continued to watch, her eyes and mouth open wide. The seconds seemed to linger as they watched and still the earth kept on rising like a miniature volcano when from the middle of the mound appeared a mole. The tiny earth encrusted creature looked up at Reg and his spade, blinked then reversed back down the channel that it had just dug. Reg brought the spade down hard on the mouth of the mound, but he missed hitting something metal instead making the impact reverberate up through his arm, he instantly dropped the spade and held his wrist dancing about on the spot. Two doors along a rear bedroom light went on and the occupant pulled back the curtain. Reg ducked as Kathleen saw a bedroom window open.

'I told you it was just that bloody cat from over the back Agnes, now can we please go back to sleep.' The window closed and the light was extinguished as Reg picked up the spade and began digging once again.

He flinched and was poised ready to strike when a cat did appear and jump down from the fence top having come from the direction of where the man had opened the window. As curious as it was customary the cat sat under a nearby bush to watch. Kathleen wondered if the cat was watching for the mole too.

Reg continued to dig and remove earth for another ten minutes before his spade head suddenly hit something solid. From the dull thud it sounded wooden. He dropped to his knees again and in a flurry of activity used his gloved hands to push aside the remaining soil.

Moments later he pulled a wooden casket about the size of a shoe box from the hole. Kathleen watched as Reg sat back, studied the box then prising open the lid reached inside to remove a single white envelope. Removing his gloves he pulled out a folded sheet of paper.

To her surprise he crumpled up the note, threw aside the spade, picked up his gloves and left the property walking back down the side of the garage. Moments later she heard him slam shut the car door and the engine start up. She waited until he had reversed and driven away before going around and into Aunt Maud's garden to see what it was that he had unearthed.

She picked up the sodden note to read what was written:

'I knew that one day Reg your curiosity would bring you here and that Aunt Maud would help you dig up her garden patio. We used to share secrets in the beginning when love flourished, but as time went by my mistrust of you grew stronger and now we find ourselves enemies. I will find your precious book and then when I hold it triumphantly aloft you will be powerless to see what destruction I can and will unleash!'

Kathleen took a small plastic bag from her pocket, folded the note and slipped it inside the bag. It had now become evidence. She did think about taking the box, but it was best left where found. At least now she had something to show William Jenks.

Looking at her watch it was just seconds past twenty past one and far too late to make a call, although she felt the need to tell and show somebody. Scrolling down through her phone contacts she let the number ring. A sleepy voice at the other end answered.

'Are you alright, are you safe?' asked Matilda.

'Yes, I'm fine and I am really sorry for waking you and I know that it's late, but I have something important that you need to see.'

Chapter Thirteen

Holding the plastic bag containing the written note in her left hand as she studied short message Matilda sipped at her coffee with the other. She used the back of her wrist to suppress a yawn.

'And he just left the property without making any effort to replace the box, earth or slabs.'

Kathleen was glad of the coffee as it warmed her insides. 'That's right. I got the distinct impression that Reg wasn't entirely a happy man. There was even a local tomcat watching who seemed to be grinning.'

Matilda suddenly shivered. 'That's odd,' she said as she shook her shoulders and head. 'The hairs on the back of my neck have just stood on end as somebody or something moved through me.' She handed back the evidence bag.

Kathleen looked beyond the kitchen window, but the rear garden was in a blanket of darkness. 'My guess is that it was Aunt Maud.'

Matilda shivered once again. 'Well I wish that she'd move on and a bit sharpish, only my extremities are reacting and it's no use feeling excited without Albert being here. Which brings me nicely around to William Jenks. How did it go last night?'

'It was a nice meal and we've arranged to have another.'

Matilda was expecting more. 'And that's it, that's all you have to say, that you're having another meal together?'

'More or less yes… we talked a bit about the case, about Emma Scott-Jackson and I kissed him before he left. Then an hour later I followed Reg Smith.'

'You kissed him, did he respond?'

'Well of course he responded, he's a man isn't he. He seemed to like it.'

'Why discuss Emma Scott- Jackson?'

'Besides the note that's why I came to have coffee with you. I was wondering what you could tell me about her.'

Matilda rubbed her upper arms where they had goose bumped.

'There's not much to tell really. She was the only daughter of a greengrocer and her mother worked in a primary school as a secretary. Emma was academically gifted and she found school an easy experience unlike me. She was good looking and also annoyingly good at sports too. Despite having these up top there wasn't much in the loft except hay. Albert liked me, but most of the boys went after Emma.'

'I didn't know her well back then other than she was good at running and the hurdles.'

Matilda scoffed. 'My boobs would jump up and down like a pair of active ferrets under my tee-shirt and I'd end up falling over the hurdle rather than straddling it. The only time that the boys really cheered and gave any encouragement was at the annual swimming gala where I was always selected to do the back crawl. Top surface must have resembled a pair of killer whales surfacing for air.' They both laughed remembering the numerous whistles.

'So was Ernest on the scene back then. I don't remember him being at our school?'

'He went to an all boy's school. He would meet Emma over the park after lessons ended. She knew how to wiggle her rear as she walked down the corridor, she still does.'

'And was Ernest and Cyril Pringle friends?'

'I'm not entirely sure although I guess Cyril must have attended the same school as Ernest. Albert would have known.'

'And Penny, where did she fit in?'

'She was in Emma's year group. When Ernest asked Emma out on a date, Cyril did similar with Penny. The four of them were always together, they seemed inseparable.'

'And the falling out, when did that take place?'

'You sound like the police.' Said Matilda.

'That's what William says.' They chuckled.

'I first aware of the argument between them through Albert. He came back late one evening from having been to the snooker club when he told me about a heated confrontation that had occurred between Ernest and Cyril. We would see them at the dance hall, but after a while both couples stopped coming. They only saw one another, Emma and Penny I mean when I started the spiritual group again.'

'Who died first, Ernest or Cyril?' asked Kathleen.

'Ernest, Cyril and then Albert in that order.'

Kathleen did sound the police as she continued. 'So why the animosity at the spiritual reading over Cyril's abilities as a mortuary attendant?'

'Emma accused Cyril of not presenting Ernest at his best when she had to formally identify the body.'

Kathleen seemed slightly bemused. 'And that was it. It seems very trivial, but Ernest was dead. How exactly was he supposed to look, like he was going to a black tie evening?'

'In essence I think it was just the shock of Emma seeing Ernest dead, really dead. Cyril was always so particular about his work and Ernest was his best friend, he would have taken extra care to make Ernest look good for Emma. Shock can do unusual things to the mind under moments of stress and unexpected circumstances.'

Kathleen remembered the spiritual evening and the tension in the air. 'She more or less accused Cyril of having an affair when he should have been at work.'

Matilda sighed and nodded. 'Yes she did. Although again I would say it was more frustration than any real hatred. In time, time will heal and of the two men Ernest was the one with a wandering eye.'

Kathleen rinsed her coffee mug under the hot tap. 'So Emma blamed the closest thing to her for Ernest's demise, in this case Penny.'

'That's about the size of it.'

'But...' started Kathleen, 'blame can also produce unusual emotions, such as murder.'

Matilda looked up her mouth slowly opening. 'No... I see where you're going with this and disagree. Emma is angry, hurt and missing Ernest the same as we all miss our loved ones, but she and Penny were best friends.'

Kathleen however wasn't so easily swayed. 'Diminished responsibility in a time of an unbalanced mind are reasons enough to tamper with the rigging at a stage rehearsal and make it look like an accident.'

'Proving that would be somewhat difficult.' Replied Matilda.

Kathleen held up a finger. 'Maybe that is where a certain detective sergeant we know could help.'

Matilda rinsed her cup then reached down for Ermintrude's cat bowl giving it a wash too. It was time to change the subject. 'I tried calling Elizabeth last night, but there was no answer.' She placed the bowl on the drainer. 'You need to listen to the voicemail as there are background noises and Elizabeth... well let's just say that she sounded odd.'

'In what way?'

Matilda continued. 'It didn't sound like Elizabeth, but somebody else, another woman disguising herself as Elizabeth.'

Kathleen took her mobile from her pocket and let the phone ring until the ansamachine kicked in.

'You're right, that's not our Elizabeth.' Her brow took on lines as she pondered why. 'Why would she get somebody else to record a message, she was always so particular about getting a message just so. I think we should go to the flat and see what's happening for ourselves.'

Matilda nodded in agreement. 'Yes we should.' She suddenly placed a hand over her chest, over her heart. 'I have this feeling of dread too Kathleen, a feeling that has been affecting my sleep and dreams. Something has happened to our friend. I feel it like a twin would feel if something had happened to the other.'

Kathleen placed her hand over Matilda's. 'I've had similar. I think we should visit Elizabeth's flat and then hold another group meeting only this time invite William along.'

Matilda wasn't sure. 'Having a policeman in their midst might not go down so well with the others attending?'

'I'll make sure that he comes along in disguise. It would give him the opportunity to see who is around the table and why. There is a link somewhere Matilda, a link that both you and I are missing. Maybe William as the outsider would find it.'

Matilda shivered again only exclaiming that this time it was a different shudder. 'That time it felt like Albert, not Aunt Maud.'

Kathleen pointed at Matilda's chest where her nipples were on show. 'And I suppose that he did that too!'

Matilda looked down quickly covering herself. 'I wouldn't have thought that ghosts could do such a thing.' She looked at Kathleen. 'They've always been uncontrollable. When I was younger they would send out the wrong signals to men standing in a bus queue or sitting at a red light. Albert said I was just expressing myself naturally like Eve had when she met Adam.'

Kathleen laughed. 'Well they certainly send out some kind of signal.'

'They're not traffic lights that flash red and green,' exclaimed Matilda. 'You're lucky, you don't suffer like I do.

Kathleen surveyed her own chest. 'I'm not sure, but I think mine were flashing between red and green last night. It must have sent out a mixed message to poor William sat opposite.'

Matilda shook her head in dismay. 'So do I ring round and send out the invites?'

'Yes, make Reg Smith the first and I'll talk with William.'

'Okay, I'll do it as soon as we've been round to Elizabeth's flat.'

*****

They rang the doorbell several times getting no reply so Kathleen promptly knocked on a neighbour's door. An elderly man answered.

'I don't give to charity, dogs, cats, tigers, the rain forest, donkeys, elephants or any bloody polar bear. It's enough of a struggle to keep me head above water and the wife alive.'

Kathleen produced her identity as a private investigator. The man squinted and sniffed as he pulled his head back having barely read the details.

'So what's the law want with me?'

'Not you... the lady who lives door, Elizabeth. Have you seen her recently?'

He scrutinised Kathleen then Matilda admiring her chest before hoisting up the waistband of his trousers. With another sniff he turned and called out. 'Edna have you seen anything of Liz from next door?'

The voice of a female from a room nearby replied. 'No, she's away or so I believe, gone abroad I think Terry the postman said.' A woman, although much better dressed than that of her husband appeared sporting bright mauve tints in her hair. 'I am sorry... Stan can be so suspicious with callers, we get a lot you see and nearly all foreign saying that they have the wrong address or that they're collecting for charity.'

'We understand.' Replied Matilda. 'Elizabeth is a friend of ours and we were getting concerned because we've not heard from her.'

'I saw Terry delivering the other day. He told me that Elizabeth had said to him that she was going to Jerusalem on some sort of pilgrimage. Funny though as I never saw Liz as the religious type.'

Matilda and Kathleen looked at one another then back at the woman. 'Do you know if she was going with anybody?' asked Kathleen.

'No, I couldn't really tell you, although I think she left very early one morning. I saw somebody get into a waiting taxi, but they had on a dark hat and clothing to match, and it was very dark outside. I assumed that the person getting inside was Liz.'

Kathleen smiled. 'Okay... well thank you for your help, both of you.' The husband sniffed, turned and walked back down the short passage. 'We'll wait until she returns from her pilgrimage and see the holiday photographs.' Moments later the door closed and they heard the husband mutter under his breath *bloody foreigners.*

At the head of the stairs Kathleen stopped to look back.

'Right that settles it, come on we're going inside Elizabeth's flat. I want to have a look around. Elizabeth has never been abroad or indeed that adventurous.'

'That's illegal,' Matilda exclaimed her eyes darting left and right expecting to see the neighbour's door open once again.

'It's nothing of the sort. It's called looking out for a friend.'

Selecting a bank card from her purse Kathleen deftly slipped it down between the door and the wood jab. With a gently persuasion of her shoulder the door opened. Matilda stood open mouthed.

'I never knew that it was that easy.'

'A trick of the trade.' Replied Kathleen adding a grin. 'Come on quickly... let's get inside before we're seen.'

Inside the flat was silent, empty and not even a spider moved as they searched the rooms. Each had been left clean and remarkably tidy. Kathleen checked the laundry basket.

'That's a bit personal, isn't it?' said Matilda as she walked past the bathroom.

'It tells me two things, if Elizabeth is still around and secondly if she's had anybody staying here.'

'How?'

'Some men don't always take their dirty underwear home.'

Matilda didn't ask apprehensive about the reply. 'She has a lot of books in her bookcase. I didn't know that Elizabeth was into ancient history.'

Kathleen accompanied Matilda into the living room. 'No, me neither...' She picked up a copy. It fell open at the crusades where a thin stranded page marker had saved the page. Kathleen was about to close the book when something in italics caught her eye. 'Oh Jesus...' she exclaimed, 'Matilda look, take a look at this...'

Matilda felt her jaw drop and her heart pick up a beat as she read the short inscription *'The Order of Tintagel Knights'*. Together they sat on the settee, reading and turning the pages. 'Why would Elizabeth be so interested in the Order?' she asked.

Kathleen rubbed her chin as she thought of a reply. 'I'm not entirely sure, but there's a strange atmosphere here in this flat. I felt it the minute we entered.'

'Me too,' Matilda agreed hesitantly. 'I think we should leave.'

'Alright,' Kathleen agreed, 'but not until I've photographed this page. I want to show it to William.'

Kathleen was about to replace the book when Matilda suddenly grabbed her arm.

'Look…' she said pointing to where the morning sun had moved across the top of a glass coffee table. Roughly scribbled in the dust was a single word *'help'*.

Kathleen knelt down so that she could examine the word sideways on. 'Whoever wrote this used the end of their finger knowing that the natural oil in the pores would leave an impression upon the glass.' She took another photograph. 'This will make William's heart race.'

Matilda suddenly clutched her chest. She gasped loudly then sighed before closing her eyes. 'Matilda are you okay?' she enquired.

Kathleen saw the colour drain from Matilda's face.

'It's Elizabeth… it was her spirit,' she opened her eyes once again. 'It just passed through me.' Matilda looked anxiously at her friend. 'I recognised her face as she did so.'

'Did she say anything?'

Matilda nodded. *'Yes… get out!'*

132

'Right... that's it, I'm going to see William. In the meantime you get back and begin making the phone calls. We need to summon assistance from the other side. This mystery is getting bigger by the day and we're going to need help.

Chapter Fourteen

'And what exactly would you like me to go as Fagin or Sherlock Holmes?'

Kathleen grinned. 'Don't be facetious, by the time I've applied a little make-up not even your own mother would recognise you.'

William Jenks studied the downloaded copy of the page from the book and the photograph of the word *'help'*.

'This doesn't entirely mean that Elizabeth is in trouble, there could be an innocent explanation. Maybe it was written as a subconscious message to herself.'

Kathleen gave a shake of her head. 'I believe that it was a cry for help William. Matilda had a real funny turn as we was about to leave the flat and she's not given to theatrics. She told me that Elizabeth had passed into spirit.'

'And did you feel it too?'

'Something passed through me, a cold shiver as though an entity was trying to make contact, but Matilda experienced much more than me.

William studied the page in the book again.

'I asked a curator at the local museum about The Order of Tintagel Knights. At first he wanted to know why I needed to know. When I told him that his response could help in the investigation of a recent murder he was less hesitant. In a nutshell, the order is an ancient group of people who belong to a secret society for the preservation of antiquities, not necessarily religious, but most certainly of historical value.'

'Like the knights Templar,' added Kathleen.

'More or less, although very secretive. The impression that came across was that they would do anything to protect their identity and quest.'

'Including murder?'

William was pensive as he looked at Kathleen. 'No... quite the opposite. From what I had been told they are a peaceful Order, but they have enemies who would kill. My take on their stance is that the Tintagel Knights would sacrifice themselves rather than submit to torture or give up a secret.'

Kathleen produced the evidence bag with the written note. 'Can you have this run through your fingerprint machine and see who, if anybody jumps out at us?'

William asked how she had come by the note and so Kathleen told him, leaving out nothing including the cat who had watched Reg.

'You had luck on your side that the owners of the house and Reg didn't see you peeping through their garden hedge.'

She grinned and there was a sparkle in her eyes. 'I know, but a private investigator has to take risks occasionally and besides it's all part of the adrenalin rush.' He stared at her as she looked back at him. 'What...?' she asked.

'And the page from the book at Elizabeth's flat dare I ask how you got in?'

Kathleen however had an excuse ready on the tip of her tongue. 'I thought that I heard a moan from inside the flat so I entered to save life and limb.' She knew that if she stared at him long enough eventually William would look away, she was right.

'And whose prints do you hope to find on this note?'

'I'm not sure. Instinctively I would point the finger of suspicion at Abby Smith, but at present I am happy to keep my options open.'

William leaned forward on his desk top. 'This morning while you were committing the offence of breaking and entering I was going over the investigation reports concerning Derrick Buckworthy.' He opened his desk drawer and pushed over a copy of the report to her. 'It was the same as I remembered from before, however you have a read and tell me what you see, if anything. Your keen eye might see something that was overlooked at the scene.'

Kathleen read through the report painstakingly digesting each sentence, picturing the scenario in her mind. When she had finished she pushed the report back across the desk. 'Besides the stick of lipstick found on the back seat and the tyre tread imprinted on Derrick's head I can't see anything that was missed.'

William took an envelope from his top drawer. He spread the contents, photographs of five dead men across the desk top. Each corpse was naked.

'Take a look that their shoulders Kathleen. Can you see that each of the deceased has the same mark in exactly the same place. Not quite a tattoo, more an incision scar made with a very sharp instrument. Initially it looks like an old wound, but on closer examination it bears the hallmarks of being either self-inflicted or that the recipient had help in putting it there. Roman legionaries had similar marks.' He pushed the report back for her take a second look.

Kathleen checked again. 'Under physical marks, scars, skin blemishes and tattoo's there's nothing recorded.'

'That's right.' They checked the other four reports on each of the other dead men. None had been recorded for any.

'One administrative error you could excuse as a clerical oversight, but certainly not five.' Said Kathleen.

William nodded agreeing. 'Right again. These reports have either been tampered with or the marks are protected.'

Kathleen was astonished. 'Surely you don't suspect the coroner?'

William responded with a shrug of his shoulders. 'Who better to have in The Order of Tintagel Knights, but a coroner who could protect members of a secret organisation, not discounting a police officer.'

Chapter Fifteen

Like the previous occasion the invited guests shuffled into the room occupying the same seats that they had sat at a week previous only now there was an extra chair positioned next to Kathleen Lee. The tall stranger to the group, a man who occupied the chair was dishevelled, although smiling to each sat around the table he immediately eased any concerns or suspicion. Matilda was sat in her normal seat at the other end of the table. As soon as they were all seated and settled she dimmed the lights using her foot pedal.

'This evening we are pleased to have a new attendee join our group. His name is William and his recent loss brings him to our table in the hope that he will find answers to recent difficulties.' Once again William looked down both sides of the table smiling at the faces all focused in his direction. The only person not smiling back was Reg Smith. Kathleen looked at Matilda knowing that she too had noticed. Matilda kept the connection going.

'Since our last meeting I have been getting all sorts of different messages from the other side, some I have understood, others have been a little mixed, but that's because loved ones are eager in coming through.'

Hiding his smile behind the palm covering the lower half of his face William could see how Matilda was good at capturing the attention of her respective audience. With the exception of the man sat between the two women to his left. He recognised Emma Scott-Jackson and Penny Pringle. William watched as Reg smith's interest went left and right, then up and down the table.

'The messages that you've been receiving, has one been from my Derrick?' asked Margaret Buckworthy. William averted his interest from Reg to look left at the large lady in the floral dress and cardigan.

Matilda replied enthusiastically. 'Do you know Margaret, I do believe that one of the messages was indeed from Derrick. We should all hold hands now and let us see if we can make contact again.'

Margaret immediately joined hands with Arnold Peabody and Harold Harrison. She liked the feel of their strong hands in hers and it recalled a time, many years back when she had been about seven years of age walking around the playground holding the hands of two little boys who had been her friends. She would tell them a story as they walked. One of the boys had been Derrick. How he had always loved listening to her ramblings. Much later in life she had written them down and sent them off to be published in a weekly women's magazine.

Matilda closed her eyes suggesting that everyone do the same. With the exception of William, Kathleen and Reg Smith everybody else closed their eyes. Kathleen felt the warmth and energy flowing through William's leg as he sat next to her. She looked his way raising her eyebrows. With a turn of his eyes he indicated that Reg was watching them. Kathleen winked making Reg looked elsewhere. Did he see her looking through the hedgerow in the rear garden she wondered, it was possible. William saw Matilda take in a deep breath.

'The energy is getting stronger,' she expressed, 'I can feel it.'

'*Oh good…*' Margaret muttered, speaking out aloud feeling the two men squeeze her hands. She crossed her feet as her hands were otherwise occupied. Matilda opened one eye to see that Margaret had hers closed.

'There's a man coming… and he has a dog.'

Arnold and Harold felt the pressure increase through their fingers. 'It's my little Charlie and Derrick,' she eased back with holding their hands, much to their relief. Margaret was a strong man physically.

'Derrick wants to say that he is sorry Margaret.' Margaret opened her eyes to see Matilda looking directly at her.

'Whatever for Derrick, we had no secrets when you was alive.' She noticed that the man sat opposite was looking at her. Reg Smith unnerved her, but she focused her attention back to Matilda.

'Derrick is telling me that he did have secrets. Confidences that he could not reveal, but that his secrets almost certainly caused his death.' Kathleen and William watched as Margaret's eyes opened and her mouth gaped.

'*Tell me, was it another woman Derrick?*' demanded Margaret her fingers once again intensifying the grip of the men on either side.

Matilda sighed. 'No, it was nothing to do with a woman. Derrick just wanted to say sorry for all the times that he had left you alone at the weekend, but his trips away were of a necessity.'

'What necessity?' invited Margaret, her eyes narrowing suspiciously.

Matilda hesitated. 'He will only say that they were in a good cause.' Margaret appeared somewhat displeased with his reply. Matilda continued. 'Derrick tells me that you should move the chest of drawer aside, the one in the corner of the spare bedroom and there you will find a loose floorboard. Check underneath where you will find a surprise, something that will help keep you comfortable for the rest of your days.'

Margaret frowned. 'What is it Derrick... what will I find there?' Margaret noticed that Reg Smith seemed keenly interested in her message. For once he was smiling. She didn't give him one back.

Matilda let out a sudden gasp surprising everyone and making those closest to her jump. Either side to where she sat Harold and Penny gave her a reassuring squeeze of her hand.

'What is Matilda,' asked Penny, 'is it bad news?'

Matilda looked towards the other end of the table looking directly at Kathleen and William. 'I am terribly sorry. I have just seen somebody walk past the table, somebody that I once knew.' She expelled the excess air from her lungs.

At the other end of the table Kathleen gripped William's hand feeling the same spirit walk through the room. He looked her way. *'Later...'* she whispered.

Going left to right Reg Smith was watching. Matilda returned his gaze.

'The connection with Derrick has gone, but I have an elderly lady here now. This message is for you Reg.'

Feeling their eyes burning into his soul Reg forced himself not to look keeping his focus on Matilda only. 'Aunt Maud I assume?'

Matilda grinned. 'She's nodding which tells me that it is...' Again there was a hushed silence as Matilda interpreted the message. 'She tells me that finding Abby is imperative.' Matilda moved her stare from Reg to Kathleen and William. 'Aunt Maud tells me that Abby has to be stopped.' Matilda shivered as a cold breeze swept through her body. She was aware of her nipples rising. Watched by Ermintrude, the cat checked the corners of the room.

'Is that it, is that all,' asked Reg, 'doesn't she have anything to tell me?'

Matilda tried to think of something to dispel the cold running through her body which was covered in goose bumps. 'No, I am sorry Reg, but she's already gone. She only came through to give you that one message.'

Reg couldn't contain his frustration. 'That's like saying the last pint of milk has turned sour and I need to buy a fresh bottle.'

Matilda shrugged her shoulders. 'I am sorry Reg. The other side dictate the agenda and we can ask if there is anything else, but when they turn their back and walk away it signifies that they've nothing else to say on this occasion. I think Aunt Maud means for you to find your wife.'

Kathleen watched as the cheeks of Reg's face lost their shape. 'Well she sent me on a wild goose chase the other night. I will have to consider the next journey that I go on very carefully.'

Kathleen's knee nudged William's. She raised her eyebrows sensing something significant had just happened. Matilda suddenly turned her attention to William.

'I have a lady coming through now, she's not particularly very old although not that young. She's calling out a name... it's your name William.'

William looked up at Matilda as surprised as Kathleen. This wasn't meant to happen and she didn't expect him to receive a message. 'Is she saying who she is...?' he asked.

'Oddly enough she hasn't offered a name. She is however telling me that she is very proud of you, of what you have achieved in your life. She tells me that she watches over you!'

Kathleen squeezed his leg. *'Not too closely,'* she whispered.

William smiled back although genuinely astonished that somebody had come through. 'Can you describe her to me?'

Sat shuffled closer to William, *'this should be interesting!'*

'She is not unattractive. She has long hair and freckles over the bridge of her nose.'

William responded with a knowing nod. 'Jessie, my late cousin. She was in a riding accident, the horse bolted and threw her.'

144

'Jessie is smiling at me and she is pleased that you remember her. She tells me that you said such lovely words at her funeral. She thanks you.' There was a pause as Matilda listened in. 'She has one last message before she goes William. She wants me to tell you that not everything is as it seems. You should take care as there is danger coming your way.' Matilda breathed in. 'Jessie wants you to look after your friends and keep them close by you.'

'*I like the last bit,*' Kathleen added. He smiled at Matilda feeling Kathleen's knee knock his.

'Wait,' cried Matilda she's turned back around. 'Jessie likes the lady with whom you have just met. She tells me that will be many more associations, adventures with this lady.'

Out of the side of her vision Kathleen looked at where she had stuck the false beard next to William's ear, some of the adhesion was coming slightly loose. She hoped that it didn't just suddenly fall away. Using the foot pedal to heighten the illumination in the room so that she could see into the corners of the room Matilda turned her focus to Emma Scott-Jackson.

'We have another strong presence this time, a man.' Matilda felt the expectant energy from Penny Pringle flowing through her hands. She gave the hand a reassuring squeeze. 'Soon Penny, they are waiting patiently. The man coming through is Ernest.'

Emma immediately opened her eyes.

'Ernest wants you to know that he is still around in spirit. He is however saddened that you have let his death mar a good friendship. His death was expected and in some ways unavoidable.'

William and Kathleen looked at Emma Scott-Jackson.

'I'm not sure what you mean Ernest... expected in what way and yet at the same time unavoidable. You make it sound like the death clock was tolling in your direction that fated day.'

Kathleen saw Matilda raise her eyebrows in surprise. 'Ernest tells me that soon all will be revealed. He asks that you don't bear grudges and he sends his love Emma. He's waving as he steps aside.'

'Is that it?' Like Reg, Emma had expected more. She leant forward to see Penny Pringle looking at her.

'Goodness they are very active tonight,' remarked Matilda wanting to keep the channel of communication open.

'Malcolm is standing behind you Arnold only there's no point in turning around because you won't see him, but you will feel his hand on your shoulder.' Arnold almost leapt out his seat when he did. When he had regained his composure he too had a message for Malcolm.

'I've been thinking over what you said at our last meeting Malcolm. I am not quite ready for another adventure just yet, but I promise to keep my options open for the future.'

Matilda nodded her approval. 'Malcolm is smiling Arnold.'

'Do you know who it was that stole your shoulder bag,' Arnold asked, 'only I had a visitor the other day from a person who would be interested in knowing. Several actually?'

The room was silent as Matilda waited patiently for a reply.

'All Malcolm can tell you Arnold is that is wasn't there when the ambulance arrived.'

Once again Arnold felt a hand rest upon his shoulder. 'Never mind Malcolm, I am sure that one day it'll turn up.'

'Malcolm is going Arnold, but he sends his love and wants you to know that he'll stay close.' There was a tear in the corner of Arnold's eye, but Margaret Buckworthy came to the rescue with a tissue produced from the inside of her brassiere, it was still warm when Arnold wiped his eye.

Waiting for the room to settle once again Matilda continued.

'Goodness they are still queuing with messages.' Even Matilda seemed surprised as everybody held hands again. She encouragingly squeezed Penny Pringle's hand.

'Cyril is coming through Penny...' she paused momentarily, 'he says that you shouldn't be so stubborn. You should relax and let everything wash over you, take notice of the stars at night and the birds flying during the day. He's concerned that you are dwelling too much on the past.'

Penny however was quick to defend herself. 'But I have heard such nasty rumours Cyril, about you being involved elsewhere. Please tell me that they're not true?'

Matilda saw Penny lean forward to look at Emma Scott-Jackson who was shaking her head vigorously from side to side.

Matilda breathed in deep. 'Cyril tells me that the rumour are unfounded. Ye, he did occasional see another woman, but it was merely regarding a mutual interest that they shared and that there was no hanky-panky.'

Penny's shoulders sagged with relief.

'Was she an actor in the play?' she asked.

This time Matilda shook her head from side to side. 'No, she was important to the...' the message suddenly trailed away causing everybody to look at Matilda. She looked at Penny Pringle who was sat opened mouthed awaiting the arrival of the next word.

'Important to what...?' asked Emma Scott-Jackson.

'I don't know... he's gone. Cyril turned around suddenly and stepped into the shadow. He never finished the sentence.' William saw Reg Smith turning to look at everybody sat around the table including himself.

'Will he return?' Penny asked desperately.

'My spiritual intuition tells me not today, not this evening, maybe some other time.'

Penny Pringle exhaled and addressed the room putting to bed any wild speculation.

'He did that to me soon after we were engaged. I suspected him of seeing another woman, but Cyril denied it,' she scoffed, 'don't most men.

Anyway, I followed him one night to the other side of town and what a route he weaved as though he knew he was being followed. Down near Exeter Terrace where the shadows are much darker than the rest of London he disappeared. It was as though Cyril had become a ghost.'

It was at that moment that Ermintrude had decided she had heard enough, with an elongated stretch arching her back she jumped down from the chair by the window making the floorboard creak. The room burst into an echo of cries and shrieks as the cat bolted.

'My pussy does that whenever the lights begin to flicker,' Penny admitted holding onto her chest, 'I'd swear that it was Cyril come back to haunt us!'

Matilda patted the back of Penny's hand offering reassurance. 'The other side doesn't haunt Penny dear they only return to the living world to offer comfort and solace. If you've felt Cyril around you then that is a good thing. Remember cats and dogs are very perceptive of any spiritual presence. They have a sixth sense that is so much more acute than our own, that's why the ancient Egyptians worshipped both so much.'

Fanning the front of her face Penny Pringle felt a wave of menopausal warmth flowing through her body. 'I worship my pussy and she's all that I've got left now.' William was glad of his false beard as he managed to stifle a laugh feeling the kick from Kathleen connect with his ankle.

Matilda's expression became very serious. It made her sit up straight.

'I have a lady here, a lady that I know.' Matilda felt the hairs on the back of her neck stand up on end. 'She has a message for you Harold. She

149

tells me that you should take a restful holiday, a cruise would be good, but you need to get away. Somebody is coming and they mean to harm you.'

Harold was surprisingly calm. 'Is it mother?'

'No, not this time Harold... it is somebody much younger. She says that the danger grows ever present with each hour that you stay.'

The colour suddenly drained from Harold face as he realised that the message was serious. 'Okay, I'll go... tell her I will book it tomorrow, I'm overdue some leave.'

'Do you know who it is Harold, who it was that is telling you this...?' asked Margaret Buckworthy.

'Yes, I do and when she gives advice, it should not be ignored.'

Chapter Sixteen

'Well what do you think?' Kathleen asked William, standing close to his side.

'It was an interesting evening. I was surprised at how many messages were received although some threw up some questions too.'

'Like what?' Kathleen asked. Matilda was bemused by their interaction as she boiled the kettle for coffee.

'To begin let's take Margaret Buckworthy, she sent her stories to a women's magazine. Commendable and a very good way of getting noticed, although I get the distinct impression that her persona is not quite what it seems. When Derrick had his accident, she wasn't as upset as I had expected her to be.'

'That's just the policeman in you. You're all suspicious and of everybody.'

William grinned. He liked the fact that she might find him mysterious. 'And magazine stories often depict a hidden message.'

Matilda made the coffee. She was in favour of William's doubt. 'I am never quite sure how to take Margaret. One day she can be extraordinarily friendly and the next she can so easily give you the cold shoulder.' William nodded in agreement.

'And then there is the question,' he continued, 'as to why Margaret never asked how Derrick's secret brought about his death.'

'Hey, that's right... I picked up on that too.' Said Kathleen. 'You'd think that she would have wanted to know what the secret was, that was so important and why he died.'

Again William gave a nod. 'Gut reaction, instinct or whatever, her not asking increases the level of suspicion that she knew about his death.'

Matilda stopped sipping her coffee. 'Although Margaret can blow hot and cold, I don't think she's a killer, a murderer.'

'Maybe not,' replied William, 'but she had her eye on Reg Smith a lot during the evening.'

'So did Emma Scott-Jackson.' Added Kathleen.

'Yes, but perhaps for different reasons.' Quipped William. Kathleen smiled, she knew that William was being polite having only just met Matilda.

'And what about your late cousin coming through at the end.'

'Yes, that was a surprise.' William appeared pensive as he remembered her. 'Jessie was always so full of fun and laughter. We would play a lot together as children. I was saddened and shocked when she died having

152

been thrown by her horse. Jessie lived for riding and she was the all-embracing country girl, loving everything to do with nature and the countryside.'

'What do you think she meant when she told you that 'everything is not as it seems'?'

William breathed in filling his lungs. 'I'm not entirely sure. My initial thought was that she was telling me not to jump to assumptions.'

'A bit like Reg Smith,' added Matilda.

'More or less,' replied William. 'I noticed that he was very preoccupied in taking everything in this evening. Like Margaret Buckworthy I got the impression that he was here for other reasons.'

'Digging up Aunt Maud's patio strikes me as very suspicious. Reg Smith has a hidden agenda yet to be unravelled.' Kathleen responded. '

William took the seat next to Kathleen and opposite Matilda. 'Maybe he had an inkling what was buried in the rear garden, but he needed to make sure for himself.'

'It seemed a lot of bother and waste of energy digging to find only a note in a wooden box and he wasn't too pleased when he left.'

'Don't you feel the same sometimes when a case comes together and you close the file and there is a distinct lack of satisfaction as though something else is missing.'

'Sometimes,' Kathleen replied as she added a spoonful of sugar.

William turned his thoughts to Matilda. 'And you went almost as white as a ghost earlier this evening when somebody walked through your vision. Was it somebody you knew?'

Matilda pulled the cup away from her mouth as she stared back at them. 'The face that I saw belonged to our friend Elizabeth. When we went to her flat, Kathleen and I both felt that there was something wrong. Apparition's don't normally appear in a vision unless they're of the dead.'

William turned to look at Kathleen. 'Are you okay, you've gone quiet?'

'I was only thinking. Every time I think about our visit to her flat I am drawn to the conclusion that the answer to Elizabeth's disappearance lies somewhere inside her home.'

'I couldn't get a search warrant on the basis of a hunch.'

Kathleen nudged his shoulder. 'I know, but if we think that Elizabeth is in spirit then we could enter her home legally on the grounds of saving life and limb.'

'But you just said that you think she's dead?'

Kathleen winked at Matilda. 'We think that, but nobody else knows that... do they.'

'I think this time I had best accompany you. My warrant card might help fend off any awkward questions with the neighbours.'

Kathleen put her arm through his and gave it a hug. 'See... I told you that he would agree.'

William looked tentatively from Kathleen to Matilda then back to Kathleen. 'You two had this all planned long before we even sat down at the table to hear messages from the other side.'

Matilda pointed at Kathleen. 'Blame her if you have to blame anybody. In my opinion she's been working amongst the shadows for far too long. Some of the ideas that she comes up with scare me, let alone those on the other side.'

Kathleen laughed, squeezing William's arm. 'And with good reason I'd say, judging by recent events and the mixed messages coming through. I have never known the other side to be so busy.' She turned to William. 'Your interest in the case must have been heightened by what took place earlier?'

William smiled back at them both. 'I can't deny that I am intrigued. Looking around the table none would make good poker players. Eyes when open were darting left and right and across the table at the person opposite. Everybody who attended has a secret to tell and yet nobody wants to be the first.'

'Except poor Penny.' Added Matilda.

William agreed. 'I'd go along with that, although she's still not quite convinced that Cyril wasn't involved elsewhere. Amateur dramatics can evoke conscious desires in the weak willed.'

Kathleen was amused. 'Have you ever done amateur dramatics?'

'Only at school. We did Romeo and Juliet. I had a bit part, but I fancied Juliet at the time. In later years I met her in the street as a patrolling officer. She had four children.'

Kathleen laughed and was joined by Matilda. 'Conscious desires almost got you in trouble!' William joined in the laughter.

'Going back to Margaret Buckworthy I would have liked a peek under the floorboards and seen what was hidden beneath that will keep her in a lap of luxury for the rest of her days. My guess is that Margaret went straight home and got the jemmy from the shed or garage.

William took a sip of his coffee before going on.

'Then we had Aunt Maud coming through for Reg Smith, our dark man of mystery who watches everyone and never misses a trick. Reg Smith is loaded with secrets. He sought you out Matilda because she seeks answers.'

'And to hear the messages that the others get come through.' Kathleen added. 'He could be into blackmail.'

William shook his head rejecting the suggestion. 'No, I think Reg Smith is too smart to be involved in anything as shady. He is searching for something much deeper than just money or treasure. I've a feeling that Reg is searching for answers to a greater mystery.'

'That's deep...' Kathleen replied, 'how do you arrive at that conclusion?'

'You say Reg knows your friend Elizabeth and now she's done a disappearing act, perhaps taking the ultimate journey to the other side. Reg might too be searching for something in her flat as well.'

Matilda liked William and he was not what as she assumed he would be, abrasive and without feeling, instead he was the opposite, friendly and instantly agreeable.

'I'm guessing that you've given thought already to what Jessie told you said to you and with regards to Reg Smith?'

Kathleen looked waiting for a response.

'I guess I am in a way. Reg strikes me as an intelligent man and not given to particular whims or fancies. He has a quest that he needs to fulfil.'

'The Order of Tintagel Knights.' Matilda replied.

'Maybe, although asking outright wouldn't do you any good because they're all probably sworn to secrecy.'

Kathleen looked on dubiously, she still didn't trust Reg Smith. 'Go on, who's next?'

'The message from Ernest to his wife Emma about his innocent meetings with another woman. Again we have no name although according to Ernest, any fraternising with the enemy was all above board and that he nothing to be ashamed about. What interests me is who he met, when and where and how his departure from this life was expected.'

'We all die one day. That is the only thing that we do get right in this life,' Matilda added.

William grinned, he liked Matilda's philosophical approach. 'Yes, I know, but Ernest meant it in a different context as though it belonged to a prophecy.'

Kathleen's keen mind was whirring fast. 'You think he knew his killer, don't you?'

'I think he knew that at some time he would be killed. Not necessarily that he knew who would engineer his demise. That point definitely needs exploring deeper. I would also like to know about the bad blood existed between Emma Scott-Jackson and Penny Pringle. That might throw up some answers.'

'Or more questions,' Kathleen responded.

William nodded launching into another. 'Then we have Malcolm Swift and his missing shoulder bag. If it was indeed murder, then the killer took the bag possibly knowing what was inside.'

Kathleen was quick to reply. 'Hidden evidence. The notepad with details of the five dead men, the book of contacts and the digital camera.'

'Yes, each could be as valuable as the other. Had we had possession of the shoulder bag and contents I don't think we would have such a mystery on our hands.'

Matilda was thinking of the wall safe and that finding the key could give her some answers and possibly a legacy to keep her in the lap of luxury for the rest of her days.

'Next and like Ernest, we have Cyril who also confesses to have had secret meetings with another woman, although giving the reason as a mutual interest…'

'Don't all couples when they are attracted to one another?' joked Kathleen. William smiled keeping the conversation specifically about Cyril.

'Indeed although I've a feeling that the mutual interest we are talking about somehow connects this group.'

Matilda wondered. 'Including Elizabeth.'

William nodded pensively. 'Yes. And finally we have Harold who has a young woman come through only not his mother, but a mystery woman who he claims should not be ignored. The more I think about it, going to Elizabeth's flat should definitely be our next course of action.'

'We should leave it until everybody is in bed.' Implied Matilda not wanting another encounter with Elizabeth's odd neighbours.

Kathleen raised a clenched fist. 'We should strike whilst the iron is still hot, that's my motto.'

Chapter Seventeen

They arrived to find a majority of the properties in the road already in darkness including the residential block where Elizabeth lived, or had lived as may be the case. Looking up at her second floor window the trio were unsettled to see a light on in the flat.

'I don't remember touching any light switch, do you?' Kathleen asked Matilda.

She shook her head anxiously. 'No, I definitely didn't touch any.' They were still looking up when a shadow passed across the ceiling in the living room.

'Well there's definitely somebody inside,' said William as he reached into his pocket, 'come on we'd best go up and see who.'

Once again using her bank card Kathleen successfully unlocked the catch on the flat door, grabbing hold of the handle before it sprang away and announced their entry.

'You've mastered that technique well,' whispered William.

'She could do that when we were at school together,' Matilda replied, 'it would get us back into the gym in the evening where we'd have the whole place to ourselves.' William grinned and raised his eyebrows at Kathleen. Every day he was learning something knew about her. He volunteered to go in first having put on his leather gloves.

'Try not to touch anything,' he advised.

Kathleen scoffed. 'Fat lot of good that'll do us now. We've already plastered the flat in our fingerprints.'

'Well stay close behind.' Putting his forefinger to his lips William gestured for them to be extra quiet as he could hear somebody moving about the other side of the door leading into the living room.

'Do you want me to go into the kitchen and get the rolling pin, I know where Elizabeth kept hers?' Matilda said in a hushed voice.

William rolled his eyes. 'No… a weapon only invites a defensive attack.' He put his hand over the door handle turning it sharply and stepped inside. 'Reg, what the hell are you doing here?'

Kathleen burst through the open space followed closely by Matilda. 'I knew there was something fishy about you!' said Kathleen.

Reg ignored the insinuation. 'And who might you be?' Reg asked looking directly at the man standing before him.

William produced his identity card. Reg saw the badge before he scrutinised the information typed on the card.

'I had a suspicion at the meeting earlier that you wasn't who you said you was. Was the disguise really necessary?'

'Consider it as part of my strategy to get to the bottom of a murder investigation. Now perhaps you would answer my question and explain what are you doing in Elizabeth Marlow's flat?'

'And do you know of her whereabouts?' added Kathleen.

Reg looked first at the private detective. 'No, I don't know where she is and I am as concerned as you to know where.' He looked at William. 'And to answer your question, that is why I am here to see if there is anything here that will take me to her.'

'That doesn't explain the charade and why you've been coming along to the spiritual meetings?'

Reg nodded realising that they were due an explanation.

'Before I answer that may I suggest that we all sit down and put aside all suspicion.'

They each chose a seat whereupon Reg who was closest to William asked. 'I knew that one day my past would catch up with me, but before I divulge who I am and the other reason for my being here so late at night, I need your assurance that anything discussed within these four walls goes no further.' William said that he would honour the request. Reg turned his attention to Matilda and Kathleen. 'And as for you two ladies, it is in your interest to agree as well.'

'Is that a threat?' Kathleen wanted to know.

'Indeed not my dear lady, but matters of importance and possibly national security could be at risk here.' Matilda felt her eyes opening a little wider.

'When I came to your house Matilda it was with a genuine purpose. I did need to have Aunt Maud come through from the other side and tell me what was hidden beneath her patio...'

Kathleen interrupted. 'Well you didn't appear to be very happy with what you found. I know because I watched you raise the slabs and find the wooden box.'

'I know... I saw you watching me.'

Kathleen remained steely eyed. 'How?'

'Because I followed you both to the restaurant and later I knew that it was you when you parked your car at the end of the road. I've been hiding in shadows long enough Miss Lee to know when I'm being followed. I would also suggest that if you decide to stand behind a neighbours rose hedge do so without wearing a gold necklace and pendant. I saw the flicker of yellow metal when the neighbours light came on.'

'Why didn't you make yourself known to Kathleen?' asked William.

'I'll get to that soon enough sergeant, but suffice to say that what I thought might have been in the wooden box was not exactly valuable in momentary terms, but in the wrong hands it could priceless.'

'What are you... a spy or criminal?' Kathleen asked. William was convinced that she had what it took to be good in a police interrogation.

Reg grinned watched by Matilda. 'I've been called many things Miss Lee including a spy and thief, but I assure you that I am neither.'

'Well maybe now is a good time to explain who and what you are?' William interjected.

Reg nodded at the three persons sat opposite and on either side. 'Remember, nothing leaves this flat... is that agreed?' Matilda, Kathleen and William agreed. 'Have you ever heard of The Order of Tintagel Knights?' he asked.

Kathleen responded first. 'No, but it was written on the reverse side of a photograph that was discovered recently.'

Reg smiled. 'That is a start at least. May I ask where it was found?'

'In my late husband's garden shed.' Matilda replied.

'You don't seem very surprised Reg,' said Kathleen, 'and especially as you feature in the photograph!'

'As a junior scout leader, yes I remember seeing the photograph once before.'

'In my husband's garden shed?' asked Matilda wondering when exactly.

Reg soothed her concern raising both palms. 'No Matilda, I saw the article and photograph first amongst the pages of a local newspaper. A reporter did a piece for the paper on the borough scout movement. He came along to our evening meeting, asked questions then took the photograph.'

'So you knew all the scouts in the photo?' asked William.

'Most of them yes.'

'So this Order of the Tintagel Knights what's it about?' asked Kathleen.

Reg breathed out very slowly as he assembled his thoughts. 'A very long time back, long before the crusades of the tenth century there was a secret order of men. A group selected from noble knights and warriors to preserve the secrets of man.'

'But Tintagel wasn't built until mid-twelfth century,' she added. William was impressed by Kathleen's historical knowledge.

'You're right Miss Lee and before that building project took place there were several other names that were used by the Order. Times however were dark and nothing could be taken for granted, there were many assassins around, waiting to unravel the secrets hidden by the Order by whatever means necessary. The Order did all that it could to protect its members, but humans have many remarkable attributes, but torture is not welcomed by any.' Matilda looked shocked as she looked across the room at a framed photograph of Elizabeth in her ski outfit.

'So you're in the Order?' asked William.

Reg felt his heart begin to race knowing that his reply would bring about his possible downfall. 'I am a Regional Protector.'

'Which means what exactly?' William pursued seeing that it had clearly caused Reg some angst to divulge his true identity.

'I'm a high ranking knight and oversee others in the order within my region. We meet in secret, very rarely I hasten to add due to the constant dangers that exist globally.'

Matilda surprised herself when she asked, but she felt it was necessary to know. 'Was my Albert in the Order?'

'Yes, he was a grand knight.' Matilda's jaw dropped as her mouth fell open in astonishment.

'And the others in the scout photograph – Cyril Pringle, Ernest Scott-Jackson, Malcolm Swift and Arnold Peabody, what were they?' asked William.

'All Knights of the Order and they each took their responsibilities very seriously. Being a member of our order is one of the best kept secrets in the world and not just in this country.'

'Exactly how high does this Order go?' asked Kathleen.

'As high as you would imagine Miss Lee. We even have a member of royalty in our Order although you understand that I cannot divulge who of course. There are several government minsters, judges, nurses and teachers. We also have many others, each with a role to offer, engineers, farmers, nurses, police officers and the list goes on and on.'

'That's an impressive membership.' William agreed looking back at Reg. 'So why did you follow us to the restaurant?'

'Because I knew that you didn't trust me, especially you Miss Lee. I too needed to know more and I've acquired a keen nose for suspicion and I can smell doubt in a person.'

Matilda couldn't stop her sudden outburst. 'She was like that at school Reg, always snooping about. Kathleen has a nose for trouble.'

William grinned. 'Really... it's a trait that's stayed the distance by the looks of it.'

Matilda wanted to know more. 'My Albert, a grand knight, that sounds important and yet he was nothing special, merely a civil servant. Albert was a peace loving man who enjoyed tinkering about in his shed, making homemade wine and football.'

Reg endorsed her sentiment with a nod. 'Albert was indeed a peaceful man, but none the less he was an important member of our Order Matilda and he had control over at least fifty knights in the surrounding Home Counties.' Matilda looked impressed as she placed a hand over her chest in admiration.

'So what was it that you expected to find under the aunt's patio?' William asked knowing that Kathleen was about to ask the same question.

'A long list of names.'

'Containing what exactly?' Kathleen wanted to know.

'An important list... and undoubtedly a valuable asset. You see that list contains the whereabouts and possibly names of our rival group, the Hashyshan.'

Kathleen's expression changed. 'An ancient order of assassins from around the twelfth century made up of Syrians, Turks and Persians. I read about them when I was at university.'

Reg was impressed as was William and Matilda. 'Your studies serve you well Miss Lee.'

'And the Hashyshan, do they still exist,' she asked, 'only it was my understanding that they had disappeared, disbanded after the ruling authorities had executed most of its members?'

'I am sorry to say that it does, through the sons of sons and so forth. Down the centuries the reign of terror has never been far from our door and strong family ties within the Hashyshan has seen their treacherous tradition of terror remain as a warning to the civilised world.'

Matilda suddenly jumped in her chair as a cold shiver passed through her body.

She apologised. 'I am sorry, but something dark and definitely evil walked through me. Usually the spirits of the dead give comfort only not this time. This presence was the very essence of everything bad.'

Reg agreed and he advised accordingly. 'We should all be extra careful and vigilant after tonight, danger lurks from every shadow.'

'That's cheerful to know,' added Kathleen. Reg however was unmoved by her stance.

'Like me and my fellow defenders, their Order is made up of ordinary people, but listen to me when I say that they are anything but ordinary, they are highly trained killers.'

'Did they kill my Albert?'

The expression on Reg's face changed as the lines softened. 'It is very likely that they did Matilda. I am so very sorry.' Matilda was grateful for his honesty.

'And the others, Albert's fellow scouts what about them, did they come into contact with the Hashyshan?' asked William.

'Obviously I have no definite proof regarding any of their deaths, however based on what I know about the Hashyshan it could be that they were instrumental in their demise.' William noticed that Reg had chosen his words carefully.

'And is there an estranged wife on a Greek island Reg?' asked Kathleen.

'Yes, Abby is my wife.' Reg looked directly at Matilda. 'I owe you an apology dear lady. It is true that I have not seen my wife for some time now, but she is there with a purpose in mind although I am not quite sure what exactly and the fisherman is a cousin. For all I know she might have changed her name or her appearance.'

Matilda nodded understanding. 'Hence the urgency to establish from Aunt Maud what was hidden under her patio?'

Reg smiled. 'You are very perceptive Matilda and you possess similar qualities to that of Albert. He would have been proud of you.' Reg paused and took in extra air to fill his lungs. 'Abby held the rank of Court Messenger in our Order, I suppose you would call her a latter day secretary. At some time and even I am not sure when she changed her allegiance to that of the Hashyshan. She has become a very dangerous woman within their organisation.'

'And where does Elizabeth fit in with all of this...?' asked Kathleen.

'Elizabeth is a knight in our order. She keeps records of our secrets, coded locations, names and dates. I am really worried about Elizabeth as she has not been seen or heard of in weeks.'

'It was Elizabeth who I saw in my vision at the spiritual meeting Reg.' Reg closed his eyes as he contemplated the worst.

'Do you know where Elizabeth kept the records?' William asked.

'We did, but they had been moved. We hope by Elizabeth as she updated certain pages. The missing ledger is a great concern. That is why I came here tonight hoping that I would find either the ledger or a clue as to where I might find it. The ledger of secrets is greatly sought after by the Hashyshan. Abby knew that it existed, but her rank did not permit her to know where it was kept. It is imperative that I find the *Book of Records* and keep it safe.'

William rose from his seat. 'Then I suggest that we make some coffee and we begin looking around. After tonight perhaps you and I Reg can get together our heads together regarding recent events and see if we can make some missing connections.' Reg agreed that it was a good idea. 'And please call me William and let's dispense with the formalities.'

'Is your name really Reg…' asked Kathleen, 'it's not Sir Galahad or anything equally romantic?'

Reg grinned. 'Nothing as gallant I'm sorry to say, it is as I told Matilda and just plain old Reginald Augustus Symion Smith.'

'Just one more question,' asked William, 'have you any idea what was in Malcolm Swift's shoulder bag besides his digital camera, books of contacts and notepad?'

'Malcolm was a very pro-active knight in the Order and he used his position as a freelance journalist to keep us abreast of current events locally and up and down the country. He was also useful knowing journalists abroad. Some mysteries although investigated never reach the tabloid press due to government pressure or state security measures. Malcolm would delve deep and find out why. His was one of our most important field intelligence officers. What was in that shoulder bag could very well contain a wealth of knowledge. To the Hashyshan it would be like opening up a treasure chest. Malcolm had close contact with Elizabeth and together they would let us know if danger was coming our way.'

'We have probable motive,' Kathleen said, as she flicked through a large volume of a world atlas. William and Reg both agreed as Matilda entered the room with a tray of coffee. 'Black I'm afraid as there is no fresh milk in the fridge and she was also short of biscuits in the cupboards.'

Reg was quick to volunteer. 'There is an all-night store down at the corner, I'll pop down and get us some it won't take me no more than five minutes to get there and back. My stomach has been rumbling like an express train all evening.'

'Do you want me to come too?' asked William.

'No, you stay and protect the ladies Sergeant. I will only be a few minutes and I need a new packet of cigarettes.'

Chapter Eighteen

'He's been longer than five minutes,' said Kathleen checking her watch.

William went to the window to see if he could see Reg. 'Yes he has,' he replied William, 'too long. I'm going down to check on this corner shop.'

Kathleen closed the drawer that she had been rifling through. 'I'm coming with you. Matilda you stay her and guard the fort. You can let us back in rather than my having to keep using my credit card.'

'Oh okay...' Matilda wasn't keen on being left by herself, but she saw the sense in her staying behind. Her next thought had her grab Kathleen's arm. 'Hang about, how will I know it's you on the other side of the door and not some assassin from the Hashyshan?'

'You'll know it's us if you look through the letterbox!' They left with Matilda adding the security chain.

'Is she always this nervous?' asked William.

'More or less. She's been worse since Albert died.'

'That I can understand. I don't suppose hearing about the Hashyshan from Reg helped any. Matilda's probably doing the sums right now and adding up that Albert and the others were killed as a result of their allegiance with the Order.'

'The way Reg described them, they'll stop at nothing to get what they want.'

William didn't reply. There was no need and they both knew that stopping at nothing to succeed meant death to anybody who stood in their way. When they arrived at the all night supermarket they were surprised to see that there was nobody inside except the shop assistant who was playing with his mobile phone stood behind the counter.

William stepped back outside scanning in either direction. 'That's odd and we didn't pass anyone on the way here.'

Kathleen's suspicions were immediately elevated. 'Odd in that he tells us who he is and why, then does a runner.'

William wasn't convinced and ready to give Reg the benefit of the doubt. 'I'm not so sure. I got the impression that Reg had a great deal on his mind and wanted to offload to somebody.'

'Okay I get that, but why us?'

William gave a shake of head as he thought why. 'Maybe the burden of being the protector has become too great to bear and Reg needs help, perhaps a way out. Just because he is protected by the Order doesn't rule him out from being depressed, suicidal or suffering another form of mental anguish.' They were on their way back to the flat when William heard what sounded like a moan. 'Did you hear that?' he asked.

Kathleen pointed ahead. 'No, but I saw a cat run across the road ahead, something startled it.'

Once again a low agonised moan came from the other side of a nearby privet hedge, they ran around to find Reg lying on his back clutching his chest. Even in the shadows they could tell that he had been stabbed and that Reg was in a bad way. William instantly reached for his mobile phone.

'Stay close to me...' he advised, 'this wasn't a random attack.'

'The Hashyshan...' Kathleen replied as she stood up to look at the street which appeared deserted. In the background she could hear traffic noise, but nothing else. She knelt down again alongside William as he finished talking to the emergency services. 'Reg doesn't look good.'

William agreed. 'No, he doesn't.' He suddenly leant down much closer to Reg. 'He's trying to say something, but the blood is clogging his throat, help me support him.'

Kathleen did as she was asked noticing that the sleeve of William's shirt was already smeared with blood where he had removed his jacket. Seconds later she looked at William having heard Reg struggle to say something. *'He's trying to say Matilda.'*

Instantly William was on his feet. 'Stay with Reg until the police and ambulance arrive Kathleen, you'll be safe and they'll be here any minute now.' With that he was running back in the direction of the flat.

Kathleen supported the injured man's head as best she could, but the life was draining fast from Reg and his eyes were already beginning to stare at the night sky overhead. A moment later Reg went limp as he closed his eyes and accept eternal sleep. Kathleen gently lay his head on the front lawn wiping her hands on the uncut blades of grass. 'I am really sorry Reg, I guess none of us should ever judge a book by its cover.'

Kathleen stood up as the ambulance rounded the corner and came to a halt where they saw her waving. Several marked police vehicles followed lighting up the adjacent properties with their flashing blue lights. Kathleen took her identity from her jacket pocket and stood aside for the paramedics to do their bit.

'Detective Sergeant Jenks called it in. He's already searching around for the perpetrator.'

She didn't want to tell them that he might be back at the flat, not until they'd had chance to check through all of Elizabeth's personal effects. Having heard in which direction Jenks had run, two of the three marked units attending quickly followed.

*****

Back at the flat Matilda heard the sirens. Rushing to the window she saw the blue lights illuminating the street a short distance from the junction. Down below she saw a man running towards the service road of the flats. Her first thought as she backed away from the window was that the shadowy figured belonged to the Hashyshan.

Having exhausted her search of Elizabeth's spare bedroom cum study Matilda went to the kitchen to look for something heavy to use as a weapon. She was searching the floor cupboard when she suddenly felt very heady, the feeling inside her scalp a mix of fear and something that she had felt recently. She held her hand to her brow believing that she was going to faint. Seconds later she lowered her hand and turned holding the pastry rolling pin in her free hand as instinct told her that somebody or something was standing behind her.

The figure moved towards her. *'For goodness sake Matilda do close your mouth that was always a bad habit of yours.'*

Matilda Closed her mouth then promptly opened it again. 'Elizabeth, it was you that I saw in my vision.'

Elizabeth sat herself down at the kitchen table. 'Well who else do you think it was, Greta Garbo and will you put that rolling pin down. Who was you expecting a deranged escapee from the local mental institution?'

'No...' Matilda replied taking the chair opposite, 'although when I felt somebody standing behind me I did think it could be an assassin.'

'You've been talking to Reg.' Matilda nodded.

'They killed Albert and the others.' Elizabeth momentarily closed her eyes in a gesture of sorrow before she opened them again. Matilda continued. 'I never would have imagined that you could be involved in anything so dangerous.'

Elizabeth laughed. 'Some days, the events that took place would have made your toes curl Matilda.' She let her eye lids flutter before going on.

'Although the end of my life could be best described as premature. That I regret, but if I had to choose I would do it all again. It was exciting besides worthwhile.'

'But all those secrets Elizabeth, it must have been very dangerous. Wasn't you frightened, I'd be petrified.'

'Sometimes, but so were many others. I was a calling that I had to fulfil and of course there were the men. Such brave and valiant knights.'

'Including my Albert.' Matilda stopped the rolling pin from moving as she moved catching her knee on the leg of the table. 'Along with Ernest, Cyril and Derrick, and we think Harold Harrison, not to mention Reg Smith.'

Elizabeth's eyes were full of sorrow. 'Alas poor Reg has sadly joined our ranks here tonight on the other side.'

Matilda felt her jaw drop once again. 'He went to the corner shop for milk, a packet of biscuits and some cigarettes. Kathleen and William have gone to make sure.'

Matilda watched as Elizabeth gave a shake of her head. 'Reg is no longer in your world Matilda. He fought his attacker in the street below valiantly, but the shadows that move do so quickly and without warning. They are skilled in the art of death.'

Matilda clutched her chest. 'Kathleen and William, are they okay?'

'Yes, Kathleen is with Reg and the other, the policeman is coming back to you make sure that you are safe.'

Matilda kept her hands on her chest. 'Am I in danger Elizabeth?'

'Not this night you are not, but you should be cautious Matilda. The Hashyshan move only ever in the shadows. You will neither see nor hear them until they are upon you and the first that you will know is when you feel their breath on your neck. They also have a quest which as yet remains unfinished.'

Momentarily Matilda was unable to react. 'But, I know nothing of your secret organisation, the Order of Tintagel Knights or about my Albert being a grand knight what could I possibly tell the Hashyshan that they don't already know?'

'You possess an extrasensory perception that can communicate with the other side. This interests the Hashyshan and they could use you to help fulfil their evil destiny. For centuries now they have been trying to destroy our organisation, murder our members and unravel the secrets that we hold hidden safely away.'

'Are they always so violent, can they not just come to a compromise?'

Elizabeth rubbed the back of her neck as she replied. 'They are not only assassins, but skilled in the art of medieval and modern torture.'

Matilda felt the excess saliva drop down the back of her throat. 'I'll bear that in mind.'

Elizabeth lent closer. 'I came to speak with you this evening Matilda because I need you to do something... something very important.'

'Yes... what?'

'I need you to take down the framed painting covering the safe and put the grandfather clock in its place. The Hashyshan must never find the safe.'

'Alright, I can do that although I must tell you that I can't find Albert's key to the safe?'

'I know, Albert put it somewhere where nobody would suspect it would be hidden.'

'But the deeds to the bungalow are supposed to be in the safe, so are my jewels.'

Elizabeth grinned. 'Albert gave me a message to tell you that the bank manager has them.'

Matilda felt her head droop as she left forth a sigh. 'At least they're safe.' She removed her hand covering her bosom. 'How did you die Elizabeth only your neighbour the one with mauve tints said that you were in Jerusalem on some sort of pilgrimage?'

'That's right and you could describe it as a pilgrimage of sorts, but the Hashyshan had me cornered shortly after leaving a bar one night where I had met one of our Israeli members. He managed to slip the net and escape their trap, but I didn't know the area well enough. I got caught.'

'Did they hurt you?' Matilda asked expecting the worst.

'Surprisingly no... well not really. After they dragged me to a disused warehouse they drugged me with Sodium Pentothal, a truth drug. What they didn't know was that I had been taking a muscle relaxant for pains in my back which resulted in an aggressive reaction between the two drugs. My heart couldn't cope and so it stopped beating much to the annoyance of the Hashyshan. They never got the chance to torture me or have me reveal any of our most treasured secrets.'

Matilda was both saddened and relieved. 'I am sorry that you're dead, I will miss you, but I am so grateful that they didn't get the chance to hurt you.'

Elizabeth smiled. 'Thanks.'

Matilda felt her heart suddenly beat fast. 'Albert and the others they were killed by the Hashyshan weren't they Elizabeth?'

'I'm afraid that they were Matilda. You see for centuries the mysteries surrounding the secrets of the ancient world remained unknown to mankind, but our eminent members, scientists, physicists and mathematicians helped to unravel each, one by one. What they discovered could even to this day destroy nations overnight, perhaps bring about the destruction of mankind. The Hashyshan would welcome this apocalypse whereby they could begin again and rule the world. They are an extremely ruthless group who are desperate to get their hands on the hidden secrets, each one recorded in the Book of Secrets. Long has the Order kept them safe, moving the book to a different location every so often and only a handful in the order know where. Albert was one such knight who knew, but he told the Hashyshan nothing before he died.'

'My Albert was so brave. Why he only worked for the civil service in the...' Matilda pulled up short the realisation suddenly dawning upon her.

'Yes…' continued Elizabeth, 'in the National Archives Department. Ideally placed where Albert could keep track of important movements concerning archived records, items of national interest and some never to be disclosed state secrets. From a young boy Albert had already been chosen by Reg to join the civil servant and the order.'

'You mean Albert, Ernest, Cyril and Derrick had all been recruited by Reg when they were in the scouts?'

'Yes… young boys showing adventure and promise always make excellent knights.'

There came a sudden and anxious knocking on the front door of the flat as William arrived. Remembering what Kathleen had said about looking through the letterbox he bent down and raised the metal lid. William called out trying to keep his voice down low although with enough momentum to suggest the urgency and attract Matilda's attention. *Matilda, hurry up and open the door… it's William!'* He sounded like a puffing steam train that was running out of steam as he had been running hard and then climbed two flights of stairs. He was relieved to see her walk down the hallway towards him. Removing the security chain Matilda pulled the door open and stepped aside as William entered, checked the landing then closed the door again.

'Who was you talking too?' he asked.

'Elizabeth Marlow, only she went as soon as she heard you at the door. I already know about poor Reg Smith. It was the Hashyshan, they got to Reg before he had chance to escape.'

William nodded and agreed. 'They'd be top of my suspect list.'

'Is Kathleen safe?'

'Yes.'

'Did Reg suffer?'

William was surprised that she had asked. 'He was stabbed in the chest, but I think his main concern was elsewhere knowing that death was creeping up fast.'

'Elizabeth told me how the Hashyshan torture their victims before they kill them. That's why I asked. They used a truth serum on Elizabeth only I can't remember the name, but it sounded like sodium penthouse.'

William grinned. 'I think you mean Sodium Pentothal.'

'Yes, that was it. They injected poor Elizabeth with it, but the reaction with medication that she had been taking for a bad back gave her a heart attack. She died before they could extract any information from her.'

William began to smile, but he thought better of it. 'That was very sad that she died and so young, but at least the Hashyshan didn't hurt her.'

'That what I said.'

'Did Elizabeth say anything else, anything significant?'

'I asked if Albert and the other men had been the victims of the Hashyshan. She believed that in all probability they had each met their fate at the hands of the assassins.'

William placed his hand gently on her shoulder for reassurance. 'After seeing Reg Smith tonight, I am of the same opinion Matilda.' He looked at the doors on either side of the hall. 'Have you found anything yet?'

'No, just lots of books, but most of them have been written in Latin although it's all double Dutch to me.'

'We might need to come back another day, preferably when it's a lot lighter and maybe bring along some officers to stand guard at the door. Right now I think we should turn out the lights and secure the flat then go find Kathleen, she'll be wondering where we are.'

'She can handle herself,' replied Matilda, 'she has black belts by the dozen or at least two that I know about.' William grinned to himself as he pulled the door shut. Martial arts had never interested him, but Kathleen might need it if the Hashyshan came visiting.

Chapter Nineteen

The man knelt down on one knee before the woman with his head slightly bent forward as a mark of respect for her recognised status. His right hand was flat across his chest.

'And you are completely sure that he had nothing on him?' the woman asked.

'No my lady, I checked twice. There was no book.'

Abby walked around the kneeling man.

'Maybe on this occasion Hashem you were a little too hasty in your actions.' She placed a hand on his shoulder standing behind him. 'Although I do not question your loyalty as you have proved your worth to the Hashyshan on many occasions and I can forgive you this one discretion. Another opportunity will present itself soon. Maybe we should pay the medium a visit and seek her help and if her meddling friend intervenes, deal with her as you see fit.'

Hashem lifted his head to let her see his smile. 'Thank you my lady. There is also a man, a policeman I think.'

Abby exhaled long and hard as she gathered together her thoughts. 'What is it with these fools, we eliminate their number and yet others immediately take their place. You would have thought that killing all five would have sent a message and that our quest for the book should be taken seriously.' She walked over to the window staring out at the passing traffic and pedestrians. 'Do whatever is necessary Hashem only let them live until we have a chance to extract what they know. Maybe from this latest trio we will know the location of the book.'

'Very good my lady... is there anything else?'

Abby moved away from the window to face Hashem. 'Will you need any help?' she asked. She looked directly into his eyes which were focused upon her, his expression impassive and only his eyes grew more intense. Behind his stare she recognised a flicker of indignation.

'Not this time my lady, but it is kind of you to consider the risk that I take.' Hashem stood, lowered his head once again then left the room. The discussion was at an end and he had his orders. Soon he would deliver all three to her.

Abby watched him leave the room and very quietly pull together the large oak doors. The church had once seen many visitors serving as a place of worship, but long discarded by the church authorities it had been acquired through an agent and was now the headquarters in London of the long forgotten Hashyshan. Absorbing the wondrous moon beyond the window as it masked her face she stared up at the glowing orb feeling that at last they were getting close.

'Soon we will grasp what is rightly ours. Destiny will be ours as written. Soon we will rule this planet and eliminate all who oppose us.' She raised both arms and let the white light absorb her completely.

Standing the other side of the door the assassin could hear her chant echo in the empty chamber. Turning silently away he walked towards the outer door. It was not right that a woman, a lesser mortal should be giving him orders, Not right that he should take all the risk and he despised living under the roof of an old English church. One day soon however he would be the one in charge and then things would be very different.

Chapter Twenty

Sharing a bottle of wine in preference to coffee, the three of them sat around the kitchen table thinking over the events that had taken place that night. Kathleen was the first to break the silence.

'Losing Elizabeth and now Reg, this has just become a lot more sinister.'

'That makes seven dead,' Matilda added, 'and each one we knew. I can feel their souls shivering through my bones as they wander the afterlife wondering about their sacrifice.'

Sipping his wine William was pensive.

'The Book of Secrets seems to be the ultimate prize in this case. A prize that the Hashyshan will kill for, using any means or method at their disposal.' He looked at the two women staring at him. 'What...?' he asked.

Kathleen spoke again. 'Do you remember when I first came to see you William, you had a nagging feeling in your gut that these murders were linked and yet you had neither the evidence nor the reason why to connect each case, well now we know why and Matilda has made the connection through Elizabeth and Reg. Recent deaths were made to look like an accident to keep the Hashyshan secret. How many others down the centuries have they killed I wonder and more recently though the decades. The Hashyshan come and go as quick as the moon can hide a shadow. Even I feel wary about their presence.'

'They've certainly become more dangerous,' William agreed aloud. 'I will have installed a personal attack alarm in both of your properties. At least then I'll know that you are safe.'

Kathleen pulled aside the clasp of her shoulder bag pulling from within a commando knife, a metal knuckle duster and a small tin of mace spray. She laid them out on the on the table top.

'You should be carrying the same whenever you leave the house,' she advised Matilda.

Matilda looked shocked. 'I wouldn't be seen dead with the armoury you carry around with you.'

'You will be dead if you don't...' Kathleen replied. 'If I'm stopped by the police I have a legitimate reason for carrying each. The knife I have to help cut somebody free from a seat belt in a serious road traffic collision and the knuckle duster in case I have to smash a window to save life or limb.'

'And the mace?' asked William picking up the knife and examining the blade.

'It has proved very effective time and time again with seriously unhinged guard dogs.'

William shook his head incredulously. 'Cutting through car seat belts and smashing a pane of glass to gain entry wouldn't wash in court or with a judge and jury.'

Kathleen laughed as she picked up the wine bottle topping up their glasses. 'It has before now so why not again.'

'When exactly?' William asked as Matilda lowered her eyes in disbelief.

'I was attending a Christmas dinner and dance last year and dressed to the nines, wearing a short above the knee evening dress with stockings and suspenders. Halfway through the evening I spotted a man on the far side of the room, a slippery customer who I had been on my case load for over three months. When he left he must have sensed that he was being followed because he started to run. Well naturally I gave chase and eventually three stone lighter than him I caught up with him. He was handed over to the police, but he claimed that I had assaulted him in the chase and threatened to kill him. The case went to court.'

William was hiding his smile behind his glass. 'And...?' he asked as Matilda took a gulp of her wine.

'The assault as he claimed was when I threw my high heeled shoes at the back of his head. It was a good throw and they caught the side of his head causing a small cut just behind the ear. The threats to kill were a figment of his imagination, pure fabrication. The knife that I took from my bag was for my protection and to help persuade him that he needed to give himself up to the police.'

William looked amused. 'Do you always take a commando knife and a tin of mace to a Christmas dinner and dance?'

'Have you ever tried repelling the amorous advances of a drunken wolf after a night of free drinks and a flash of cold blue steel next to the goolies soon sobers them up quicker than a cold shower.'

'That is why she didn't get asked out a lot when we were teenagers,' added Matilda. 'Boys used to think that we were the odd couple.'

William stopped sipping his wine. 'Why...?'

'Because she would go around with a flick knife hidden down the side of her knicker and going through the punk era I had my hair cut short down one side.'

William grinned. 'I would never had thought of you as an anarchist.'

'I wasn't. It was more peer-pressure and the fact that my dad's cutters slipped when mum was trying to style my hair.'

'And Albert, did he like your new look?'

'He was a practicing skinhead at the time.' Matilda replied.

William looked puzzled. 'Practicing, in what way?'

'We'll he liked the doc martins, the rolled up bottom jeans and the red coloured braces, but he was torn between Billy Idol and David Bowie so he had his hair shaved at the sides and left spiky on top.'

'He looked like an aggressive Sonic to me,' Kathleen added.

William was amazed. 'But back then, he was a Knight in the Order and looking after the nation's interest.'

Matilda shrugged her shoulders. 'I didn't know that, but I guess the Hashyshan wouldn't have given him a second thought or look, dressed like a punk.'

Kathleen giggled. 'If Edward Heath had sported a spikey top rather than his normal pushed over from one side look then perhaps the Hashyshan might have noticed Albert.'

'All the same it was hardly inconspicuous.' William took another sip looking at the two women. 'Although I suppose in hindsight,' he went on, 'it was a genius disguise. Who in their right mind would think that a punk rocker with orange hair could really be a Knight of a secret Order keeping safe the treasures that they had hidden.' He paused momentarily. 'And the others were they Bowie fans by any chance?'

'Come to think of it, they were except Ernest who liked Marc Bolan and had like him a mass of cork-screw hair.' Said Matilda thoughtfully remembering when they met over the park. 'The boys formed a band called *Saracen's Revenge*. That they would practice generally on a Tuesday and a Thursday at the local church hall then perform at gigs on a Saturday or Sunday evening. They were quite good and had a following. Ernest was the lead singer.'

William nodded. 'They had an apt name. Have you got that photograph handy of the scout troop?' he asked.

Matilda fetched the photograph from a shelf in the larder where it was hidden behind the bread bin. 'Are you looking for anything specific?' asked Kathleen.

William studied the faces of the other boys and senior scouts. 'I'm looking for anything unusual. Have you got a magnifying glass Matilda?'

She returned with a large convex glass handing it to William. 'I can't find anything better. At one time Albert collected stamps, but he got bored with all the foreign duds and so he sold some of his collection taking up carpentry instead.'

'I would like to look through any albums that he did collect and you have left over.'

'Why,' inquired Kathleen, 'are you thinking of becoming a philanthropist?'

'No, but stamps are a good source of sending information and what you see in the movies isn't far from the truth. Microdots hide a multitude of sins.' William scanned the photograph carefully looking at each individual. He pointed to one particular member standing at the back, three away from where Reg Smith was standing. 'There...' look at that lad,' he pointed so they could see, 'he has a darker skin than the rest and he definitely looks oriental.'

'So did a quarter of the school,' added Kathleen.

'I agree.' He turned the lens of the magnifying glass so that she could see as well. 'But, look at the interest shown by the foreign lad who is turned sideways and looking at Ernest Jackson.'

'But he could have been distracted by something at the side of the room.' Kathleen argued.

'I agree, but to me he looks like his focus is set on Ernest and not the others. I would dearly like to know who he is...'

Matilda asked for the magnifying glass so that she could look. After a few seconds she looked back up. 'He was in our year group at school. Do you remember him Kathleen, his dad owned the tailors shop around back of the High Street.'

Kathleen took the magnifying glass and scrutinised the boy's face. 'I remember it... Mustafa Fashions and you're right... Musty as he was known was in our year.'

'Musty Mustafa, are you sure that was his name?' asked William.

'Yes, only it was Mohammed Mustafa, but everybody at school called him Musty.'

'Why?'

Matilda answered. 'He always seemed to have chalk dust in his hair. When the boys played football they would shy away if he went to head the ball in case they got showered with dust.'

'Do you know what happened to him after he left school?'

Matilda nodded. 'He joined the post office as a postman.'

Kathleen flicked her forefinger and thumb together loudly. 'Where he could keep track of correspondence going in and out of the country.'

'Precisely.' William agreed.

'So he would know everything,' Matilda piped in, 'everything that Albert and the others had received and handed to Elizabeth.'

'That's about the size of it.' said William. 'Do you know if his father still owns the tailors?'

Both women shook their heads and Kathleen took up the story. 'No, old man Mustafa died a couple of years back. Another of his sons took over the business, but they trade mainly in wholesale stock now, buying and selling Middle Eastern artefacts. It's like going into Ali-Baba's treasure trove when you enter the Mustafa Emporium. The smell of incense alone is intoxicating and you must know the one that we mean. The staff are nearly always out back in the courtyard where they have a small coffee business and lots of treacle pastry. The air is thick with either essence of spices or apple hubba bubba pipes.'

'A Shisha Hookah,' William corrected.'

Kathleen nodded enthusiastically. 'You smell it walking past the emporium sometimes. It smells like camel dung, pure sh...' she didn't get chance to finish before Matilda quickly intervened. 'Would anybody like a piece of fruit cake only I'm feeling a little peckish?' she asked. They both said that they would so Matilda left the room to go fetch it.

'And she doesn't keep the cake in the kitchen?' William mumbled to Kathleen.

'No, Matilda stores her cakes in tins and outside in the old coal shed where she says that the cold brickwork helps keep the cake ingredients that much more moist and fresher.'

After five minutes of her leaving William checked his watch putting it to his ear to make sure that it was still ticking. 'She's been gone a long time just to fetch a cake?'

They pushed back their chairs rushing from the kitchen to find the coal shed door wide open and the cake tin lying on the floor where it had been dropped. There was no sign of Matilda.

Kathleen still had hold of her commando knife. *'I'll kill every last one of the Hashyshan, if they harm Matilda!'*

William did a quick sweep of the garden checking the darkest corners and behind tall bushes, but she wasn't there. He was relieved that she wasn't having found Reg behind a privet not far from the corner shop. 'She's definitely not here,' he said returning, 'let's check inside, just to cover all options.' William looked around upstairs whilst Kathleen checked the ground floor. They came together at the bottom of the stairs where it was obvious that Matilda was not on the property. William was about to call the station when Matilda's land line telephone started to ring on the hall table. Kathleen grabbed it answering on the second ring.

'Hello!'

A foreign voice spoke into the mic at the end. 'I will not repeat myself so listen very carefully.'

Kathleen however was incensed. *'If you hurt my friend, I will find you and hurt you more!'* William took the receiver from Kathleen before she made the caller angry.

'This is Detective Sergeant Jenks. What have you done with the owner of this property?' his voice was controlled and calm. He could hear the calling breathing into the mic.

The caller replied. 'It is good that I talk to a man. Where I come from women are considered inferior and not worthy of making important decisions. I would rather negotiate with a man.'

With her ear glued to the receiver Kathleen wanted nothing more than to reach down the line, drag the owner of the foreign voice back and beat him senseless using her knuckleduster. William shook his head to indicate that it would not help.

'What do you want?' William asked.

'The book, only the book.' The caller requested.

'Book... what book?' William thought it best to stall for time and play the innocent.

'The book containing the records of course. The Book of Secrets that Reggie Smith was looking for when he left the flat to go to the shop to buy cigarettes.'

'Did you have to kill him?' Kathleen cried out standing next to William.

'He would not help. He refused to answer any of my questions and my mistress... she is ruthless, she demands answers and quickly.'

'So you answer to a woman. That must be difficult knowing your culture?'

There was a momentary pause as the caller contemplated the inference, choosing his response carefully. 'One day she will no longer be in charge and I will look after our needs here.'

'Here, meaning London?' William inquired.

'Yes.'

William put his hand over the speaker. *'At least we know that she's not that far away and that she is still in London.'* Kathleen smiled and responded with an encouraging squeeze of his arm.

This time the caller was insistent. 'So the book… you bring it to me and then I let the woman go, yes?'

'The thing is we didn't find the book. We didn't know that it existed until earlier this evening. We don't even know what it looks like or where it could be hidden.'

Hashem wasn't interested in excuse. 'You have twenty four hours to find it. I will call you again on this number tomorrow night at the same time. Have it in your possession, or else I will hurt your friend.'

'Wait…' said William, *'how do we know that you've not murdered the woman already?'*

Hashem placed the receiver next to Matilda's mouth. 'Hello Kathleen…' was all that he permitted her to say before it was hastily pulled away.

'Now you know that she is unharmed for the present. Twenty four hours or she will not survive to see the dawn of the next day that I promise you.' The line went dead and William replaced the receiver.

'He's gone.'

'What are we going to do William the Hashyshan are trained killer. They will mercilessly torture poor Matilda and she can't stand the sight of blood let alone her own.'

William was drumming the top of the telephone. 'First we need to have a trace put on this phone and then we should think about obtaining a book.'

'But we don't have the Book of Secrets.'

'That's right, bur our kidnapper doesn't know that. First thing in the morning we need to visit the public library and I need to speak to the librarian.'

'I doubt they'll be a member of the Order and remember the clock will be ticking.'

William seemed confident that he had a plan. 'A library is full of books Kathleen and many more archived that people never get to see or read. There has to be some underground stockroom that is old and dusty where we could find ourselves an old looking book, one printed in Latin and which would take days to decipher. If we had such a book that we could hand over, it would give us more time to negotiate Matilda's release and prevent her being hurt.'

Kathleen threw her arms around William's waist and hugged him tight. 'Thank you and we should move the grandfather clock as well.' She pulled back, but didn't let go. 'Matilda is built for comfort, not speed, so if we do succeed and rescue her don't bank on her running fast.'

'So I've noticed.'

Kathleen found his lips and kissed him. 'Will you stay with me tonight please? I know that I am well prepared for any eventuality and armed to the teeth, but neither my black belt nor the certificate in survival training will count for a lot if some determined assassin climbs in through my bedroom window.'

William smiled as he kissed her again. 'In which case we had best lock up here, leave out extra cat food for Ermintrude and head to my place hoping that they're not already there.'

Chapter Twenty One

When the woman walked across from the shaded corner of the room Matilda looked up. She was astonished to find that her head felt heavy resting upon her shoulders where she had been sleeping whilst unconscious. Adjusting her eyes to the hazy light where a single shaft of sunlight was streaming in through a dirty window she was aware of a hand reaching forward to hold her chin in a vice like grip.

'I always find it irritating when women snore in their sleep.'

'I only do that when I am nervous,' Matilda replied, 'at least that was what my late husband would tell me.'

The woman disturbingly stroked her forefinger along the underside of Matilda's chin then coursed down between her cleavage making Matilda follow, her eyes opening wider as the other woman's hand stopped.

'Am I going to be physically abused like what happens to sex victims in horror films?'

The woman laughed out loud. 'Not unless you want that to happen.'

Matilda's bosom went up and down like a spluttering engine piston. 'Not particularly, but I thought it was important to ask... that was all.'

The woman took her hand away. 'I would have thought that it was more important to ask why you are here and what we intend doing with you.'

Matilda tried flexing her fingers, but her wrists had been bound together behind the chair back. *'You're Abby aren't you?'*

The woman had stopped pacing back and forth in front of Matilda. 'I take it that Reg has told you everything?'

'Not a lot.' Matilda lied. 'Was it you who killed him?' Abby was surprised at how cool Matilda was taking being kidnapped and held captive.

'No, it wasn't me personally. I no longer besmirch and get my hands dirty if I can help it. I have others to undertake such task. My role here is to think things through and delegate.'

Matilda stared at Abby, her gaze full of loathing. 'Did you give the order to have my Albert killed?'

Abby looked to a corner of the room where it was dark. 'Do you miss him Matilda, do you miss your knight in shining armour?'

Matilda replied angrily. 'Of course I miss him, Albert was my husband.' Matilda changed tact. 'What was it that you buried under the patio at Aunt Maud's?'

●

Abby grinned in response. 'So Reg did tell you some things. I replaced a list of the protectors with a note of my own. Annoyingly though the list wasn't just written in Latin, but it has an encryption that has yet to be broken.'

Matilda afforded the moment a smile. 'So how did you know about my Albert?'

Abby pulled up a chair from the side of the room before placing it before Matilda the back rest set forward. She leant forward resting on her forearms. 'This way you cannot kick out at me and I can demonstrate that at present you are in no danger.' Again she looked towards the darkened corner. 'We had our people follow Albert day and night. Eventually with your husband's help we made a vital connection and knew a lot about all five men that were involved. We in the Hashyshan know them as the protectors although you probably know them as The Order of Tintagel Knights.'

Matilda could feel the blood coursing through the sinews in her arms. She wanted to break free and strangle the woman sat opposite her.

'My Albert was a good man, a decent law abiding citizen. He stood proud for injustice and he would help those who needed help the most.'

Abby smiled as she gave a shake of her head to indicate that she disproved of Matilda's unwavering loyalty and love. 'Some of his moral stands could be judged to have been misguided in the wake of those members that he followed.'

'You mean keeping the secrets of the world safe. I would have thought his life worthwhile and to oppose evil.' Matilda was frustrated and the room appeared to be getting hot and stuffy as she noticed dust particles drifting aimlessly in the air accentuated by the sunlight. She did wonder if her last remark had sealed her fate.

Abby repositioned herself on the seat of the chair as she considered Matilda's reply.

'Evil can be described best as wrongfully immoral. We seek to make a better world, whereas your husband and his knights defended old practices, kept ancient secrets that in themselves could be judged to have been inappropriate. Time alone changes Matilda and so do opinions.' Abby rubbed the underside of her chin thoughtfully. 'I didn't think that we would reach this point so quickly, but now that we have we might as well continue. Tell me, what do you know about such secrets?'

'Nothing. I didn't even know about Albert as his involvement with the Tintagel Knights.'

'Who beside Reg told you about the Order?'

Matilda's thoughts were racing through her head. Telling her captor that Elizabeth had come to her in a spiritual vision was hardly likely to be believed. 'Reg told me... that was until you had him killed.'

'My late husband's demise was necessary. The fortunes of war Matilda and throughout the centuries certain sacrifices have been necessary to maintain a balance. Call it the rules of the game.'

'Not a very nice game.' Matilda added. She thought that she heard a movement somewhere else in the room, but she couldn't be sure because it was so dark in the corners despite the shaft of sunlight.

Abby continued. 'Albert was a Grand Knight in the Order and his position carried a lot of weight, a responsibility unlike some of the lesser protectors. He would have been party to knowing where the secrets were kept and where the book was kept. You've been married a number of years and as his wife he must have told you something about his other life?'

Matilda shook her head quite adamantly. 'No, as I've already told you he went to work, came home and in the evening would have his tea, perhaps spending time pottering about in his shed where he'd tinker about with his wood and tools. On alternate Saturday's he would go football if the team were at home and occasionally he would meet his friends to play snooker and enjoy a pint together. Albert was as far as I was concerned a simple man with simple needs.'

Abby could feel the unseen tension rising.

'And when you thought that he was at football or playing snooker that is when the Order would meet. I have to admire their tenacity, never meeting in any one chosen venue. We have skilled members in our organisation, but even they would lose track of your husband and his friends at times. Nowadays however we use GPS trackers which makes our task that much easier.'

The fact that the Hashyshan had failed made Matilda smile. 'Alas the fortunes of war Abby, but why tell me all of this unless you intended killing me.'

Abby chuckled. 'That as yet has been undecided. Tell me, did you ever go down to his garden shed?'

'No... not many women that I know trespass on a man's private domain and Albert would steer clear of the spare bedroom where I did my sewing and made patchwork quilts.'

All of sudden the figure of a foreign man stepped away from the darkened shadow in the corner of the room. He had something draped over his arm. In the shaft of sunlight Matilda recognised was he was holding.

'I made that quilt cover especially for Elizabeth's bed. It was a birthday present.'

Abby nodded. 'What interests us and what we want know is where you acquire the material from. Was it bought from a store locally, did you get it on line or was it given to you by Elizabeth?'

Matilda frowned wondering why they wanted to know. 'Elizabeth supplied the material and I put it together. She didn't tell me where she had got it from, but I do remember thinking at the time that it was beautiful, woven in silk with an interesting pattern and the embroidery was so skilled. I thought it might have been from somewhere like Florence as Florentine silk can be centuries old.'

'And the inscription in the pattern, do you know what it means?'

'No, it's all double-dutch to me. I just about master my own language.'

Abby reached out and gently ran her hand over the quilt. 'It's Latin although a very old version probably dating back to before Christ and around seventy five BC. We have had our scholars looked at the pattern and inscription. They have deciphered parts, but not all of it.'

Matilda sucked in air, astonished that she had touched something so valuable. 'You mean that there's a secret message hidden amongst the text?'

'Yes.'

'No wonder Elizabeth kept it close by her.'

Abby nodded. 'Precisely. That demonstrates also as to what lengths the protectors will go to protect their precious secrets. Did you make any other quilts for anybody else Matilda?'

Matilda was wry in replying knowing that she had made several in fact including one for Penny Pringle another for Sylvia Burtonshaw, two for Emma Scott-Jackson and even one for Arnold Peabody. On each occasion the material had been supplied by Elizabeth.

'Yes, I did make some others. They were mostly mail order clients and people that I never met. They would send me material in a specific pattern that was desirable to them and other cut-offs were purchased locally from a haberdashery shop.'

Abby stared at the man who had taken to standing close to Matilda. 'That is disappointing to hear. Did you keep a record of the orders and where they were sent?'

'No. I only made the items, Albert liked to deal with the business end of the order. He would wrap them and send them out with an invoice. He was always so much better than me at wrapping our Christmas and birthday presents.'

Matilda turned to look up at the surly foreigner who was staring back at her. Where her hands hand been bound behind the chair back it had exaggerated her chest. It was impossible to know what he was thinking although she didn't like that his dark eyes were intently staring at her cleavage. 'Was it you who killed my Albert?' she asked to distract his thoughts. The man however remained tight-lipped and continued keeping guard.

Abby answered for him. 'Hashem has had occasion to deal with many men and some women in his time. He does not need to know their names, only their movements. He is a loyal and very trusted servant in our organisation.'

'I don't know if he understands, but I don't like the way that he keeps looking at me.' Matilda replied hoping that Abby would connect with her feminine concerns. 'And you mentioned women, what women... do you mean like Elizabeth?' it had slipped out before Matilda realised, but her level of concentration had been hampered by Hashem leering at her.

Abby grinned first at Matilda then Hashem. 'You see, the approach has to be slow like that of a creeping snake before it bites its victim.' She

208

focused solely on Matilda. 'Yes, like your friend Elizabeth, or should I call her the protector of the records. Hashem and others went to Jerusalem to bring her back, but she ended her life before we could talk to her.'

'Torture you mean!'

Abby laughed. 'I can see that some of the things that Reg told you were mere fantasy on his part. We prefer to discuss matters before we have to consider or introduce extreme measures.'

'And what about my life, what is going to happen to me...' Matilda asked, 'will I fall from the window of a building or be pushed in front of a tube train?'

Abby pushed the chair away as she stood. 'You see what I mean. Reg used poor judgement in telling you about our methods. I've not made up my mind what to do with you yet, only part of me believes that you are innocent whereas the other part tells me that you are hiding something. Perhaps introducing a little truth serum will help loosen your tongue.'

Hashem stepped obligingly forward with a syringe, he jabbed it through the fabric of Matilda's dress and inserted the serum into her arm, moments later the room began to spin.

Chapter Twenty Two

The sound of the birds singing outside the window woke Kathleen from her fitful slumber. She had expected to see William lying beside her, but the ruffled sheet where he had slept as badly as her was cold and empty. Swinging her legs out and under the duvet cover she was searching for her underwear when William returned carrying two mugs of coffee.

'Good morning sleepy head, I took the liberty of making us both coffee. I wasn't sure if you'd be awake yet. You've had a restless night.'

Kathleen stretched her arms as far as they would reach ignoring that she was naked.

'You were just as fidgety.' She caught the aroma of the coffee as he put it down beside her. 'Coffee is a good start to the day and I like seeing you first thing.' He leant forward connecting with her lips.

'And I like waking up next to you also.' William sat on the side of the bed. 'Any other time I would get back in with you, but with Matilda's welfare at stake it's a little too distracting.'

Pulling her legs back up and covering herself with the duvet Kathleen nodded although the disappointment was hard to hide. 'I know, but the sacrifices I make in the name of friendship.'

William sipped at his coffee. 'They'll be other times.'

'I hope so.'

They were making small talk and drinking their coffee when with her free hand she suddenly gripped Williams arm.

'What is it?' he asked.

'It's Matilda... I know it.' She put down her mug. 'I felt her spirit walk though me.'

'Is she in spirit?'

'No, but she's drifting... floating.'

William took a wild guess as to why. 'They've probably given her sodium pentothal.'

'What are we going to do?' Kathleen still had hold of his forearm.

'Right now, there's not a lot we can do until we find out where they are holding Matilda. We should get ready and be outside when the library opens. Finding a very old book written in Latin is essential to use as leverage against Matilda's release.'

Kathleen knew his plan was the only option available.

'What if they have an expert who can read Latin, they'd soon see through the deception?'

William was stroking the unshaven stubble on his chin. 'I'm not that far ahead yet, but let's take one thing at a time. We'll think of plan B nearer the time of the exchange.'

'And if we don't?' she pushed.

'Then we improvise taking the Hashyshan by surprise. Something that they would not be expecting.'

Kathleen looked at the clock. It was only seven minutes past seven.

'The library doesn't open until ten during the weekday.' She flicked back the duvet cover. 'Can we at least cuddle up again and work through your plan before we take a shower!'

*****

They were the first in through the revolving door at the library where William had produced his warrant and offered a brief reason why they needed to have the use of a very old book. Suspiciously the female librarian wasn't entirely convinced. 'And can the library guarantee that we would get the book back Sergeant?'

William decided to be honest. 'Probably not Miss Lake, but consider your generosity as the book being used to save somebody's life.'

'And we mean that literally,' added Kathleen.

Virginia Lake tapped away at the computer screen. It had not been the start of the day that she had envisaged when she had left home around nine that morning and walking the short distance to the library. Scrolling down the Latin records she found an archived book that might help.

'Do you have a library ticket?' she asked pushing her spectacles back up the bridge of her nose.

William pulled a card from his wallet whereupon the librarian scanned it through her records. Virginia Lake held onto the card. 'This belongs to a man named Harrison A. W. and he owes the library a two pound fine for an overdue book on bird watching.'

William nodded, digging into his jacket pocket where he produced two one pounds coins. 'Adam is a friend and he asked that if I was passing would I mind calling in and paying the fine.' Kathleen was rapidly becoming impatient with the bespectacled librarian and her time wasting, but William sensed as such putting his free hand in hers. 'I've not got my library ticket with me, but please accept Adams. He'll pay any futures fines on the book we need today.'

Virginia Lake dropped the two coins into the penalty box which was screwed to the desk top. She wrote down the reference number of the book that she had found on the screen. 'I'll be back in about five to ten minutes. It's housed at the far end of the archive store.'

Kathleen watched as the librarian headed for a door on the far side of the public reading room. 'Anymore officialdom and I would have made her see the errors of her ways.' William just smiled. 'And who exactly is Adam W. Harrison?'

'Just a young man that I know. At present he's serving an eighteen months prison sentence.'

Kathleen was intrigued. 'Eighteen months, what for exactly?'

'Indecent exposure.'

'That's sound a bit harsh just for dropping your trousers. Normally it's a shaming in court, a telling off by the magistrate who issues a stiff fine.'

'Adam would have got exactly that, but the lady that he exposed himself to on the day just happened to be our lady mayor.'

Kathleen grinned wickedly as she tried to visualise the moment. 'I bet the po-faced old hag had to hold onto her ticker when she saw Adam's thingy dangling. I should think the last one that she saw was officiating at the starting line of the charity donkey derby last summer.'

William nodded. 'That was where the incident took place. The race was about to start when Adam ran onto the course. It made page five in some of the nationals. His sentence might not have so severe had the magistrate not been a friend of the mayor.'

'Did you arrest him?'

'No, he was picked up by a passing patrol who saw him go into the library.'

'The same day?' Kathleen inquired.

'Later that afternoon. Adam had told the officers that he wanted something to read in the cells.'

'And where is the book now, the one that cost a two pound fine?'

William picked up the library card that Virginia Lake had left on the counter top. 'Back at the station in the property office. We promised to keep it safe until Adam's release.'

'So he knew that he was going to be arrested?'

'Oh yes, Adam likes the publicity and the notoriety. He told Robert Shawhead, the arresting officer that the thrill of the chase excites him and that he can't help himself.'

Kathleen laughed. 'I bet old droopy draws Madge Matthews has the picture of the start of the donkey race framed and hanging on her office wall.'

William didn't say as they saw the librarian coming back with a rather small although somewhat thick looking book. Virginia Lake laid the book down on the counter top and using a duster removed a cobweb.

'You're in luck as previous librarians had not bothered to stick a loan label on the inside of the cover.'

William checked the cover and the contents. 'This is perfect, thank you.'

'Shall I add a comment to Mister Harrison's record to say that he took the book out on loan?' Kathleen smiled at the librarian. 'You're catching on fast Miss Lake.'

Sitting in the coffee bar they studied the content of the book in greater detail. William was pleased to see that none of the pages had been stamped with the library logo. 'This is really good,' he said, 'I think we might just get away with it, at least until we have Matilda somewhere safe.'

Kathleen nodded. 'Do you mean a safe house?'

'We have one that we use. Even some of the officers don't know of its location.'

'Matilda wouldn't leave Ermintrude behind.'

William closed the book and sniffed the cover. It smelt old, musty which was good. 'I'll arrange to have one of our patrols pick her up. Ermintrude will enjoy the long garden and apple trees.'

Kathleen leant forward and kissed his lips. 'Thank you. The book, it does looks old and authentic with its leather cover. For all we know it could have been written a thousand years back. Do you think it'll fool the Hashyshan William?'

'It's all we have to offer.'

They looked at the people passing by the coffee bar knowing that any of them could belong to the Order of the Tintagel Knights or indeed the Hashyshan. Kathleen looped her arms through William's. 'It's scary really,' she replied. 'I've had some dangerous, risky assignments in my time as a private investigator, but I have never come across anyone like the Hashyshan. They're on a completely different level.'

William squeezed her hand. 'Me neither.'

Kathleen suddenly closed her eyes. 'Matilda is sending vibes my way again. I see a large room with a shaft of light coming through a dirty window. She's okay, but her head is spinning. Beyond the window there's a spire of some sort, like a church.'

'In your vision is there anything distinctive, like a billboard, a known building or sounds?'

Kathleen kept her eyes closed. 'No, all is see are birds sitting on the window cill, looking through the glass.' She suddenly applied more pressure to her grip on William's arm. *'There's a woman coming out of the shadows... wait, wait she looks familiar.'* Kathleen opened her eyes. *'It's... its Elizabeth and she knows that Matilda is in trouble.'*

'Has she come to help?' asked William keeping a watchful eye on the other customers nearby who were thankfully engaged in their own conversations. Kathleen replied. 'She's talking to Matilda, telling her to be strong and to fight the drug.'

Chapter Twenty Three

Abby stepped forward to pull open an eyelid before turning to Hashem.

'Just how much sodium pentothal did you give her, she's mumbling incoherently like a babbling young child?'

'The usual amount,' Hashem replied, annoyed that his actions were being questioned.

Abby slapped the side of Matilda's cheeks twice with her fingertips to get a response, but Matilda was already away somewhere else. *'Matilda can you hear me?'* she asked.

Like an automatic clockwork mannequin Matilda suddenly opened both eyes making Abby take a wary step back. She repeated the question. *'Matilda can you hear me?'*

'Albert put the fruit in the freezer after removing the skins!' Matilda replied.

'Forget the bloody apples,' Abby was fast losing her patience, 'tell me where did Albert hide his secrets?'

With a smile creasing her cheeks Matilda responded with a riddle. 'In the safest of places where spiders cannot crawl nor air can escape.'

Abby turned to look at Hashem who could only shrug his shoulders. 'Yes, but where exactly.' Abby asked.

Matilda was still smiling as her eyes tried to focus on one particular point in the room. 'Secrets kept in a safe place, where a safe key cannot be found.'

'What safe, where is the safe?'

'The one without a key.' Matilda mumbled.

'A combination safe?' Abby probed.

'You'd need a stick of dynamite to blow it open, but like the king's men the wall would come tumbling down.'

Abby sighed. 'And where exactly would I find this safe?'

'Where Ermintrude sits in the sun.'

Abby again looked at Hashem. 'Who the hell is Ermintrude?'

'I do not know mistress.'

Abby focused back on Matilda. 'And where would I find Ermintrude?'

Matilda's attention was drawn to a corner of the room where she thought she had seen a flicker of light appear. 'When it's dark, she sleeps under the stars.'

Abby stood, arched her back where recent arthritis had started to cause her problems. She changed her question. 'Why were you at Elizabeth Marlow's flat last night?'

'Because we had a coffee morning arranged, only Elizabeth didn't turn up.'

'Did you go to the flat looking for a specific book?'

'What book, there were lots of books?'

'*The Book of Records, the Book of Secrets...*' Abby replied adding particular emphasis to secrets.

Matilda felt her head was less fuzzy. 'No. Like I told you, we went because we were concerned for Elizabeth.'

Standing behind Hashem where neither the assassin nor Abby could see her Elizabeth smiled at Matilda, she was doing well under pressure.

Once again Abby brought her question around to Albert.

'When Albert peeled the apples before he cooked them, where did he store them, did they go in a pie or pantry?'

The memory of Albert peeling apples made Matilda smile. 'He never added enough sugar. I was always telling him another spoonful otherwise they'll be sharp.' Matilda looked at Hashem. 'As sharp as an assassin's knife.'

Abby sighed long and hard, the stupid woman wasn't playing ball and her answers were confused. Soon she would let Hashem and the others deal with the clairvoyant. She was contemplating her next move before she lost all face and respect with Hashem when Matilda rolled her head once then fixed her gaze beyond the centre of the room at seemingly nothing. Opening her mouth she asked a question of her own, not looking at either of them.

'Did he...' she asked, 'only I could never get that damn lid to open, it had a faulty catch?'

Hashem checked around the corners of the room, but there was nobody there. He felt his skin crawl when Elizabeth passed through.

'There is nothing mistress.'

'Then who is she talking with...' Abby asked her brow creasing as she thought hard. 'I've a feeling that we have another visitor present, a visitation that we cannot see and from the other side.' Immediately Hashem drew a closed knife from his pocket and flicked it open. Abby held her hand out to indicate that the knife would not be of any use. 'Let her ramble on, we might learn something useful.'

Matilda was still nodding when they turned their attention back to where she was sat. Hashem checked to see that her bonds were still secure.

'Somewhere cold, yes...' Matilda continued. 'And Ermintrude knows you say. I bet she does, the little devil.'

Abby looked at Hashem. 'The mortuary attendant... of course. He would have had access to many cold fridges. You should go there later when there is nobody about and check the insides. Pay particular attention to any hidden panels. A mortuary would be an ideal place to hide secrets.' The assassin nodded accepting the task.

Elizabeth spoke to Matilda. *'Concentrate hard Matilda and channel all your thoughts across to Kathleen. She is with William and she can hear you. Tell her about the freezer. She'll know what to do.'*

Abby whispered something in Hashem's ear and moments later he left the room.

'Concentrate hard Matilda,' Elizabeth begged. *'The assassin has orders to look at Cyril's place of work, but soon Abby will think through other possibilities and she will consider looking in the freezer. Kathleen and William need to get there before the Hashyshan.'*

*****

Sitting in the coffee shop Kathleen suddenly opened her eyes wide. Letting go of Williams's arm she reached down for her bag.

'Come on William, bring the book we have to go to Matilda's home.' They ran from the coffee shop and back to where William had parked the car.

'Why the urgency?' he inserted the key in the ignition.

'I'm not sure how much Matilda has revealed under the influence of the truth drug, but she told me through her thoughts that there's something important hidden in her freezer.'

He engaged gear and released the handbrake. 'Like what?'

'I'm not entirely sure as her thoughts were jumbled and I kept getting the feeling that a third party was talking as well. For some reason I keep seeing water although I've no idea why and what water has to do with a freezer.'

'Maybe because somebody turned the power off and everything inside is melting into a pool of water.' He turned left at the junction before increasing speed once again.

Kathleen was shaking her head. 'No, it's not that kind of water... I keep seeing fish.' Checking his rear view mirror he saw a police car turn the last junction and approach them fast. 'I bet Ermintrude could tell us.' He was still watching in the mirror when the blue lights on the police vehicle were activated. Kathleen turned to look as the two tone siren also sounded.

'What are we going to do?' she asked.

'Go faster,' William replied as he depressed the accelerator pedal, 'they'll check the registration and see that the car is registered to me.'

Sure enough a minute later the two tones ceased, but the police driver left the blue light running.

'Good, they've realised that I'm going somewhere in a hurry. Now they'll follow, we could do with some extra muscle in case the Hashyshan are already there.'

*****

'Where's your assassin gone?' asked Matilda as she watched Abby pacing back and forth. The effects of the drug were wearing off and Matilda's head felt much clearer. She liked it that her adversary unacquainted with all the facts. Elizabeth was watching too and smiling.

'He has a little errand to undertake for me, but be under no disillusionment only he will return and depending upon what he finds will decide your fate.'

Matilda stared back at Abby. 'I would have thought that, that had already been decided. You and your organisation are hell bent on evil and destruction. One day the tables will be turned and you'll be the ones facing fear. You'll live an eternity in the darkness.'

Calmly Abby smiled and gently stroked Matilda's cheek. 'You are more plucky that what I expected you to be and neither as daft as I had imagined. None of this would have been necessary had Albert been more co-operative and exposed the whereabouts of the book.'

Matilda retaliated defending her husband. 'My Albert was a Grand Knight in the Order. He would have sacrificed himself before he told you anything. Albert was a chivalrous man.'

Abby came in close so that her face was only inches from that of Matilda's. 'He died as a result of his honour. I respect him for that, but it was unnecessary. You need not do the same.'

Matilda didn't reply, instead she watched Elizabeth follow Abby around as she paced the floor.

'Do you find it cold in here?' Abby asked as she rubbed her arms which had goose pimpled.

'No, not necessarily. Maybe the ghosts of those you have had killed are walking over your grave.'

Abby grinned.

'I admire your bravado and you've certainly more gusto than some of the men in my organisation. I should however warn you that Hashem is an expert at extracting information and he takes great delight in pushing the boundaries of his skills to experiment with the pain threshold of an individual.'

'Are you trying to frighten me?' asked Matilda.

Abby appeared vexed by the reply. The captive was much more resilient than the others even when threatened.

'Frighten you, no I am merely advising you Matilda.' Abby continued to circle in a wide sweep. There was definitely a presence in the room with them both only she could not detect who. 'Our organisation has survived for centuries and in that time we have learnt a lot including the art of torture. Nothing, I hasten to add as crude as used by our forefathers and their cruel methods, but modern adaption is just as effective. Nowadays we like to inflict pain using a power drill or electricity.'

Surprisingly Matilda leaned forward on the chair in an attempt to show her captor that she was unafraid. 'I'm not frightened of dying and by whatever means. You see... I know that soon enough I'd be with Albert again.' Stood behind Abby, Elizabeth was nodding emphatically, a signal that it would happen.

'And what about your friends, the private detective and the policeman. What if they were both to meet with an unfortunate accident, would that not be a stain on your conscience?'

Elizabeth gave a defiant shake of her head.

Matilda was just as bold. 'She knows how to handle herself and he will see through you. Plans have already been drawn to bring you and your organisation down.'

Abby laughed although it was tinged with doubt.

'Now you do sound like the others. Let's hope that when I make the next call Matilda that your friends have the Book of Secrets.'

Chapter Twenty Four

Both cars pulled up and parked outside of Matilda's home with William and Kathleen immediately exiting their vehicle pleased that they had back up.

'We're really glad that you decided to join us,' William declared recognising both constables.

'Are you expecting trouble sarge?' asked the uniformed passenger as he closed his door.

'Quite possibly only the person turning up is no slouch and will prove to be a formidable opponent. It's also certain that he's a suspect in a murder investigation, quite possibly several in fact.'

Kathleen noticed that they were both armed as one of the officers placed his hand over his holster. 'We're ready and willing, and our glocks can stop most things on the move.'

'Do we have a description?' asked the driver.

'No, but he is likely to be of foreign extraction.'

They removed their firearms and checked that the safety locks were in the unlocked position. 'Okay, we'll stand guard if you want to go on inside.'

William thanked them as they walked down the garden path.

Kathleen led the way. 'We'll go round back only I know where the spare key is hidden.' From under a stack of empty flower pots she located the key noting the disproving look on William's face. 'It was Albert's idea in case he lost his keys and Matilda was elsewhere on a spiritual evening.'

'It's not a practice that I would recommend.' William replied.

'I know, but today it served our purpose.'

She inserted the key only to find Ermintrude waiting eagerly on the other side of the door. 'Hello darling, I bet you're starving. Mummy sent me to feed you!' Ermintrude purred loudly immediately circling Kathleen's ankles. She pointed at the hallway beyond.

'Do you want to go and have a look, you'll find the freezer in the corner of the spare bedroom. If I remember right it used to have a red velvet table cloth draped over the top. Ermintrude liked to sleep on top during the hot days in summer.'

William grinned as he watched the cat watch Kathleen open a tin of cat food. 'Why am I not surprised.' He said as he left the kitchen.

Having secured and made sure that the outside door was impenetrable Kathleen bent down and scooped Ermintrude up into her arms. 'Mummy has got herself into a little bit of trouble at the moment old girl, but Aunty Kathleen is going to get her back and very soon.' Ermintrude purred in response although she was keen to get to her food.

Pulling the dusty red drape aside William found the catch to be difficult and it needed a fair amount of persuasion to pull the lid open. When it did finally relent the lid lifted in a gust of frozen air that hit him square in the face. The contents filled half of the long cabinet consisting of various food items, mainly frozen meat, vegetables and fish.

'What am I looking for...?' mumbled William to himself as he began removing different sized packets and ice cream tubs in which were stored pork and lamb chops, chopped pieces of beef and strips of steak. He was bent over the cabinet side reaching in for the lower packets when a cold shiver passed through him.

William remained bent over the side dismissing the idea that it could have been anything spiritual, but the cool refrigerant escaping between the packaging. When it happened a second time he stopped sorting the packets, straightened up and checked that he was still alone. When it happened a third time a voice materialised in his head. '*I am looking,*' he replied, '*only I've no idea what I should be looking for...?*' The voice inside his head told him to look for the key.

Sensing that he was not alone he turned quickly armed with a bag of frozen chips. Standing in the open door way was Kathleen.

'Is that the best you could find to defend yourself with, what was you going to do beat the intruder into submission with a bag of Harrison Farm's finest potato chips?'

William dropped the bag onto the table alongside the freezer. 'It was the first thing that came to hand.' He tapped the side of his head. 'I was sorting this lot when a voice came into my head. I'm supposed to be looking for a key, only I've no idea where it could be.'

'Are there any packets of fish inside?' Kathleen asked.

'Yes, several packets of plaice, cod and haddock... even a whole salmon why?'

'Look at the fish William. Albert was a keen angler and he would take his fishing equipment with him anytime that he and Matilda had a weekend away.' William dived back into the freezer and removed everything that he thought represented fish. Nearest the bottom of the chest he grabbed the salmon by the tail and hoisted it onto the table, it was a big fish and very heavy.

Kathleen stepped forward to admire Albert's catch. 'That's a beauty, an Atlantic salmon and by my reckoning almost a metre long.'

'How do you know?' asked William.

'My dad used to take me fishing when we went on holiday to Scotland.'

'And this would come from Scotland?'

Kathleen smiled remembering the good times that she had spent wading thigh deep into a river with her father. 'Almost certainly and on the west side of the lochs.' She pulled aside the clear wrap covering the fish before taking her knife from her pocket where she inserted the blade into the belly where it had been sliced clean by Albert.

'What are you doing?'

'Albert would have cleaned the salmon before it was frozen, I'm just ticking off every possibility.' Applying pressure to the frozen flanks she managed to prise the fish apart. 'Here help me William. Keep the flanks open while I feel around inside.' A moment later a long chrome key fell from inside the fish. Kathleen was elated as she picked it up. *'Bingo... well done Albert, you crafty old bugger.'* She gave the key to William. 'I do believe that this will fit the wall safe.'

Standing alone at the junction of the road where the hedgerow was thorny enough to conceal his presence Hashem peered through the glass window of a nearby parked van. He saw the marked police car and the two officers standing guard outside of the house, his frustration growing, annoyed that his mistress had taken so long in extracting the information from the big chested woman. Had he interrogated her, it would have only taken a few minutes. Twice now his mistress had sent him on a fool's errand and he was beginning to suspect that she was trying to disgrace him and turn the other members of the organisation against him. Hashem took another look realising that it would be foolish going anywhere near the house not last until the police had gone.

Holding the key between his forefinger and thumb William was thinking out aloud. 'We should really rescue Matilda then be present when she opens the safe only there could be something inside that is personal to her, not us.'

'I doubt that,' Kathleen replied, 'Albert wasn't exactly the romantic type.'

But William was insistent. 'Ignoring his feelings, I still think that Matilda should be the one to open the safe.'

Begrudgingly Kathleen accepted that William was probably right. 'So what now?'

'I've a strange feeling that we won't have to wait long for another call from the Hashyshan.'

Chapter Twenty Five

Hashem ibn Muhammed stood before Abby his head bent low once again mainly so that she could not see the contempt in his eyes.

'That was unfortunate and extremely inconvenient,' Abby replied as her fingertips drummed frustratingly along the back of the chair occupied by Matilda, 'not only for us, but you also Mrs Barron. Now we will have to adjust our plans.'

Unable to stifle the yawn that was coming Matilda felt that the combination of the drug and the stuffy air wasn't helping.

'I'm not entirely sure myself what was stored in the freezer only I've been on a diet for the past two months and barely touched any meat or ice cream.'

'So what now mistress?' asked Hashem impatiently. Abby was surprised by his interruption, but she was deep in thought as she paced the floor so she let his outburst go unanswered. Later she would talk to him about why. Collecting her thoughts together she faced Hashem.

'If they have possession of the book then they will want to make an exchange, the woman for the book. If not they will plead for more time. How much room do we have spare in the deep freeze?'

Unconsciously Matilda's licked her lips as the sodium pentothal had made her a little peckish. Abby grinned as ran her fingertip beneath Matilda's chin. 'I wasn't implying that we were about to cook you a meal. I was only inquiring if we had room on the meat hooks for another body.'

Matilda swallowed the saliva that had amassed at the back of her throat. 'Well is there any chance of a cup of tea or a coffee, only the inside of my mouth feels like a hedgehogs arse after it's been foraging amongst the leaves all night long looking for overweight oily slugs.'

Hashem moved towards Matilda, but Abby was swift as she reacted catching hold of his arm. 'Check on the facilities downstairs first and then come back, I want to have a little girl to girl talk with our hostage... then after that you can do what you want with her.' Hashem slipped away into the shadows as Abby pulled the chair close to where Matilda was sat.

'Hashem has a foul temper at times and it's a mistake to goad him.' She stroked Matilda's cheek with her fingertip. 'You know I only married Reg so that I could get close to Albert and the others.'

'Is that why you had him killed.'

Abby chuckled mainly to herself. 'That decision was made easy for me only you see he was a mere pawn in my game. I knew that Albert and Reg worked together in the same office, on the same floor in fact.'

Suddenly a memory emerged, switching itself on in Matilda's head.

'Of course... the Christmas party. I remember now and I knew that I had seen Reg somewhere before only I don't however remember you being there?'

'I wasn't there, I was in Greece taking part in a manhunt. We were chasing down one of your husband's precious Knights, a fisherman in fact who had uncovered an artefact in the caves of Melissani.' Abby stopped stroking. 'You see it was rumoured that he had found the secret elixir of the nymphs.'

Matilda mocked. 'That's a myth written by Aesop and sold as a children's stories. A fable for bedtime reading.'

'Is it, how can you be so sure Matilda. A good many legends and myths, why even some nursery rhymes hide different messages about ancient secrets. The more innocent the message the harder it becomes to believe. Let me tell you a secret. The nymphs although not immortal lived to a very great age somehow keeping their youthful looks. If we could discover where the elixir is hidden, we could put it to good use. Think of how many bottles we could sell on the black market, why the profits alone would fund our organisation for years to come.'

Once again unnoticed by Abby, Elizabeth was present. *'What she tells is the truth Matilda. Many methods have been used to protect our secrets and some text was even written into children's nursery rhymes. Some of the authors were also past Knights of the Order.'*

The expression on Matilda's face suddenly changed. 'Why are you telling me all this... I've been dragged here by your thug, drugged and you've blatantly paraded around in front of me knowing that I could easily recognise both your faces and I now know who killed Albert and his friends. None of which bodes well for me. And now you begin telling me what secrets you have been searching for around the world. Aunt Maud doesn't want anything to do with you, she despises you!'

The thought of her elderly aunt made Abby smile.

'Ah yes, dear old Aunt Maud, she had to go too. You see she had been a suspicious old crone for quite some time and we would volunteer to use her place when she was away on one of her many cruises. Think of her bungalow as a second home, only the daft old bat annoyingly came home much earlier than expected from one particular voyage suffering from a bad stomach bug. Walking into her bedroom she found Hashem taking a shower in her en-suite. After the initial shock she was reaching for the telephone receiver when he stepped from the shower and casually wrapped the cord around her neck... you can figure the rest for yourself.'

'So again I ask, why tell me this...?'

'Because Matilda, you have a friend here in the room... somebody from the other side and unless they help locate the book then they will soon watch you suffer and join their ranks.'

Matilda was thinking fast.

'I don't feel anybody here and as you know they have no physical presence anymore. They cannot just latch onto a soul and make them do things against their will.'

Abby stood and began pacing.

'No, I guess not, but that's where you come in. We know that you have a special spiritual gift and that you converse with the other side. You've been communicating with past knights and others in the order, they're on your wavelength. Many who have gone on before you did so taking secrets with them to the grave. Think about the options available to you Matilda. You can either help us find some of these long lost secrets or I let Hashem lose on you. He likes you, I can tell and he will do things that make even me shudder.'

'I see, but what if I can't channel my thoughts and open up a line of communication, it's a two-way thing you know?'

Abby grabbed the back of Matilda's hair.

'Then you will suffer in the capable hands of Hashem and the others. They are not tolerant men and neither do they have wives, family or girlfriends. Assassins are specially picked and trained. They are men who have to find their pleasure in any way possible and you are a young, shapely and desirable woman Matilda.'

'Put like that, I guess my options are limited. I had best get in touch with the other side.'

Abby smiled as she released her hold on Matilda's hair straightening out the strands where she had held them tight. 'Even I sleep with my door locked at night.'

'Don't you have mystics of your own, somebody like Ali Baba?'

'Yes, we have mystics in our Order, but you have such close connections with your husband and probably Elizabeth. The information would be first hand, authentic to use a phrase.'

The door suddenly opened and in walked Hashem with another man, another Arab. Their eyes were dark and their souls full of menace. 'There is room mistress... downstairs!'

'Can I first have something to eat and drink only a medium needs to have energy to communicate only think of me as a radio without a power source, it would die very quickly.

Abby sighed. 'And what did you have in mind?'

'A Chinese takeaway would be good with an extra helping of cod balls.'

Chapter Twenty Six

With her hands untied Matilda eagerly tucked into her plate of food much to the annoyance of Hashem who had been asked to go and fetch the takeaway. When the time was right his mistress would join the other dead bodies hanging on the meat hooks.

Watching Matilda eat Abby made the call. It was answered by William.

'Do you have the book?'

'We do... but firstly is Matilda safe and well?'

'She is currently tucking into a Chinese meal.'

William who had his hand over the mouthpiece of the receiver told Kathleen who smiled. 'Chinese is her favourite, maybe she's just stalling for time!'

He took his hand away. 'Where do we make the exchange?'

'I would like to suggest somewhere public, but as you must realise our organisation has survived for so long by keeping our identity secret. Maybe somewhere less conspicuous, somewhere dark.'

William had an idea. 'There are a few disused underground station around central London?'

The suggestion suited Abby. 'King William Street would be ideal, but you come alone... just you and the private detective, nobody else.'

'How can we trust you?' William asked.

'You've no choice and especially as I hold the ace card.'

'Alright, what time?'

'Ten tonight when it's dark outside and most of the foot traffic had died down that way we can see if you bring backup. If I even smell or suspect that there are armed police about I will kill the woman then disappear into the night.'

William understood. 'You've done this before.'

'Needs must detective.'

'Okay, we'll be there with the book, but I want to see Matilda and unharmed.'

Abby looked across at Matilda whose plate was already half consumed. 'Don't be late William.' She cancelled the call.

Kathleen blew out hard exaggerating her approval. 'I've been to King William Street on a ghost walk, it's a creepy place, dark and full of cobwebs. How did you know about it?'

'I must have done the same walk as you.' He was thinking as he rubbed the stubble on his chin. 'They have obviously used the location before as she didn't suggest another location. The one thing in our favour is that it will be quite dark and will help us when we make the exchange. The shadows will help veil the true identity of the book.'

'I just hope it works.' They both shivered feeling the cold chill that had entered the room. Kathleen held onto William's arm. 'Don't be alarmed, but we have a visitor, a friendly.' William turned around to see a woman standing behind him. He recognised her from the various photographs dotted about her flat.

'Elizabeth Marlow.'

'Yes, that's right and you're William, I am pleased to make your acquaintance.'

She turned towards Kathleen. 'Hello old friend, it seems a long time now since we saw one another last, but I see that you've found the key. Keep it somewhere safe Kathleen where the Hashyshan cannot find it. The real Book of Secrets is hidden somewhere very safe and it's protected day and night. Albert had just come back from making sure that it was safe when he met with his unfortunate accident.'

'You mean he was murdered,' Kathleen corrected, 'we both know that the Hashyshan did it.' Elizabeth nodded. 'Have you been to see Matilda, is she okay?'

'Yes… for the time being, but the Hashyshan want to use her spiritual influence to help them locate the secrets and Abby Smith is personally looking for an elixir to give her longevity.'

Kathleen scoffed. 'Aren't most women only even the expensive perfumes and potions don't seem to work.' Standing alongside William disagreed, he considered her to be beautiful. Reading his thoughts they made Elizabeth smile.

William continued. 'They have asked for a meeting where we exchange the book for Matilda.'

Elizabeth appeared alarmed. *'You cannot give them the book… No not ever!'*

'It's okay Elizabeth, we've acquired an old inconsequential publication from the local library. It'll fool the Hashyshan long enough for us to get Matilda back safe and sound.'

Elizabeth's expression changed as she looked at Kathleen. 'He's not only handsome, but smart as well, you need to hold onto this one Kathleen!'

'There are others?' asked William. Kathleen gave a quick shake of her head. 'No, of course not… well not now anyway.'

Elizabeth grinned, Kathleen with her beauty, athleticism and spirit of adventure had never been any different although she sensed a change in her school friend as she stood alongside William. 'The place that you have arranged to meet the Hashyshan is familiar to them and they have made similar exchanges before in the underground tunnels. Tread carefully as they are devious as well as deadly.'

William acknowledged with a nod. 'I thought as much. Tell me Elizabeth are there hidden service doors along the tunnel, somewhere where they could disappear after the exchange has been made?'

Elizabeth nodded. 'Yes many and railway workers servicing the adjacent line at night would use them. They all exit into the pedestrian walkway above.'

'Are you thinking what I'm thinking?' Kathleen asked.

'Perhaps...' William replied as he refocused on Elizabeth. 'Do the Hashyshan have members of their organisation who work in the police?'

'Yes, many.'

Kathleen uttered an expletive. 'So much for trusting a policeman if you get into trouble, present company accepted.'

'Do they know that we have the key?' William asked Elizabeth.

'Hashem di Muhammed, their most valued and skilled assassin saw the police guarding the front gate. He assumed that you had found something of value otherwise you would not have had two armed officers protecting the property.'

'And the truth serum that they gave Matilda, did she tell them anything important?'

'Not really, but mainly because she doesn't know anything about the Book of Secrets, what secrets are kept safe and where.'

'If they get her to communicate with your lot... can you help,' asked Kathleen, 'can you influence what they want to know?'

'That could be difficult because our rules are strict and that we can only ever tell the truth.'

Kathleen looked surprised. 'You have rules, I thought each day up there was spent walking around some flowery garden or on a park beach talking with a friend whilst listening to music.'

Elizabeth grinned. 'Most days are, but we also have a long list of rules regarding communication with the living. We cannot just influence or manipulate any communication.'

'Oh, I see.'

'If you can tell us what Matilda tells the Hashyshan before the exchange that might help,' asked William.

'Now that I can do. In the meantime please find somewhere safe to hide the key rather than turn up to the exchange with it in your pocket. The Hashyshan are very resourceful.'

Elizabeth then looked purposefully at Kathleen. 'No tricks this evening and remember that these people are trained killers. They come and go like the wind, are rarely seen and have survived years by stealth alone. They will see if you take reinforcements below ground. Now I must get back to Matilda only I should think that she's about finished with her lunch.' With that she disappeared before Kathleen could ask any other questions.

'So where do we hide the key?' she asked William.

'I would have suggested the police station although now I'm not so sure who I can trust there. No, it has to be somewhere obscure, somewhere where very few people go.'

'A cemetery, a church or a museum.'

William grinned. 'Actually I like all three. I was wondering if you had desires on becoming a vampire, only my body is marked all over from last night!'

Kathleen stole a kiss from him. *'Sccchh, only you never know who be listening into our conversation.'*

They put everything back in the freezer except the key which they took through to the kitchen where Kathleen emptied Ermintrude's bag of fresh cat litter grit into a bucket. Putting the key at the bottom of the bag she then refilled it.

'You think that will be safe enough?' William asked.

'Well for the moment yes... until we find somewhere better and you have got to be pretty desperate to put your hand in amongst that lot!'

Chapter Twenty Seven

'I hope you realise that there is no guarantee that anybody will come through and communicate from the other side,' warned Matilda, 'the vibes have to be right and the atmosphere conducive for the spirits to feel confident and safe enough to appear. Anything in the least hostile or unpleasant and they will vanish without trace.'

Abby cleared the room so that it left her and Matilda alone.

'Right, now it's just us two girls. You are free of your bonds and I have no weapons to hand. The only furniture is this table and two chairs. No paintings, curtains or broken windows to distract them, so do you consider this appropriate?'

Matilda nodded. 'We'll soon see if they agree.' She breathed in through her nose and set her mind free of all other thoughts. To help out and show that she was about Elizabeth blew up a small dust cloud from the floor close to where Abby was sat, but where she wouldn't notice. Matilda closed her eyes hearing Abby shuffle about on her chair as Elizabeth came close to whisper in her ear. *'Okay Matilda... she believes in ghosts, now let's see what she wants from you!'*

Opening her eyes and breathing in and out Matilda sucked hard as though she had been startled by an abrupt arrival. 'I have a gathering of souls, although there are so many and none that I recognise, but a mix of men and women.'

Matilda was surprised when Abby asked. 'Is my father among them?'

'I'll ask?' she closed her eyes again rolling her head a little on her shoulders as though turning a radar beacon, when she opened them again

Elizabeth was stood alongside. 'I have a man here in the room with greyish hair, dark in places. He wears bronze coloured glasses and has a scar across the bridge of his nose.'

'Yes, that's him,' said Abby, the excitement in her voice controlled. 'Does he bring a message?'

Telepathically Matilda asked Elizabeth, *'well does he?'* To her surprise there was no reply and the room was very silent. Matilda scanned all around, but there was no sign of Elizabeth.

'Well...' demanded Abby. 'Is there a message or has he come just to mock me?'

'I'm not sure. He... he won't stand still and he keeps moving about. It's difficult when they jump about because it distorts the open channel.'

'STAND STILL FATHER!' Abby ordered. She leant forward towards Matilda. 'Did he...?' she asked.

'Yes, although he doesn't appear to be happy. He keeps looking on either side and behind him.'

'He was always such a fidget when he was alive. Ask him again why he's come through?'

Matilda did as asked and seconds later had the reply. 'He is telling me that there is treachery afoot within your ranks and that you should take care Abby.' This time she leaned forward. 'I think that's why he is so agitated, he senses danger is nearby.' Muttering as though receiving another message from the other side Matilda offered the name Hashem.

Abby sat herself up straight, her eyes set narrow and cautious. 'I thought as such... the treacherous bastard. I've known for some time that he despises me and sees himself in charge.'

Matilda could no longer feel nor see Elizabeth wondering where she had vanished and left so suddenly, leaving her to cope by herself. She wondered if the danger that Abby's father had spoken of would affect Elizabeth as well. She continued.

'Your father, he says that the book is close, much closer than it has ever been before. Soon it will be yours.'

Matilda wasn't sure if it was a message from Abby's father or from somebody else as a second shadow had joined her father. From the outline she thought it looked like Albert although she couldn't be entirely sure.

'Does he know where exactly I can find the book?' Abby stared across at Matilda, her voice unfaltering, kept low, but menacingly demanding.

'Under God's protection.' Came the reply.

Abby's stare penetrated hard. 'Do you mean that the private detective has the book... is she a knight?'

Matilda nodded sensing Albert was close by. She could feel his hands resting on her shoulders.

'Yes, she is a knight.'

Abby sighed. 'At last, tell the old fool that I am done with him!'

'He's gone... he broke the link his end.'

Abby wasn't in the least bit concerned. 'He was always a fool, a meddlesome individual. It was why I had Hashem end his life. Men can be so intolerant when women hold down a position of power. My father had once sat in this chair, once been in charge, but I could see through his faults. I will not make the same mistake.' She reached across and grabbed the back of Matilda's hand. 'Is there anyone else?'

'Yes, a woman... your Aunt Maud, replied Matilda. She watched Abby's head fell forward her chin resting on her chest. Moments later she lifted her head.

'Another old fool. What does she want?'

Matilda listened intently before relaying the message. 'Aunt Maud's message is to say that what you are doing is wrong and that the danger coming your way is to stop you.'

Abby responded by shaking her head from side to side. 'No, the quest will go on until we have unearthed every secret. Other's will take on the undertaking after I am gone, although I intend being around for a very long time. Tell the old crone that unless she has anything constructive to offer she should leave and never come back.'

Matilda watched as Abby got up and checked to see that the door was shut and secured from the inside before returning.

'Has she gone?' she asked.

'No, she has another message.'

'Well go on, tell me' Abby was obviously irritated by her aunt's presence.

'Despite the evil of your quest, she has a duty to protect you both from the afterlife.'

Abby's reply was hardly inaudible, but Matilda managed to catch the name Margaret. Abby composed herself and continued. 'Very touching. Ask her what does she know about the cave of Melissani and the elixir of the nymphs?'

The reply was instantaneous. 'That the elixir is only for the worthy.'

Matilda noticed that the messages were beginning to make Abby angry. 'I am only passing onto you what is passed to me.'

Abby rubbed the underside of her chin looking at Matilda, checking for any signs of hesitancy. 'I believe you. Now ask the old crone about the cave?

Matilda concentrated hard. 'The fishermen, they know where to find the cave,' she conveyed, 'but it was wrong to send the assassin and the elixir has been moved to another location.'

Abby drummed her fingertips on the table top as she gathered her thoughts. 'You are really not as dumb as you look. How do I know that you're not making up these messages?'

'How would I know how to describe your father, about the assassin going to Melissani and the fishermen? The messages mean nothing to me, but they do you!'

The drumming stopped. Alright, carry on, but no tricks.'

Matilda looked startled. 'She's gone... Aunt Maud's no longer there.'

'I am not surprised. When she was alive she would leave a message on my ansa-machine to say that she was at Southampton docks and about to board a cruise ship. Her constant gallivanting about the world would irritate me. Okay, who's next?'

Matilda hesitated as the shadow moved forward. 'A man... he tells me that his name is Malcolm Swift.' Matilda had expected a reaction from Abby, but expression remained unchanged.

'The freelance reporter.'

'He wants me to tell you that it will be centuries before all the secrets are known and long after you are dead.' The last part Matilda did add.

Abby laughed. 'I have survived fire, floods and pestilence. Tell Malcolm Swift that I am not afraid of his lame prophecies.'

Matilda rested both hands on the table palm down. 'Do you not recall the Four Horsemen of the Apocalypse and how they were sent down from heaven by God to patrol the earth. Each horseman representing a punishment for the way in which the people had little or no respect of life, the land and one another. God sent them pestilence, war and famine, and lastly death. The messenger's message to day is that the Hashyshan will suffer such a similar fate.'

Abby scoffed the warning. 'Four horsemen representing the four winds, the four quarters of the earth and a symbol of creation. When we have the Book of Secrets our organisation will begin to rule the earth as it was meant to be ruled, not by weak fools who have no vision, no courage and no direction.'

Matilda wasn't sure if the woman sat opposite wasn't completely mad or simply a misguided idealist, besides a kidnapper, torturer and murderer.

'He's walking away and waving goodbye.'

Abby grinned. 'You mean he knows that what I speak is the truth. And who else comes to advise me?'

'None, they have all turned their backs and leaving.'

'Noooo,' cried Abby, *'tell them to come back... I am not finished yet.'*

Matilda responded with a shrug of her shoulders. 'I am sorry, but they have gone. Three was a good number to have come through today and spiritually represented the body, the soul and the spirit. You should not have been so rude and you would do well to heed the warnings that were given.' Matilda let her head slump forward theatrically to dupe Abby into believing that the link of communication had at last been broken.

Abby stood and went around the other side of the table. 'Are you okay?'

Blinking hard Matilda made to appear that she was dazed. 'Yes, that can happen when they shut down without warning.'

Abby walked over to the window where she surveyed the view beyond the dirty windows. The day was no different to any other day and hordes of people were scurrying to and fro going about their business. Did they she wondered have any idea how many secrets there were hidden in the world, many ancient, some more recent, but how each could change all their lives. She turned around and looked again at Matilda.

'Who else amongst the wives knew about their husbands activities in the Order?'

'None that I know about and I only found out by talking with Reg. Believe me when I say that Albert's involvement came as quite a shock.'

Abby grinned. 'I bet it did. What about that snotty mare Emma Scott-Jackson, the one that struts around most of the time with her nose stuck in the air as though the smell of cow shit wouldn't dare to invade her nostrils.'

Matilda thought Abby's description was almost spot on. 'Emma was always like that although she did tell me once that her haughty posture was due partly to an old injury and had something to do with her neck.'

'And the mortuary attendants wife, what about her?' Abby asked.

'Penny is a sensitive woman and she has her crochet stitching to keep her interested.'

Abby remembered having muttered a name during the spiritual session. It was important that she drew Matilda away from the truth.

'My stick of lipstick in the back of the car certainly had Margaret Buckworthy jumping through hoops and wondering who her husband had been seeing on the sly.'

Matilda moved her hands from the table top wringing her wrists and inviting the circulation to work calmly. 'You put it there on purpose,' she accused.

'Of course I did. Her imbecile of a husband was a complete moron and what woman in their right mind would have wanted to have been involved with him.'

'Margaret loved him.' Matilda answered feeling that she had to defend Derrick.

Abby sat on the edge of the table. 'Tell me, what do you know about Arnold Peabody and Harold Harrison?'

Matilda wasn't in the least surprised that she knew all the names of her spiritual circle.

'Poor Arnold, the man was crushed by the death of Malcolm who was his live-in partner and Harold as far as I know was involved with Elizabeth Marlow.' She stopped massaging her wrists. 'Although now that she is dead there is no way of substantiating their involvement.'

Mockingly Abby smiled. 'The brave Knights of the Tintagel Order, what do you think?'

Matilda responded sensing the anger rising in her chest. 'What Arnold. I hardly think so and as for Harold, he lived with his mum until her recent death.' She hoped that her anger would demonstrate that neither man was of any interest to the Hashyshan.

'That means nothing, not nowadays and many men still live with their parents.' She slipped from the table edge and paced the floor. In fact it would provide the ideal illusion for the Order. Maybe Hashem should pay Mr Harrison a visit.'

Matilda thought it best not to react again. Being over-protective of her group would only arouse suspicion.

Abby stopped pacing near to the window. 'Your silence is intriguing. In different circumstances you would have been a useful member of the Hashyshan.'

'I could never kill anybody, I bury any dead animal that I find in the garden?'

'Including burying the book?'

Matilda could see that Abby was fishing and wasn't quite sure. 'No. As I've already told you, I don't know anything about any book.'

Abby swept aside a cobweb on the window frame as she thought about owning the book, touching it and having the secrets decoded. 'No matter, but it seems that your two friends have possession of it now.' She ran her fingertips down the pane of glass feeling the smooth texture please her imagination. 'In exchange for the book I am prepared to let you go.'

Matilda exhaled slowly. 'Where and when?'

'King William Street at ten o'clock.'

'I've never heard of it?'

'Not many have. It's a disused underground station which hasn't been in service since the turn of the last century.'

'I don't particularly like claustrophobic and draughty, dirty spaces like the underground and I have a fear of rodents which is why I have Ermintrude.'

Abby ginned watching the spider whose web she had destroyed. 'Don't worry Hashem has vowed to stick very close to you.'

Having heard his name mentioned Hashem knocked on the door. Abby unlocked it.

'Our guest here is worried that there will be rats, possibly hungry and foraging for something to eat where we intend making the exchange this evening, but I have allayed her concerns Hashem and promised that you will stay close to her and protect her with your life.'

Hashem smiled leeringly across the room at Matilda. 'It will be my pleasure my lady.' Matilda looked contemptuously back at the swarthy Arab although it pleased him to see that she was both fearful and apprehensive. Hashem liked to see the panic in his victim's eyes as they realised their fate.

'And after our meeting I have another mission for you, one that will require the use of your skills Hashem.'

He rubbed the palms of his hands together eagerly. 'My wish is your command mistress.'

The words used by Matilda to describe the three spiritual visitors that afternoon were still ringing clear in her head, but Abby had indeed survived floods, fire and many dangerous close shaves in the past, coming through all unscathed. She watched her deadly nemesis as he continued to leer suggestively at their captive. Soon she would deal with the assassin and show any in the organisation who doubted her that she still was a force to be respected. And very soon she would have the power of the book within her grasp. And soon after that she would search once again for the elixir at Melissani. There was nothing that she could not possess.

Chapter Twenty Eight

'It's certainly darker than what I remember,' Kathleen announced as she brushed aside a large tangled spider's web that had remained undisturbed for several months. Dealing with some of his own William had hold of the torch.

'I would have thought the dark didn't worry you none.'

Kathleen dug him in the ribs. 'It doesn't, I was just saying that was all.'

William stopped walking, grabbed her forearm, told her to remain where she was and not talk. Ahead of them they could hear a noise like a metallic hinge being forced under pressure. Extinguishing the beam of light by switching the torch off the tunnel was plunged into complete darkness. Kathleen held onto his arm. Putting her mouth next to his ear she whispered.

'That sounded very much like a metal door being opened up ahead. The platform can't be that far.'

'You're right. We should leave it a few seconds and move forward again. Let's see if they're there.

Kathleen squinted. 'There... do you see it William, there's a light reflecting on the bend where the track turns left.'

William saw a shadow move across the reflection. 'That has to be Matilda and the Hashyshan. Come on let's make ourselves known. I wonder how many there will be to greet us.'

'Including Matilda, no more than three or four,' surmised Kathleen, 'too many and it could over complicate the exchange.' They edged forward placing their feet carefully between the wooden sleepers which were strewn with old cans, broken bottles and large stones. Kathleen was glad that on this occasion she had William to hold on to. 'It was never this bad. My guess is that some youths must be using the disused station for smoking their weed.'

William agreed. 'I wonder how they're getting in.'

'Walking the track back from the next live station would be my guess.'

They were almost at the tunnel edge when a figure stepped out blocking their way having concealed himself in a recessed safety hole set deep into the brickwork. The man wore a shrouded mask and only his eyes were visible. As far as they could tell he had no weapons at least none that they could see.

'I made a mistake, make that five Hashyshan,' muttered Kathleen, 'maths was never my strong subject.' The masked man noticed that the man was carrying a rucksack over his shoulder. He hoped that it contained the book.

'My mistress is expecting you, you will please come this way.'

Stepping up onto the platform with their escort walking alongside they could see the group standing near to an exit corridor which had once been used by commuters heading for the escalators. They came to a halt ten feet from the group. Matilda was there, but she had a black shroud covering her head and her hands were tied behind her back. There was another woman amongst the group, she stepped forward.

'You've brought the book?'

William let the rucksack slip from his shoulder. 'We have the book, but first I need to make sure that the person under the shroud is our friend.'

Abby turned to the men either side of the other woman. She nodded and instantly the shroud was removed. Matilda blinked adjusting her eyes to the change of light. She was pleased to see Kathleen standing next to William.

'You should not have come. Albert and the others, they died to protect the secrets.'

'Be quiet,' snapped Abby as she stepped forward and reached out her hand. 'Okay, you've seen your friend, now show me the book.'

William passed across the shoulder bag. Abby pulled the cord free and reached inside removing the book from the library. In the limitation of the light she smiled, the book looked very old and like many hands had touched the cover, philosophers, scientists and even astrologers. Maybe the mystics too had their secrets recorded within. She carefully opened the cover stroking the heavy workmanship of the gold gilded edging of the pages, inside the text was undeniably Latin and written in old script.

'This will of course have to be verified by an expert.'

William sensed Kathleen breathing at his side. 'Naturally, but our part of the exchange has been fulfilled, now release our friend.'

'Before she goes free, tell me where did you find the book?'

'It was hidden in a garden shed,' Kathleen declared.

Abby nodded. 'Ingenious. Kept hidden from the enemy and under the nose of the man whose job it was to keep safe his knights.' She turned to look at Matilda. 'Despite what you think of us and our reputation we honour our agreements. You are free to go.' With another nod of her head one of the men produced a small folded knife and cut through the cord holding Matilda's wrists bound together. As she walked past she stopped and took one last look at the woman who had questioned her.

'You should take heed of what we talked about. Remember what the three told you.' Reikesh stroked the blade of the long handled knife hidden inside his trousers, it was cold and had been instrumental in many deaths. Hashem, his cousin would not have let the woman go free.

'I won't forget,' said Abby.

The trio backed away until William felt it was safe to turn and retreat back the way that they had come only now with Matilda. Watched by Abby and the three assassins the gloomy darkness soon enveloped the two women and the man, and within seconds they were no longer visible, gone.

Holding onto the book Abby turned to Reikesh. 'Have you seen or heard from Hashem?' she asked.

'Yes mistress, his task was successful.'

Abby grinned. 'Good. We let one go, but in her place we take another. Perhaps this will send a message to prove that we move in the shadows and when least expected we can strike anytime or anywhere.' The men laughed. 'Come let us depart before we are seen, I saw it in the policeman's eyes and no doubt there are armed officers in the street's above. We'll walk down the line and use the crowds overhead to escape.'

Reikesh sniffed the air, it was full of treachery, dust and soot. 'Why did you let the woman go mistress, we could have easily dealt with all three and disposed of their bodies where they would not have been found for many weeks.'

'There are occasions Reikesh when letting our enemy go free can prove very useful. Killing a policeman could cause those in our organisation who have infiltrated their ranks problems. No, we can keep an eye on him and as for the private detective, she can fall foul of men with skills such as yours anytime.'

'And the other woman, the shorter woman?'

Abby grinned. 'I've a feeling that she will lead us to other treasures which have eluded us in the past.' The men looked at one another not knowing to which treasure she meant, whereas Abby was hoping that Matilda would eventually take a holiday on a Greek island and search for the cave where the elixir was hidden. Using the crowds of theatre goers and late night shoppers they arrived back at the old church in time to find Hashem guarding his latest victim. Placing the rucksack on the table Abby walked over to the man sitting and bound to the chair in the middle of the darkened room where all he could hear was the sound of traffic going by.

'You've done very well Hashem,' she said to the assassin whose head was bent slightly forward. 'We have our prize, however if it turns out to

251

be a fake perhaps you can persuade Harold here to tell us where we might find the real book.'

Chapter Twenty Nine

Matilda was grateful for the feel of fresh air as a group of both men and women surrounded William.

'Who are they?' she asked.

'Armed police,' Kathleen replied, 'we were hoping to take some of the Hashyshan in for questioning, but William decided at the last minute that it was too risky and would place you in danger.'

Matilda smiled. She saw William point to the exit that they had used as the group headed for the door.

'They'll be long gone by the time they get underground.'

'I know, but at least William can say that he tried. With members of both the Hashyshan the Order of Tintagel Knights in the police force it'll be difficult now knowing who he can trust.'

They're a dangerous lot Kathleen and they'll do anything to get what they want.'

Kathleen grinned. 'We know, that's why William had a small tracker device sewn into the lining of the rucksack. It might work to help pinpoint their base.'

'Thank you…' Matilda said to William as he came back over to rejoin them. 'Are you sure that you're okay?' William asked as he slipped his jacket over Matilda's shoulders.

'Yes, thank you, I'm fine. But you know that they've already gone and disappeared.' She touched her chest to signifying a deep rooted sensation. 'I can feel a shadow already occupying the chair that they sat me on when they were questioning me.'

Standing alongside Kathleen also clutched her chest. 'I feel it too William. My gut tells me that it's either Arnold Peabody or Harold Harrison.'

'How do you know?' William asked.

Matilda looked around at the pedestrians as they walked on past uninterested in their conversation, but finding their presence a nuisance as they occupied the centre of the pavement. 'Because Abby Smith was asking about the members of my spiritual group. She was especially interested in Arnold and Harold.'

'She'd be interested in Harold because of his connection with Elizabeth.' Matilda nodded agreeing.

William was thinking as he guided them across the pavement to stand by the safety barrier. 'I wondered why she was so casual at the exchange. If I were her I would have brought along an expert who could have identified the book immediately. She had a contingency plan obviously.'

Matilda tugged on Kathleen's arm. 'Have you been to feed Ermintrude?'

'Yes and we left her in the capable hands of that nice neighbour next door, Beryl or Betty... I can never remember which?'

'Alice.'

'Yes, that's the one. Ermintrude seemed quite at home when I left.'

'She would be only Alice is always giving her extra little tit-bits when I think that Ermintrude has gone out to get some exercise. I was thinking only recently of putting her on a diet.'

They were about to leave when the team leader of the armed response unit returned from having searched the underground tunnels. 'They're long gone.'

'I thought they would be.' William said nothing about Harold or Arnold. 'Thanks, we appreciate your checking anyway.' They watched as the officers climbed aboard a police vehicle with blacked out windows and moments later converged with passing traffic. 'What now?' Kathleen asked.

'We should make our way back to Matilda's, unearth the key or least give it to Matilda and then she can see what's in the safe.'

*****

Ermintrude was pleased to see Matilda when she walked in through the door although she didn't want a lot of fussing, instinctively knowing that they had come back for an alternate reason and not to just make sure that was fed and safe. William and Kathleen moved the grandfather clock aside leaving Matilda to retrieve the key from the bag of cat litter. Inserting the key in the lock Matilda was about to turn it to the left when she paused.

Kathleen picked up on the hesitation. 'What's wrong?'

'I've been looking all over for this damn key and now that I have it, I need give it a twist, open the safe and all will be revealed. I'm apprehensive about what I might find inside.'

'You'll always be wondering if you don't.' William implied stepping forward. 'Would you rather that I looked.'

To Kathleen's surprise Matilda stepped aside. 'Yes, please, would you.'

William turned the key, they heard the lock click back and a second he had the door pulled open. They were surprised to see that there was nothing inside expect a single piece of white card. William took the card out, read both sides then gave it to Matilda. She looked puzzled. 'What does fifty four degrees north and one degree west mean, along with the phrase *'follow the path of the lord and he will be baptised once again'*.

Kathleen took the card from Matilda and read the hand written text. 'They're map co-ordinates, latitude and longitude. Do you have a geographical map of this country knocking about the place?' she asked Matilda.

'Yes, Albert always kept one in his study.' She stopped and turned in the doorway. 'Come to think of it he would be in his studying looking through the atlas whenever I took him a coffee or tea, morning or afternoon. If I asked why he would close the book and dismiss my question stating that it was nothing more than mere fascination. Now I know why he was looking.' Matilda left the room to fetch the atlas.

They found the page and Kathleen traced the co-ordinates. 'It's somewhere around the York area.' William studied the phrase writing it down again. 'Why are you doing that?' asked Matilda.

'I've found that at times writing something down helps as it can jump back out at you!'

'And does it…' asked Kathleen, 'has anything jumped back at you William?'

William kept on repeating the short phrase. '*Follow the path of the lord.* He certainly walked a lot on his travels so he would have used roads, many being just dirt and gravel tracks used by goats, but whatever their purpose they would help him reach his destination. A road that lead him to somewhere spiritual perhaps.'

'There are a lot of roads in and around York.'

William smiled at Kathleen before he continued with his thoughts. '*And he will be baptised once again.* Back then, between six and three BC people were baptised in rivers, whereas nowadays and here we use a font in a church.'

Matilda nodded eagerly. 'A church, the path leads to a church. On holiday we would always be visiting churches. Albert had a great fascination for them.'

Kathleen tapped the end of her finger on the atlas. 'Abandoned or still in use?' she asked.

'Either or both, it didn't seem to matter. Oddly enough whenever we did visit one, there was always a member of the church there to greet us, a vicar, curate or guide.'

Kathleen picked up the atlas and held it upside down, shaking the pages. 'I'm just seeing if anything drops out,' she replied when she noticed the curious look etched on their faces. 'Albert was canny at the best of times. He obviously thought this through and should he not be around he left us a clue. It would have been handy if he'd just said which place or church, but I guess we have to consider the Hashyshan.' Matilda took back the atlas to look. 'And don't forget that they have either poor Arnold or Harold.' She looked at Kathleen. 'We should sit down and lock thoughts, maybe we can help.' Kathleen sat opposite Matilda as William stood studying the pages of the atlas to see if anything had been marked by Albert, any hidden locations.

'Did your tracker device work?' she asked.

'Our technical department technicians are going through the computers now trying to get a fix. For some reason the tracker keeps shifting about. I'm not sure if the Hashyshan have found it or the rucksack is being used by someone who doesn't know that the tracker is hidden in the lining.'

'Then we don't know where they are being held.' Kathleen exhaled showing her frustration. 'Was there anything identifiable that would help us locate the building when you were a guest of the Hashyshan, an odd or strange noise, traffic nearby or a large clock that chimed on the hour, even the sound of a train whistles... you know what I mean.'

'Only traffic noise and the sound of people walking past below. I think I was on an upper floor as Hashem, that's the assassin, he was asked to go down and check if there was room in the cold store, room enough for another body.'

William who was stroking Ermintrude's neck looked up. 'It sounds like they've been busy!'

'We should use the crystal ball on this occasion,' suggested Matilda. 'It might help produce a location which one of us might recognise.' She went over to the sideboard bringing back to the table a ball wrapped in a mauve cloth. It was the first crystal ball that William had ever seen.

'Have you used it before?' he asked.

'No, although it was purchased from a very reliable clairvoyant who assured me that it would work when called upon.'

William watched as Kathleen and Matilda placed their hands either side of the glass orb linking the tips of their fingers so their combined energy would bring forth a vision.

'Okay... let's focus,' said Matilda. Kathleen smiled and told Matilda that she was ready. Even Ermintrude stopped purring as the energy flowed through the fingers of the two women their combined psychic abilities joining forces. 'It's working... I feel it,' exclaimed Matilda.

William lent forward as the orb began to glow with a blueish light. 'There's something happening... look,' proclaimed Kathleen looking William's way. Matilda continued concentrating as hard as she could.

'There... it's the monument to the Great Fire of London near Covent Garden,' Kathleen muttered, 'keep going Matilda, you're doing great.' The image in the orb stopped moving about coming to a halt at the junction of King William Street.

'That's South Portman Terrace,' William interrupted, 'I recognise that because when I joined the police I had to walk the beat around that area day or night. I remember there being a lot of commercial offices in the area, some that were empty including a church.'

'Which is why the windows are so dirty,' added Matilda. Both William and Kathleen looked at Matilda.

'Can you describe the building opposite Matilda,' William asked, 'I might remember something that is significant.'

Matilda closed her eyes as she concentrated keeping her hands covering one side of the crystal ball.

'I see a building, tall with black stone and many windows. There are a lot of wires going to one side of the building and a sign on the roof. It looks like somebody has painted an aeroplane on the right hand side of the sign and to the left there's a...' she paused allowing her memory to draw the image in here mind, 'there's a beach.'

'That's the Caribbean travel office. Well done Matilda, I'll get the armed response team to visit the premises opposite and if I'm not wrong, that should be the disused church. I'll have a detective go along too and he can contact me directly with what they find.'

Kathleen touched the end of Matilda's fingers with her own making her friend reopen her eyes. 'And what about York,' she asked. 'Any delay in going there could give the Hashyshan the advantage again?'

Matilda suddenly felt the energy intensify and flow through her body.

'I see another building, this time it is a church. There is a woman going inside.'

'Abby Smith?' asked Kathleen.

'No...' replied Matilda, 'a lady vicar perhaps.'

'Right, then we head north and see what we can find.' William let Ermintrude down gently. 'There are enough detectives left behind at the station to deal with any members of the Hashyshan that they find. Our priority is to locate the real book.'

Chapter Thirty

Abby walked around Harold hoping that her constant pacing would make him anxious, make him say something that he was fighting hard not to say. 'You were lovers, were you not?' she questioned her nose almost on his.

'Yes,' he cried back, *'until you killed her!'* The look in Harold's eyes was frosty and full of contempt for the evil woman who stood before him. Behind her was the man who had hit him over the head back at the house.

'You are all so stubborn in the Order, tell me... why is that Harold?'

'Maybe because we have to deal with ugly people like you on a daily basis.' Abby grinned unnervingly. She liked, even admired his pluck.

'You know that she was weak and took the easy way out.' She gripped his upper arm feeling the sinew beneath his shirt. 'You however are that much stronger and you have more fight in you.'

Harold strained forward having the bonds holding his wrists cut into the flesh. 'Untie me and you'll see how strong I am.'

Abby laughed and even Hashem allowed himself a smile. Abby exhaled as she circled once more. 'So besides being her lover what were you with the Order, a Knight, a pawn or just a starter with no responsibilities?' Hashem placed the edge of a long curved knife under Harold's chin.

Harold gulped. 'A librarian... a trainee.'

Abby gave a slight nod and the knife was pulled back a shade, but close enough to inflict pain and injury if needed. 'Good, so you would have documented, kept records of books and the like. What do you know about the Book of Secrets?'

'I have never heard of it.' Harold was quick to reply. Hashem reapplied the knife. 'Okay... okay, I know such a book exists, but I have never seen it.'

'And Elizabeth, I take it that she was your mentor?'

Harold dare not nod. 'I guess you could call her that.'

'And she never mentioned the book or told you about any of the secrets?'

'No... as I have already told you, I was a trainee. We'd not long met before you took her life.'

'You were misinformed Harold. She took her own life rather than face the torture that Hashem had planned for her.'

Harold looked up at the dark tanned man staring fiercely back at him. 'If anything she was brave. He's not the most attractive of men and I would certainly pity his mother.' Hashem drew a small blood on the underside of the chin as a warning. Abby stepped forward quickly to quell his anger.

'You can do what you wish with him later Hashem, but first let us see what he knows.'

Through the darkness Harold thought he caught a glimpse of somebody or something moving in the shadows near to the corner nearest the door, although he couldn't quite make out who or what. 'Who says that I know anything at all of any importance, I am only an apprentice librarian in the Order and as such my level of expertise is still limited. The secrets you mention has not been explained to me.

Abby felt the air was becoming stifled in the room. She could sense Hashem's frustration too. 'Are you so determined to die Harold?' she replied.

With the blade still under his chin Harold was surprisingly calm. 'If that is my destiny then it has already been written. We are only masters of our fate up to a point.'

Abby was pacing back and forth much slower than in the last few minutes knowing that Hashem would inflict more injury soon and he was expecting her to make a decision. 'What is it that makes your order so special Harold that you are willing to sacrifice your own life, after all it owes you nothing?'

'Chivalry, that and keeping the secrets safe. This world is fragile enough without the Hashyshan trying to take over control.'

Hashem immediately slapped the back of Harold's head hard. 'So you do know about the secrets and who we are.' It was Abby's turn to watch.

Harold's expression mirrored his thoughts. 'There is nobody in the order who does not know about you, your treachery, your torture and murdering ways. One day soon your day of reckoning will come and then there will be none of you left.'

Harold's defiance was admirable although stupid. Abby gently placed a hand on Hashem's shoulder before he could deliver another rebuke. 'Hardly the courageous words of an apprentice librarian Harold, more the reproach of a knight or protector.'

'What I am matters not nor the torture that I will endure. I will say nothing that will help your cause.' The figure who had been watching in the shadows stepped forward, Harold smiled recognising Elizabeth. His smile was misinterpreted by Abby.

'What do you find so amusing...' she asked, 'are you not afraid?'

'That is where we differ because we do not fear the inevitable. Death is only a part of our journey as others before me have found out. Passing over to the other side the secrets remain safe. Whatever means you employ, all your efforts are in vain.'

Hashem angrily tore the front of Harold's shirt open swiftly producing a long deep cut across his chest. Instantly the pain like that of red hot pokers searing through his flesh had Harold grit his teeth as the blood began to flow from the wound.

'That just demonstrates what I have said. You are nothing, but a bunch of barbaric amateur butchers. You've learnt nothing down the centuries and you will never find the book. It is hidden somewhere where you would never expect it to be. Your own existence is worthless.'

In her anger Abby gripped Harold's jaw, her eyes blazing. 'I will give you one last chance before I let Hashem do his worst. Where is the book and who knows of its whereabouts?'

Despite the increasing pain and loss of blood Harold laughed hoarsely, the laugh of a defiant knight as Hashem went to work with his knife. Walking to the door Abby was aware of her tenuous position which had been so strong throughout so many years, but she had failed miserably in the past forty eight hours having first let Matilda live and go, and now letting Hashem finish Harold. Taking one last look back she realised that it was time to deal with her enemies within the Hashyshan. At the head of the staircase going down to the lower floor she could hear the echo of Harold's words of defiance as his life began to ebb from his body. Descending slowly she passed two other assassins going up.

'Hashem will need help disposing of the body.'

'Yes mistress.' They lowered out of respect, but Abby felt the contempt in their thoughts as she reached the lower steps.

From the top shelf of her office she took down a small dark bottle with a cork top. From the floor above there was now only silence. Reaching out Elizabeth caught hold of Harold's hand. She held it tight as his life ebbed away and his soul got ready to begin another journey.

'It only takes a few more moments my love and then there is nothing left, but peace. Soon and like me you'll enjoy passing through walls and doors without turning any handles.'

Harold looked back at his body. 'What will they do with it?' he asked.

'They'll likely dump it somewhere extremely dark or throw it into the river. It's their normal practice. The Hashyshan have no respect for anything or anybody. You did very well Harold and like the others you died with honour.'

Chapter Thirty One

Sitting in the rear of the car Matilda suddenly gasped and held her chest, a second later Kathleen did the same.

'Whatever's wrong...' asked William steering the car into the slower lane. 'Do you want me to pull over?'

'No, it's okay keep driving,' replied Kathleen, 'it's just that we both felt it. I think Harold has gone into spirit.'

William glanced sideways. 'You mean he's been murdered like Reg.'

'Yes,' came the voice from the back seat, 'just like all the others. The Hashyshan.' William decided to pull over. He reached for his phone when the vehicle was safely in the layby and made the call.

'Go when you're ready and if you find anybody lurking about who remotely looks suspicious arrest them for anything you consider relevant, just make sure that it sticks and puts them in the holding cell until I get back!'

When the call ended Kathleen was concerned. 'Are you okay, I've not seen you angry?'

William looked behind at Matilda. 'Yes... I'm sorry, I'm just getting a little peeved with these senseless killings.'

Matilda suddenly had another dark thought. 'Regrettably there'll be another before the night is out.' She warned.

'Do you know who and where Matilda?' William asked.

Matilda closed her eyes trying to form a vision in her mind, but nothing came to help. 'No, not yet.'

Kathleen turned around in her seat to look at Matilda. 'The force is very strong with you lately.'

Matilda agreed. 'Stronger than it has ever been, I wonder why?'

'My guess is that it has something to do with Albert and perhaps Elizabeth.'

'How?' Matilda was frowning.

'You see and hear things from the other side more clearly. You are receptive to events that are taking place, like what happened to Reg and now Harold. Your spiritual guide has made you a beacon by which others can find a way over or home.'

William interrupted. 'And you think that has something to do with Albert or Elizabeth?'

'Yes. Matilda was innocent of any involvement in the Order and it was her naivety, her pure heart that helped her survive the fate normally administered by the Hashyshan.'

'Maybe, but Albert and Elizabeth... that still doesn't explain how they helped?'

Kathleen looked back at Matilda. 'Because you saw Elizabeth when you were being questioned. Albert sent Elizabeth to you.'

'How do you know that?'

'Because Albert came through to me while you were being held captive.'

William noticed the look of disappointment on Matilda's face.

'Why didn't he come to me instead?'

'Because Abby had somehow tuned herself into the presence of another being in the room, albeit spiritual. She knew that you was getting help from the other side. She must have some spiritual insight, however

266

limited. Had she believed that Albert, a once Grand Knight in the Order was present she would have made things extremely unpleasant for you until Albert had been forced to give the answers that she desperately needed.'

'And poor Harold, why didn't they help him?' Matilda asked.

William replied. 'Because it is important to keep you safe Matilda. Harold was resigned to die to make sure that you lived.'

Matilda sighed feeling the weight of what had happened thrust upon her. 'Now I feel responsible for his death.'

William placed his phone on the dashboard. 'In a roundabout way we might all be responsible.'

'How do you arrive at that deduction?' asked Kathleen.

'Because inadvertently we might have exposed Harold. Do you remember back at the spiritual meeting where we all thought that Reg was the unknown fly in the ointment, my thoughts now are that somebody else sitting around the table knew a lot more than what they were letting on.'

Matilda looked directly at William. 'You mean like the Hashyshan.' William nodded.

'Well,' Kathleen responded, 'aside from you, me and Matilda that leaves Arnold Peabody, Margaret Buckworthy, Penny Pringle and Emma Scott-Jackson.'

'That's right and call it gut instinct or whatever you like, but they're an odd bunch.'

Matilda was momentarily quiet as the conversation continued between William and Kathleen. 'So which of those four does your gut tell you is the mole?'

'*Margaret,*' Matilda mumbled.

Kathleen asked how and why. 'I know I said that your powers of communication with the other side were on the up Matilda, but that was a pretty quick deduction, even for you!'

Matilda sat forward coming her head coming between the two front seats. 'I suddenly remembered an afternoon from last year when Margaret came to see me. She wanted a spiritual reading telling me that it was urgent, although she wouldn't explain why. I agreed. After an intense hour of communication, the cards and hand interpretation we had a cup of tea and slice of cake. Albert was at work. Margaret had been very curious as to where Albert, Derrick, Ernest and Cyril had met. She wanted confirmation about the scout group and was asking questions about where they had been camping. At the time her questions seemed demanding and I did think them odd, but clients have peculiar needs and requests from time to time.'

'I would have though being married to Derrick, she would have known the answers.' Said Kathleen voicing her thoughts.

'And did they go camping often?' asked William.

'Yes, nearly every month including some colder months when the men would go away for fishing weekends, salmon or trout fishing. Albert and Ernest were exceptional fishermen and Albert would always return home with a basket of fine fish.'

'Or fish that had been supplied by the local fishmonger' added Kathleen.

William agreed and Matilda caught on. 'Oh yes I see your point. Now her questions make sense. Margaret could very well be the eyes and ears for the Hashyshan. The mole.'

'Which would explain a lot.' William said gently pumping his chin with his fist. 'She was friendly with all the other wives and she'd know a lot of the men's movement socially and professionally.'

'There was one other thing William. She lied that afternoon and I felt strongly that it had been a lie. Margaret told me that she had no siblings and yet I saw a sister in my vision.'

268

'A sister like Abby Smith.' Exclaimed Kathleen. William reached for his mobile and told the detective answering to run a background check on Margaret Buckworthy and to check registry records for a family link with a sibling named Abby or Abigail.

Chapter Thirty Two

Abby held the blue tinted bottle up to the light checking that there was sufficient contents inside before she began pouring. She had only just finished when there was a knock at the office door. Throwing a cloth over the paperwork on the desk she invited the visitor in.

'It is done mistress. Abdul and Mejia will dispose of the body where it will not be immediately found.'

Abby was feeling confident. 'That is good Hashem. Soon we will be rid of these infernal annoyances.

'So what do we do next?' Hashem asked.

His abrupt manner was not pleasing and Abby was slightly surprised at how brazen he had become lately. Hashem was almost certainly forgetting his place and becoming more intolerant of hers.

'I was working on that when you arrived.'

Hashem realised his mistake. 'I am sorry mistress, it is just that I and some of the others, we feel that the woman we let go knows a lot more than what she told us. We should have had the chance to explore the possibilities.'

Abby ignored the inference. 'Did you do as I asked and have Zahra follow them?'

'Yes mistress, at present she is following them north along the motorway.'

'Then we know that they are going somewhere. It's my assumption to find the real book.'

Hashem looked around the office it was very spartan, hardly inviting or comfortable. 'You had the book checked that the policeman gave you down in the underground station?'

Abby scoffed. 'It was a book on ancient folklore. I guessed as much, but playing them at their own game will lead us to the real Book of Secrets. Make sure that Zahra doesn't lose them.' Hashem nodded acknowledging that he understood.

Turning to the wine glasses Abby offered a glass to Hashem. 'Here, we should toast our recent successes. Killing can be such thirsty work and occasionally you need something to quench the back of the throat.' She watched as Hashem suspiciously took the glass that had been offered.

'Success mistress, but surely there is more to come?'

Abby sipped her wine. 'Indeed, but so far you have managed to severely disrupt their Order and the ones left are running scared wondering if they are next.' Her confidence and the use of his talents pleased Hashem, he obliged by raising his glass and drinking the wine. It felt refreshingly cool as it slipped down the back of his throat.

Abby watched as the treacherous Arab continued to drink from his glass. He had served her well, but the time had come for Hashem to move on and into the next life. When Abdul and Mejia returned from disposing of Harold she would have another task for them both. Looking to the top of the filing cabinet where she could see the blue bottle, she afforded herself a wry smile. Soon the contents which were deadly would begin to take effect. First came the paralysis, then the constriction of the throat closing down the vital air supply. Death wasn't instantaneous, but long enough to have Hashem know that he was a fool to have ever misjudged her.

Rolling the rounded blue bottle between the tips of her fingers she watched as his glass fell to the floor and moments later clutching his throat Hashem followed landing on his knees. When the authorities found his body near to where Harold Harrison had been dumped, suspicion would land heavily on the assassin. Abby smiled, success took many forms. Raising her glass in toast at the dying assassin she was full of positivity and soon Zahra would call with good news. Taking a step back after Matilda Barron, Hashem had been so blinkered in his outlook. Now she was about to take two steps forward. After dealing with Hashem she would call her sister and ask if she wanted to take a trip north.

*****

'We have about ten miles to go.' Replied William, every so often checking the road behind in his rear view mirror.

'Is something wrong?' asked Kathleen.

'I'm not sure, but don't either of you turn around to look. I think we might have somebody following us only there's a white car, a Toyota several vehicles back that has been with us since we left London.'

'Can you see the driver?'

William took another look. 'Yes, it's a young woman of foreign extraction.'

'The Hashyshan.' Matilda responded sitting in the back. 'I feel them close.'

Kathleen checked her wing mirror just catching a glimpse of a white wing as it moved in behind another vehicle travelling behind. 'You could lose her by increasing your speed,' she suggested.

'No, that would only tell her that we know she's there. I'll let her continue to follow us and when we get close to the York turn-off I'll give the local force a call and have a traffic unit stop her vehicle. They can improvise saying that she has a dodgy rear light, anything that will throw her off our tail.' Two miles from the junction with Askham Fields all three turned to see a marked police car stop the Toyota much to the annoyance of the female driver as she got out from the car. William quickly disappeared taking the boundary road skirting the main city.

'How long will they keep her occupied?' asked Matilda.

'Long enough. Probably ten, hopefully fifteen minutes tops which will give us enough time to be the other side of the city.' He looked sideways at Kathleen. 'Have you got that road map of York handy?'

Kathleen unfolded the map on her lap. 'There are several churches in the area, we would be better off stopping and asking one of the locals.'

William pulled up alongside a pair of elderly ladies, the kind who would attend the flowers for this coming Sunday's service. Depressing the button on his steering console he watched as the electric window next to Kathleen disappeared into the casing of the door.

'Could you help us please?' she asked as the old ladies stopped walking.

'If we can,' said the one nearest the kerbstone, 'are you lost dearie, only you're not from around here... are you?'

Kathleen gave the ladies her best smile.

'No, we're not although we've made a special trip up today to come and see York. I hear that it is a city of outstanding beauty.' She knew that bolstering the praise of their county would satisfy their curiosity. It worked.

'You must find time to see York Minster,' said the other lady not wanting to be left out of the conversation.

'We intend too,' she replied, 'although we are also trying to find a church where my friend's aunt is buried. The trouble is she cannot remember the name of the church.'

The elderly ladies gave Matilda a wave who was sat in the back of the car. Kathleen knew that they would come up trumps.

'The only clue that we have is a short phrase ladies which was written on the back of a Christmas card.'

From his seat William looked at Matilda who had raised her eyebrows and was gently shaking her head in disbelief. William however was grinning admiring Kathleen who was never short of originality. He watched as the two ladies moved closer so that they could both hear.

273

Kathleen waited until they were close enough. *'Follow the path of the lord and he will be baptised once again'*.

The one nearest the car window reverberated a fingertip against her lip as she began searching various locations in her head. Sat in the car Matilda, William and Kathleen waited for a reaction which only took seconds.

'I know...' said the lady standing behind. 'It's St Jutes and the words are painted in gold over the main door of the church.' Her companion was pleased that one of them had found the answer. 'That's right Veronica and if you remember that nice lady vicar took over recently.'

Katherine smiled. 'It certainly looks like we stopped and found ourselves the right ladies to ask.' Her flattery made them both return the smile.

'Is it far from here?' asked William leaning across Kathleen.

'You follow the road and take the third on the left then first right. St Jutes is hidden from sight, but it is the most charming of little churches. You'll see the words over the narthex.'

William asked if they wanted a lift, but the older of the two politely declined. 'No thank you, that is kind of you young man, but we we're on our way to meet a friend for a coffee. We hope you enjoy your visit to York.' They waved their goodbyes immediately engaging one another in conversation about the lady vicar.

With directions to the church it took only minutes to locate. St Jutes was as described a small parish church although with a neatly tended garden at the front and as the ladies had said above the door were the words *'Follow the path of the lord and he will be baptised once again'*. Matilda suddenly took in a sharp intake of breath. 'This is the place, the feeling is very strong. It's like the book is talking to me, calling my name.'

William turned the large wrought iron handle and pushed the door inwards. Stepping inside they were instantly met with a smell of damp.

'Old churches are always like this,' said Kathleen as she pulled the front of her jacket together as she shivered. 'I've never understood why as

274

a place of sanctuary they are so cold and uninviting. I rarely step inside any unless some poor soul is either getting married or departing this world.'

'I'll keep that in mind,' William replied as he walked between the pews to the font which was sited at the side of the altar. 'This font hasn't been used recently,' he pointed to the cobwebs around the basin and base. They turned when another voice joined in coming from the side of the church. Coming towards them was a young woman.

'That's right. My understanding is there is a shortage of babies at the moment and the parents with very young children no longer see that it is necessary to have their offspring baptised.' She came alongside her smile warm and friendly. 'St Jutes doesn't get many visitors during the day, although you are most welcome.'

To save explanations William told her who he was producing his warrant card as proof before he introduced Matilda and Kathleen. The vicar didn't appear fazed by William as she turned to Matilda and Kathleen. 'I sense however that you ladies are not police officers?'

Matilda responded first. 'No, I am a clairvoyant medium and Kathleen here dabbles from time to time. Most of her days are spent following people around.' Kathleen produced a business card and handed it over to the vicar.

'A private investigator, you are the first that I have ever met.' She offered to give the card back, but Kathleen declined.

'No, you keep it vicar only you never know when you might need my help.'

The vicar laughed. 'The good lord protects and watches over me.' Standing behind Kathleen, William grinned. 'A police sergeant, a private detective and a clairvoyant, you make an interesting trio. Are you hunting anybody in particular today or is it solace that you seek?'

'Not somebody,' said William, 'but a book that we believe might be hidden here in the church. Something of great value.'

The vicar spread her arms wide encircling the interior of her church. 'We have but one book that encompasses all Christian churches and St Jutes is a humble place of worship, unlike others in and around the city.'

Kathleen checked looking at the door to see that they weren't being watched or overheard. 'St Jutes is exactly the place where I would hide something if I had the choice.'

Sensing that they did not possess evil intention the vicar outstretched her hand towards a door from where she had first appeared. 'I think you had best come into my vestry where we can discuss this in private.' William agreed that private was good.

Occupying the four chairs in the vestry the vicar introduced herself. 'My name is Jane Kersholt and St Jutes has been my church since the end of last year, can I offer you tea or coffee?'

Kathleen was swift to respond. 'Coffee all round please vicar, each with milk and one with sugar that's for William.'

Matilda who had settled herself into her seat was gently tapping the side of her head. 'You know I remember a Jane Kersholt who went to our school. She was a couple of years ahead of us I think. Don't you remember?' she asked Kathleen, but the vicar replied before Kathleen could.

'I do originally hail from London and I thought that you looked familiar when I saw you standing beside the font. I remember you both.'

She handed the packet of sugar along with a clean spoon to William. 'We don't stand on ceremony here sergeant only normally it is only myself and the verger who use this room.'

Jane Kersholt poured the hot water into the mugs then handed them around. 'And if my memory serves me right you're Matilda Barron, and you married Albert. I am so sorry for your loss. Albert was a really good man.' Matilda replied with a smile.

'Wow... a small world,' said Kathleen sipping her coffee which was good and hot.

William jumped in. 'Did you join the Order straight from school?'

'No, I got my calling while I was at Art College.' William remained silent knowing that the effect would have her continue. 'Now I devote my life to the church and currently St Jutes.'

'We were wondering, is it only God that you serve vicar?'

Jane Kersholt had to be sure. 'I am not quite with you sergeant. The lord is my master, I serve no other.'

Matilda intervened. 'We came to look for a book and on behalf of the Tintagel Knights.' William watched for a change in the vicar's expression, but he saw none in her eyes. Jane Kersholt needed to know more before she could expose herself.

'Did you know about Albert?'

'Yes, although I only found out how he was involved recently. I'm proud that my Albert was a Grand Knight although since his death several others have died tragically at the hands of the Hashyshan.' It was what Jane Kersholt needed to hear. She put down her coffee and picked up the bible instead that lay on the desk top.

'I will require each of you to swear on the holy bible that you have not come here today with only good in your heart. If you do not I will ask you leave.'

William was the first to comply followed then by Matilda and Kathleen who without any warning grabbed the vicar's wrist pulling her forward so that her hand joined her own on the bible.

'And you swear on your holy book that you being here isn't a coincidence and that you have been waiting for somebody like us to come visiting.'

William was about to move in to pull Kathleen away when Matilda grabbed his arm. Jane Kersholt stared directly back into the eyes of the private detective. 'I represent the good lord here on earth. I carry his word to those who wish to listen and I protect his secrets. I am not the Hashyshan.'

Kathleen nodded and let go of the knife in her pocket.

'Well I had to be sure. Jane knew Albert, but that didn't necessarily mean that she wasn't the enemy. We could have walked into a trap.'

Surprisingly Jane Kersholt agreed.

'I heard about poor Elizabeth and more recently Reg. They were both brave souls and they will be rewarded in heaven, but sorely missed here on earth.'

'As will Harold Harrison,' Matilda added as she sat back down. Kathleen never ceased to amaze her.

Jane Kersholt was shocked. 'Oh no, not Harold too. The Order has lost so many good knights of late, none more important than Albert and Reg. Together they were responsible for so much. As yet replacements have not been elected.'

William stirred in his sugar. 'Is there a Master Knight?'

'Yes, although I am not high enough in the order to know who. Only a certain few in the order know his or her identity.' The vicar picked up her coffee again. 'Was you followed here today?'

'We was, but they were detained for a roadside check just outside of York. The woman following won't know that we're here at St Jutes.'

Jane Kersholt picked up her bible placing it in her lap. 'The Hashyshan will not stop until they get their hands on the Book of Secrets which is why we guard it with our lives.'

Matilda was looking up at the wooden cross that was hanging from the wall next to a book case. 'It's here, I felt it drawing me inside when I was stood outside. It was as though I was meant to come here today.'

Sat alongside Jane Kersholt placed her free hand over Matilda's 'Yes, the book is here and you were expected Matilda.'

'I wish somebody would just tell us,' interrupted Kathleen, 'I understand why all the secrecy, but getting a heads up occasionally would help. Who told you we were coming?'

'Elizabeth, the librarian. I am a woman of faith, however in the quieter moments I get visitations from the other side. St Jutes has long been the crossroads of travellers going north and south as far back as when records were first scribed. Beneath the font lies a secret chamber where we keep our important relics, scrolls and other valuable documents. If we feel that the Hashyshan could be getting too close the secrets are moved to another location by the order and the chamber is sealed.'

'That's impressive.' Remarked William.

When they had finished their coffee Jane Kersholt stood up. 'Come with me and I will show you something that very few others see or know about.'

They followed the vicar into a tower room which sat was opposite the vestry. Tied onto six stout hooks were ropes disappearing high up in the belfry above. Jane Kersholt released one of the ropes which she gave to William to hold before she turned the hook sideways. Immediately where a section of the stone wall had been inscribed with the date twelve eighty one the flag stone below began to fall away to reveal a stairway descending down. Kathleen noticed that all round the stone walls had been scratched and inscribed with numerous initials and dates. William recognised the date dug deep into the wall.

'That was during the reign of Edward Longshanks, the king of England. By all account an extremely turbulent time.'

'Your recollection serves you well sergeant. Yes indeed a very unsettled period in our ecclesiastical diary. Such was the uncertainty that existed that the secret chamber was introduced to prevent the king's men from finding what lie beneath the church. Many died keeping the secrets safe.'

Matilda who was looking into the dark abyss below muttered out loud, 'nothing much has changed then down the centuries.'

Taking the torch that sat on the small table in the centre of the room Jane Kersholt turned to look at the trio about to follow. 'I warn you that it can be rather chilly below ground and damp in places so tread carefully. It's good that you're all wearing warm clothing.' She led the way and when they were all at the bottom she pushed up on a lever which sealed the stone slab up top of the staircase. 'It's only a precaution and in case anybody enters the tower room above uninvited.' She tapped a small bell set into the wall. 'If anybody enters the tower room the door opening will activate bell. They won't hear it, but we will. Don't worry the men that built this secret chamber added a second staircase to prevent the guardians from being trapped below ground.'

'Ingenious,' said William admiringly.

The vicar held the torch beam straight and true pointing out the way ahead. 'I hope that none of you are claustrophobic as the passage narrows in some places and headroom is limited in others, although I assure you that the foundations of St Jute have stood the test of time including the bombing raids by the German Luftwaffe when they bombed York during the last war.'

'April twenty ninth, nineteen forty two,' added William again showing his interest of history. He saw Kathleen grinning. 'A keen hobby and healthy distraction from police work.' Kathleen wondered if she was a distraction too.

Shuffling through the narrow passage they eventually came across a solid oak door. Matilda had expected to see it locked, but Jane Kersholt pushed it open wide reaching inside where she flicked a switch and instantly the room was illuminated with several light bulbs.

'One of the Order must have been an electrician and he installed the power otherwise we would have brought a better source of light other than a single torch.'

Surrounding them on all sides were stone shelves each laden with a variety of different sized wooden boxes, sacks and leather document cases. Jane Kersholt spread her hands out wide. 'Before you are some of the world's most important and valuable treasures. Secrets that have remained hidden for centuries in the sake of humanity. If they were ever lost or stolen by the Hashyshan the fallout would be disastrous, possibly apocalyptic.'

'Why here, why keep them in York?' William asked.

'Founded in seventy one BC during the Roman Empire, even then York was deemed an important city, a resourceful divide between the north and south of England. Ecclesiastically it was seen as the northern province of the church. The Roman ninth legion built a fortress alongside the River Ouse and York Minister is built on the very foundations of that fortress. Our foundations are solid sergeant and will stand strong for centuries to come. Hidden beneath the font where life is baptised, it seems apt to keep the secrets safe.'

Jane Kersholt flicked open the pages of a dusty book pointing to a scaled down drawing.

'Seen and recognised as a centre of trade throughout the land, York was awarded a royal charter by King John, and thus the city became an important thriving province that grew in stature as did the number of churches, both big and small. St Jutes is still recognised as one of the smaller original buildings of worship, but with its location near to York Minster and the underground crypt it serves the order ideally. Ignored by tourists and even church elders, we have managed to keep our secrets here for a good many years without attracting any unwanted interest.'

'Do you know where the Hashyshan have their stronghold in Britain?' asked Matilda.

'Here, there... everywhere. It is difficult knowing who is in their organisation as they have so many and even some who have infiltrated senior posts in government, most senior of the public services and they almost anywhere.' Jane Kersholt looked away from Matilda and at William next. 'Including the police.' He told her that he had only found that out himself recently. Moving across to the shelf furthest from the door the vicar moved aside several boxes and from a narrow hole carved into the stone wall she removed a wooden box. Gently laying it down on the table she pulled open the lid and unfolded the cloth protecting the contents.

'The Book of Secrets,' she revealed.

Matilda stepped forward. 'I won't touch it, but can I place my hand over the cover?'

'Of course.' Jane Kersholt moved to the side.

Just as she would perform Reiki with her clients Matilda stroked the air above the book feeling the energy permeating upward. She closed her eyes and felt a coldness climb up through her body as the energy increased.

'What is it?' asked Kathleen coming alongside.

'Somebody from within is talking to me.'

William peered at Jane Kersholt. 'Is that possible?' he whispered.

'Yes, the book has been described as a catalyst for untold energy. Some have even described it as having magical powers. Me personally, I believe that it is the work of the almighty. Contained within the contents is said to be recorded the final resting place of the Arc of the Covenant. Can you imagine what power would be unleashed in the hands of the Hashyshan. It is why grand knights, the keepers and the librarian are such important positions in the Order. As far as I know the Book of Secrets has lay here undisturbed for several hundred years.'

Matilda shocked them all with her outburst. *'The book cannot be moved.'*

'But the Hashyshan Matilda they could be close.' Kathleen replied. 'What if there were two cars following us and not just one. William cannot dispel or plan for every eventuality. A second car might be at this moment sitting around the corner from the church.'

Folding the cloth back over the cover of the book Jane Kersholt closed the lid of the box. 'Then we should put the book back in its rightful place and seal the hole with another stone.'

'Do you know what else is contained within the book,' asked Matilda, 'I ask because I felt many voices wanting to talk to me?'

'From my limited knowledge of the contents, I have been told that explorers with the right co-ordinates would find the lost city of Atlantis, unravel the unique truth regarding the Bermuda Triangle and what happened to the crew of the Marie Celeste. Others would search and find where the Inca's hid their gold and why the Egyptians left a small narrow shaft looking up at the night sky. Was it as many believe so that the soul of a dead pharaoh could join his ancestors in heaven or did the window have another meaning, maybe a link to another outer source that governments try so hard to keep from us. So much is contained with the book that it would take years to decode.'

'Outer space lifeform.' Said William. 'Now that would certainly blow some minds.'

'Indeed yes sergeant or aliens as we aptly name them. Kathleen grinned at William's suggestion of little green men.

'But surely if the Hashyshan did get to the book, the destruction that followed would destroy them as well.'

'Mad fanatics never look that far ahead. They are only interested in total domination of today and the next day. Anything beyond that is deemed reasonable risk and irrepressible.'

'Has it, the book ever been deciphered, translated? Matilda asked.

'Scholars and scientists, many eminent men and women such as Aristotle, Einstein, Marie Curie, Giosafat Barbaro the Italian explorer to name only some have seen the book. Each was a member of our Order. Throughout time there has been much speculation and intelligent argument that some of the secrets are too preposterous to be in the book, but ignorance without fact is a fickle argument. With the invention of technology comes enlightenment and addendums have been added as more evidence is discovered. Fortunately for the Order, our explorers work for the good of all and not just the few.'

Jane Kersholt went and stood alongside Matilda.

'Some of the world's most famous people throughout time have been members of our secret Order although many less known have held very important roles, men like Albert.' Matilda smiled back at the vicar and thanked her.

'So what happens now,' asked Kathleen, 'we know that the book exists, but in order to keep it safe it has to remain here. What comes next?'

'Now you know, you have to become members of the Order. Surely you realised that we cannot let you just leave here today knowing what you know now. You will have to attend a meeting with the High Order and be initiated through a swearing in ceremony.'

Kathleen reached inside her pocket once again. 'No balls in the bag then with one being a different colour?'

Jane Kersholt grinned. 'No, our Order doesn't adopt such unorthodox methods. We only see the good in a person's soul and know them to be true. We invite them into the order through fair means.' She looked directly at Matilda. 'Of course it does help when one or two members can convey and receive messages from the other side occasionally.' Kathleen didn't say that she could do the same.

'And where does this take place, this initiation?' asked William.

'Midnight in the grand room at the Magdalen Hall College.'

'In Oxford...' William replied.

'Yes. The college is one of the country.'

'Isn't that a bit risky, holding the initiation in a college?' stated Kathleen.

'Not entirely Kathleen. Under the pretext of an evening dinner of old theologians we hold the swearing in ceremony at the end of speeches and events. Nobody except members of the Order are present.'

Matilda suddenly turned quickly looking back towards the door where she felt a presence walking towards them. Taking the knife from her jacket pocket Kathleen armed herself in readiness. It wasn't until the uninvited figure entered the light that the four of them relaxed.

Chapter Thirty Three

When Harold walked into the room closely followed by Elizabeth, Kathleen discreetly closed and dropped the penknife back into her pocket. 'Dammit Harold you gave us quite a start.'

She was however pleased to see her late friend, although the look of concern in Elizabeth's eyes was unsettling. 'This isn't social visit though... is it?'

Harold shook his head. 'Unfortunately not, we've come to warn you.'

'About the Hashyshan?' asked Matilda.

Elizabeth slipped her hand into Harold's. 'Don't fall into the trap of becoming complacent and never underestimate the Hashyshan. They are powerful and have useful resources everywhere.'

'Like Margaret Buckworthy?' William added. Elizabeth and Harold both nodded.

'We thought as much,' said Kathleen, her sarcasm evident to all. 'She's played us all for fools. The bewildered, grieving widow and wondering whose lipstick it was found in the back of the car as Derrick lay mortally battered and broken in the driver's seat. She was instrumental in his demise and all the while she was stringing poor Matilda along.'

Elizabeth sucked together her lips. 'She fooled me too Matilda. Did you know that she's the half-sister of Abby Smith?'

William introduced himself. 'We had our suspicions and treachery is never alone. As you rightly said they are powerful and have help.'

'They know about the book, they've seen it.' Said Jane Kersholt. '

Elizabeth went across to where the stone at the back of the shelf had been replaced. She checked to see that it looked right. 'It's good that they have.'

Jane stood next to Elizabeth. 'I was just explaining about the ceremony when you both appeared.'

Harold grinned acknowledging her comprehension of how replacements needed to be introduced and sooner rather than later. 'They make worthy participants.'

'As long as we don't end up cannon fodder, I'm game.' Said Kathleen.

William chuckled. 'Think of all the new adventures and mystery's that you would be investigating Kathleen.'

'Would I get paid?' she asked.

'It depends upon the merits of each investigation. Generally expenses are paid for overnight accommodation and travel, but what we do is for the good of common decency and humanity. Most members have full-time occupations, whereas you do is your day job.'

Kathleen laughed. 'Common decency and humanity. Funny, I hear that from so many wives who want me to follow a wayward husband around, day and night.'

Elizabeth took up where Harold had left off.

'Becoming a valued member of the Order is no different. The only difference is that very often you cannot tell who the enemy really is... people like Margaret Buckworthy.'

'Maybe people in my own department,' William amplified.

Harold agreed. 'You would do well to stay alert and be aware of the people around you at all times sergeant. Like Elizabeth, I let my guard down for a single moment and... well you know the result.'

'So what do you suggest we do now?' asked Matilda.

Elizabeth replied. 'Do exactly as Jane suggests. First return to London and go about your normal routines. Attend the swearing in ceremony and Matilda consider holding another spiritual evening. Play along as though nothing has changed only make sure that you invite Margaret Buckworthy.'

'That's a very good idea,' William agreed. 'At present the evidence that we have in relation to Derrick's death is very thin on the ground, but Matilda might just be able to coax something from Margaret that will help trip her up.'

'And what about you,' asked Kathleen looking at Harold and Elizabeth, 'will you come along?'

'We will certainly be at the swearing in ceremony, but the queue for spiritual evenings is always so long, it's not always possible to reserve a place.'

Kathleen laughed. 'You make it sound like a Boxing Day sale.'

'So when is the next ceremony scheduled to take place?' William asked.

Jane Kersholt was still smiling at the thought of the spirits queueing when she replied. 'It's pencilled in for the end of this week. I'll phone ahead and tell the grand inquisitor.'

Elizabeth reached forward and touched William's arm. 'Your colleagues have let the woman go who was following you. She has continued to search the area.'

'Is she anywhere close?'

'Close enough?' Elizabeth replied.

'Then we would be wise to get clear of St Jutes and make sure that Jane is safe.'

Without saying goodbye Elizabeth and Harold vanished as easily as they had appeared. Jane Kersholt took the trio back along the narrow passage to the stone staircase, none had heard the bell ring. Standing alongside the passenger door she bade them all a safe journey home.

'Will we see you again?' asked Matilda.

'I am sure that our paths will cross again soon Matilda, if only for spiritual inspiration although my healing is slightly different from yours.' The two women smiled at one another sensing that a bond had already been formed. They said their goodbyes and left. William took a different course back through the streets heading away from St Jutes.

'Do you know where you're going?' asked Kathleen sat alongside.

'No, but I have a pretty good sense of direction and generally follow my nose.'

'That's just as well,' Matilda interrupted, 'because that same white car that was following us before is behind again.' William checked his rear view mirror. He indicated left at the next junction.

'Where are we going?' asked Kathleen.

'To find ourselves a carpark close to York Minster and like the old ladies who gave us directions suggested we go visit the cathedral. Let the woman following behind see us check under the cathedral pews that should give the Hashyshan something to think about. Then having laid a false trail we should find Betty's Tea Room and partake of afternoon tea. I don't know about you, but adventures make me really hungry.'

Sitting in the back seat Matilda smiled to herself, William was exceptionally cool in a crisis. She also recognised that Kathleen was fast becoming besotted with the police detective. Maybe something good would emerge from taking so many dangerous risks. Like William, Matilda was hungry.

Chapter Thirty Four

Abby took delight in watching Hashem suffer as the poison continued to flow through his body paralysing muscles and closing down vital organs. Lifting his chin she wanted the dying assassin to know that she was more decisive and deadly than he had imagined.

Turning his head towards her desk she smiled. 'Had you been more patience Hashem you would have sat in that seat behind the desk one day. Had you been more shrewd you would have acted before I did. You see I disposed of my predecessor wanting his responsibility, his chair. You should have done the same.'

Hashem could only glare at the woman who was gloating in his agony.

'I also found you desirable, but I could never trust you. Having succumbed there was no telling what you would have done when the euphoria of passion was still hazy.' To show that she had once wanted to touch his skin Abby ran her hand down the front of his shirt to caress his muscular chest. 'Now I will have to just imagine what it would have been like.'

Hashem coughed as she removed her hand.

'One day Allah will avenge me and tear your soul apart. One day others will come for you!'

Abby laughed as she poured herself a fresh glass of wine.

'Before she left to follow the policemen and two women I had a long chat, a girl on girl conversation with Zahra. She is a skilled assassin like yourself. She shows promise and she has vision, unlike you Hashem. Zahra is happy to kill and take orders from a woman. When she returns she is going to be at my side and become my second in command.'

Hashem growled, but the effort hurt his chest.

'Zahra is my cousin, she respects me. If she knew that you had poisoned me she would deal with you. She would cut out your heart.'

Again Abby laughed. It echoed around the small office and deep inside Hashem's head.

'You fool, the poisoned wine was Zahra's idea. As I said, she had lots of promise.'

Hashem's eyes started to moisten as he realised that he had been so treacherously betrayed.

'I will be avenged.'

Abby shook her head vigorously.

'Not in this lifetime Hashem, you see I've had others watching you for some time now. When you went to Jerusalem with Abdul and Mejia they had orders to kill you after you had interrogated the woman and found the information that we needed, but when she died taking her own life they were confused as to what to do. I decided to let you live until I had the evidence that you wasn't instrumental in her death. The Hashyshan needed to know that you weren't after going it alone and wanting the book for yourself.'

This time Hashem ignored the pain that was crushing his organs and making his chest feel like it was on fire.

'I am not a traitor, I am an honourable man.'

Abby grabbed his wrist so that she could kiss the back of his hand.

'Then do the honourable thing and die. Soon Abdul and Mejia will dump your lifeless body amongst the mud and waste in the river where the police will think of you as just another junkie overdose.'

Hashem tried desperately hard to reply, but he was broken and unable to gather together enough breath to utter even a sound. Abby let his hand fall to his side.

'Now it is time for you to meet your Allah. Goodbye Hashem.'

She walked calmly towards the office door smoothing down her trousers before closing it quietly behind her where Abdul and Mejia were patiently waiting.

Chapter Thirty Five

'Well what do you think about that,' Matilda said as Ermintrude lapped up her cream from the bowl, a rare treat and worth listening to her owner prattle on about her visit to York. She heard the name Hashyshan mentioned and how the three of them had found a treasure more valuable than anything else, but right now at this moment in time the only treasure that Ermintrude was interested in was the contents of her bowl.

Matilda was still talking when she felt a cold shiver sweep down her spine as somebody or something kissed the back of her neck.

'When will you ever stop talking to that cat,' said Albert as he sat down opposite his wife.

Matilda gasped, swallowed hard fighting back the tears that were forming. 'Oh Albert, why didn't you tell me that you were a grand knight.'

'There were many times that I wanted to tell you Matilda, but you were always so busy doing this and that and you were so happy that it seemed a shame to interrupt with something that could destroy the safe bubble that you lived within. To become a member of the Order is a serious business and will demand that you keep secrets that can never be divulged. Unnaturally, you have to become suspicious of everybody even when you visit the local shops. Had I told you about my involvement it would have made you very anxious. You could have suffered emotionally

Matilda looked at her husband, Albert appeared younger and he had less lines across his brow. 'I am a stronger person now than I ever was Albert.'

He smiled. 'I can see that.'

The smile left Matilda's face. 'Who else was in the garden when you was at the top of the ladder Albert?'

'Margaret Buckworthy, a foreign looking man and Abby Smith. Margaret's half-sister. They were the Hashyshan Matilda.'

'I've met Abby Smith. Tell me... is Malcolm, Derrick, Ernest and Cyril with you?'

'Yes, they're all here. They were going to come too, but I though too many might be overkill and I wasn't sure that you'd be decent.' Albert's chivalry made Matilda smile. He had always been so protective of her.

'They too had accidents.'

Albert nodded agreeing. 'Yes and like me they each had a visit from the Hashyshan.'

'We found the Book of Secrets Albert.'

'I know Elizabeth and Harold told me. You were wise to leave it hidden in St Jutes and the police sergeant is a good man and shrewd as well.'

'Did you know that the Hashyshan also kidnapped and drugged me, but I resisted and told them nothing Albert?'

'I know Matilda and you were very brave. It was another reason why I could not tell you about my involvement with the Order. If they had suspected that you were party to my responsibilities they might have kidnapped you before I had met with my accident. Somehow I had to protect you.'

'I would never have thought of Margaret Buckworthy as the enemy and certainly not a killer.'

'Derrick had his suspicions. He would tell us about Margaret when we went away on our fishing weekends. Little did he realise that Margaret was planning for him to have an accident.'

'Why have you not come to me sooner Albert and why didn't you tell me where the key was hidden?'

Albert's shoulder's drooped in an apologetic manner. 'Again it was only meant to keep you safe and away from any harm. Ermintrude knew that I came to see you when you slept, but she promised to keep my visits a secret.'

'When you see Reg, can you convey to him that I am so very sorry insomuch that I didn't trust him.'

'He already knows.'

Matilda felt her shoulder droop. 'Oh Albert, tell me what do I do... what would you do?'

Albert responded with one of his considerate and confident smiles.

'That's another reason why I had to come and see you Matilda. Come Monday evening you will be initiated into the membership of the Order. You will soon understand that whatever your role you will have many friends and look upon them as your extended family. The order also needs you too Matilda.'

'But why me, I am nobody special Albert?'

'Oh Matilda, you are very special. You can communicate with the other side which would prove to be a very valuable link with past members. As long as your role remains a secret and hidden from the Hashyshan you will remain safe. I can't see them bothering you again as they had their chance and realise that you know nothing of any significance. Let Abby Smith believe that you are nothing more than a simple clairvoyant. Keep your journey ahead simple.'

'But Albert... I am simply only a Clairvoyant. You would sit in the other room remember and help me when we had paying clients.'

Albert smiled remembering their evenings together. 'That was true of then however now you have been given full insight into our world. Those much higher than me recognised your potential.'

'But the assassin, the evil Arab he makes my skin creep.'

'Oh you don't need to worry about him, he's dead.' Matilda sat opposite the ghost of her dead husband her mouth slightly open trying hard to comprehend the gravity of everything.

'So many people die on either side, isn't there a peaceful solution to stop the violence?'

Albert shook his head. 'No, it has to be this way Matilda. For centuries the Tintagel Knights have found and looked after the secrets, whereas the Hashyshan have kidnapped, tortured and murdered in response. The division of morals and decency has long been lost throughout.

'A long time ago around the fifteenth century there was a meeting between the elders of each Order, but alas the Hashyshan can never be trusted and they thrive on treachery and deceit. Many of our elders who went to the meeting were tricked and slaughtered as they arrived. The lucky ones who managed to avoid capture or death, escaped to warn the Order. They vowed then never to trust any of the Hashyshan ever again and it had remained the same until now.'

'The Book of Secrets, does it really contain historical facts and figures that could be catastrophic in the wrong hands?' asked Matilda.

'It is the most valuable book throughout the whole of our world.'

'Including the bible?'

Albert stroked the back of Ermintrude's head making the cat purr. 'The Book of Secrets are the secrets as written in the bible.' Matilda looked on the colour in her face changing. Albert continued with his explanation. 'When the bible was written, particular text made reference to certain events, some say miracles. Where exactly the power evolved is contained within the book, although not obvious. It would take highly intelligent scholars to unravel the hidden text.'

'And what about God, did he write any?'

Albert responded with a nod. 'The bible is his prophecy. Written in Hebrew, translated into Latin by scholars and then interpreted by those that protect it.'

'But St Jutes, here in York. Is it really that safe?' Albert looked at Matilda acknowledging that she was a beautiful woman although he had never realised just how beautiful. She was also intelligent.

'St Jutes was chosen because jute was the choice of woven cloth of the old world upon which Jesus was laid to rest after his crucifixion. It seemed an appropriate place to keep safe the book. The Hashyshan have always believed that the Book of Secrets would be hidden somewhere much more spectacular.'

'Like York Minster or the Vatican.'

'It was in both at one time centuries ago, but not even the Swiss Guard could defend their territory from the onslaught of the Hashyshan. The elders in our order deemed it was best to keep the book somewhere less conspicuous, less attractive.'

Matilda was curious. 'Does the queen know about the book?'

'She knows that such a book exists, only she doesn't know where neither. The less people who know, the more it remains a secret and they themselves are not at risk from the Hashyshan.'

'And the Pope, the American President?'

'Likewise, although Pope Vincent is more sceptical than our queen.'

'And what of Jane Kersholt the vicar of St Jutes. It seems an awful lot of responsibility to be thrust upon one woman.'

'Jane took over the reins at St Jutes at the end of last year, although before that she was in the field so to speak and as a practicing vicar she was a valuable pair of eyes and ears. If there was a suspicion that a member of the congregation or somebody in the community was a member of the Hashyshan, Jane could be relied upon to deal with them.'

Matilda looked shocked. *'You mean kill them.'*

'Such things we never ask. All that we need to know is that the matter has been dealt with and by whatever means available.'

Matilda looked back at Albert wondering if he had ever killed anybody. One half of her wanted to know whereas the other didn't. 'I could never kill Albert. I have to close my eyes when I cut a slab of steak.'

'No, I don't suppose you could, but we both know somebody who could.'

Matilda took an intake of extra air. 'You mean Kathleen.'

Albert nodded. 'When she becomes a member of the Order, she will be initiated as a knight.'

Matilda pointed to her chest. 'And me, what will I become, her lady in waiting?'

Albert laughed. 'No. You will be known as the High Sorcerer.'

'I'm not a conjuror, I relay messages from the other side... not do magic.'

Albert suddenly started to fade away as his time was almost up.

'Wait,' cried Matilda, 'there's more I need to know... to ask. Please Albert don't go...'

A voice like the echo trapped in a long tunnel called back. 'I will return another day, but now I need to lie down Matilda I am very tired.'

Once again she felt the cold shiver, rubbing the goose pimples from her bare arms. When she next looked the room was empty and Albert was gone. Only Ermintrude contentedly snoring disturbed what would have otherwise been silence. Matilda was wiping the tears from her moistened cheeks when the door bell sounded. Sliding the security chain into place she tentatively peered through the letterbox. She was instantly met by another set of eyes looking in.

'Will you stop messing about Matilda and let me in... it's bloody cold out here and I need something warm to drink.'

Matilda removed the security chain and opened the door. Kathleen barged her way past and stood inside the hall where it was a lot warmer. 'What do you think I was the Hashyshan assassin?'

297

'No, he is already dead,' she replied.

Kathleen stopped rubbing her palms together. 'How do you know that?'

'Albert just told me.'

'Albert...?' Kathleen looked to the end of the hall expecting him to be standing in the doorway.

'He came to see me.'

'About anything in particular.' Kathleen asked.

'To confirm about Margaret Buckworthy and other things.' She looked at her friend wondering if she could or would really kill the enemy. 'How dangerous it could be after we are sworn in and that I am needed.'

'Dangerous maybe, but how precisely are you needed?'

'Because they need me to communicate between worlds.'

Kathleen was already heading towards the kitchen. 'Is Albert still here?'

'No, he disappeared just before you rang the doorbell. He was tired.'

'How in heavens name can a ghost be tired?'

Matilda shrugged her shoulders. 'I don't know. I guess coming back a long distance can be exhausting.'

'Besides you was there anything else important?'

Matilda switched on the kettle whilst Kathleen stroked Ermintrude.

'He said that the Book of Secrets was the most important book in the world and that it had been translated from the teachings of Christ. It was written firstly in Hebrew and then into Latin. Hidden with the text is a code.' Kathleen seemed impressed. 'Tea, coffee or something stronger?' asked Matilda.

Kathleen responded with a nod. 'Did he mention me?'

Matilda shook her head sideways. 'He said that come Monday evening I would be initiated as the High Sorcerer and you a knight.'

Kathleen added milk and sugar to her mug.

'You know,' said Matilda, 'that if we go through with this Kathleen, there would be no turning back afterwards. We would be committing for life.'

Kathleen poured the hot water into the two mugs stirring together the contents with the coffee grains. 'I know. I've been giving it some thought on the way over. I am not sure that I could make that kind of commitment. I have my private investigations and there could be a conflict of interest at times. The two allegiances might clash.'

'And what about William,' asked Matilda needing to know to whom she could rely upon, 'what is his view, is he ready to devote his life to the order?'

'Yes, he fine with it. He told me that he can serve the Order from within the police and still uphold his day job without worrying about either responsibility. His only reservation is knowing who to trust.'

Matilda nodded remembering Albert had said the same thing about her visiting the shops.

'I would have thought that you could get around any conflict. You'd make an excellent knight. It would be like a full-time adventure rolled into one for you.'

Kathleen sipped thoughtfully at her coffee. 'I'm still not sure. It could seriously compromise an investigation. What if I was secretly following somebody who was supposed to be having a clandestine relationship and they turned out to be a member of the Order. My turning up trumps could expose them to the Hashyshan.'

'That's all the more reason to join the Order. You would have inside knowledge and be able to eliminate any risk.'

Kathleen blew the frothy bubbles from the top of her coffee. 'I guess you're right and William said much the same. We've walked ourselves into the right can of worms this time Matilda.'

To her surprise Matilda was smiling.

'I suddenly feel different Kathleen. I am more confident and with my new found spiritual prowess I am beginning to understand more. I am also ready to follow in Albert's footsteps.'

Adding an extra spoonful of coffee Kathleen stirred it in. 'Do you think it'll work with William and me?' she asked.

Matilda was surprised that Kathleen was asking.

'It will if you give him a chance. Previous men that you've dated didn't really stand a chance.' She tapped the side of her friend's handbag. 'The armoury that you carry around with you is enough to scare any man away.' Matilda paused before continuing. 'Although William is different though, he is thoughtful, he thinks like you think and he has that taste for adventure. The only difference is that he thinks it through where you can go in all guns blazing.'

'I'd like a family.'

Matilda sat open mouthed as the revelation sunk in. First Albert now this. She watched as Kathleen closed her jaw.

'With William?' Matilda asked.

'No, I was thinking the local rugby team... Yes, of course William.'

'A family, wow children... that's a big commitment and a bit sudden. You've only just met him.'

'We talked about it in the restaurant the other evening and I got the distinct impression that he is ready to settle down as well.'

Matilda swallowed what she had left in her mouth feeling the warm coffee sink down past her chest. 'You have never discussed a family before.'

'I know, but the old body clock is ticking on and I'm not always going to be able to go scrambling across rooftops. There will come a day when I'd be happier picking up a little one from nursery than taking unnecessary risks.' Kathleen suddenly looked up from over the top of her mug. 'We have company.' Coming through the door of the kitchen Elizabeth occupied the spare chair next to Matilda.

'This is just like old times when we would go to the café after school for a powwow.'

'I would make you a coffee,' Matilda offered, 'but I only cleaned the kitchen floor earlier.'

Elizabeth grinned back. 'Very funny although I heard that we have a dilemma brewing.'

'Can you eavesdrop all conversations?' Asked Kathleen.

'Only the troubled ones. Most conversations we dismiss as general chit-chat.'

Kathleen was relieved to hear it. She looked at Matilda. 'Did you call her?'

'I needed back up. This has turned into a serious moment and needs to be thought through carefully. I thought having Elizabeth here would help.'

Kathleen sighed. 'You two always did stick together if ever I came up with a new plan.'

Elizabeth reached across the table and touched her friend on the arm. 'Having a family is some plan Kathleen and children will take up so much of your time.'

'If I don't do it now, I never will and the body will be too old.' She hoisted up her breasts under her top. 'I don't exactly have the assets that you possess Matilda. You could breed a herd and not notice it.' Matilda looked down at her chest unable to see her waist. She would dearly have liked to have had a family with Albert, but he was always making excuses. She understood why.

Kathleen sensed that they were both staring back at her.

'Okay trepidations aside I know that I can juggle the two things together, be in the Order and have a family.'

'Which brings nicely around to William,' said Elizabeth. 'Would you be happy with him fighting crime out on the streets and keeping eye on every suspect who he believes could be the Hashyshan while you stay at home and look after a baby. Won't you miss the cut and thrust?' Matilda thought about the last statement which went someway to answering her previous question. Did Albert know that Kathleen had injured, maimed or killed.

Slowly the nods of acceptance came from Kathleen. 'Okay, what if I wasn't a knight, but say the new Librarian. Looking after the records, a baby and William shouldn't prove too much of a challenge.'

This time Elizabeth nodded. 'That was exactly what I had in mind.'

'I would need some help mind you only I tend to lose shop receipts quite easily.'

'I will be around to help. The other side is peaceful, but every so often the silence can be a little overwhelming. The men play bowls most days or sit around chatting as they deal the cards. Women tend to care for the gardens. Nothing much changes.'

'And Albert, does he play bowls?' asked Matilda.

'He's the team captain. His team is currently top of the league.'

Matilda looked at Ermintrude who had just finished stretching. She wasn't sure if the cat was yawning or laughing. It was funny because alive he had never shown any interest in sport. 'Would Kathleen be safe if she became the Librarian, they got to you?'

'My demise was partly because of Reg and to a certain extent, exacted revenge from Abby Smith.'

'You mean if you'd not been seeing Reg romantically, you might still be alive?'

'Something like that. She murdered her most successful assassin earlier today. Abby is a very dangerous woman and her intelligence should not be underestimated.'

'But we would have you and the others around to help. Like when you came to me after I had been kidnapped by the Hashyshan.'

Elizabeth indicated that she would. 'As the High Sorcerer you would be greatly protected.

'Will the order win...' asked Kathleen, 'will they defeat the Hashyshan?'

'That is a question which I cannot really answer. Some battles are won, some are lost. We find secrets, we lose some. Like a game of chess, not every move can be calculated. Somehow we have managed to stay one step ahead.'

'And the Book of Secrets.' Added Matilda.

'St Jutes is situated in Gods own Country and there it should stay. My time is almost done here and I am getting rather tired. I will watch the ceremony come Monday, but you should familiarise yourselves with the history of York. Roman rule to Scandinavian invasion and Celtic law has influenced our Order through the centuries.' Like Albert she started to fade away until she was gone.

'That had me on edge when Albert did that,' Matilda admitted, 'although I guess we know what happens next.'

'Will you be alright if I leave you alone here tonight?'

Matilda smiled as she chuckled. 'I've a feeling that the Hashyshan will leave me alone for the meantime and I know that Albert's about somewhere.'

'Good, I'm heading over to see William only there are some things that I need to discuss with him.'

Matilda watched waved as Kathleen's car pulled away from the kerbstone. She shut the front door and applied the security chain. Sitting in the hallway behind Ermintrude was busy cleaning her paws. 'Right girl,' said Matilda, 'it's time to have a root around the cupboard before the next meeting. There is something that I need to find, something that I have not used since I was a young woman.'

Chapter Thirty Six

The afternoon that they had spent in York had turned out to be a game of cat and mouse with the woman watching their every move periodically reporting back to Abby Smith. Exposed to the elements they could see her getting wet as the rain continued to fall admiring her pluck from the comfort of the tea room where they devoured warm scones, toasted sandwiches and two pots of tea. The journey back was uneventful and on the outskirts of London they lost the woman tailing behind.

'She had a wasted journey,' said Kathleen looking behind.

'Not necessarily,' replied William, 'any intelligence is better than none. Abby Smith knows that we didn't just travel to York for a jolly.'

Sat in the back of the car Matilda had too much to think about to worry about where or when they had lost the woman tailing. Come the end of the end they were heading out on another journey together.

Heading west out onto the A40 William checked his rear view mirror for the first twenty miles, but his diversionary tactic of swapping over cars with a friend seemed to have worked, to make sure he pulled into the next available layby and let the traffic clear before pulling out again.

'Are you sure?' asked Kathleen.

'Yes. The road for the last two miles has been relatively straight and anybody following would have shown up like a beacon on a dark night. We've made two stops so far and they've both been clear, I would say that we can enjoy the journey without having to be concerned about the Hashyshan.'

'William's right and there is nobody tailing us.' Said Matilda occupying the rear seat again.

Kathleen turned around ask how she could be so certain.

'Intuition.'

That was good enough for William. 'If Matilda feels safe, I know we are.'

The swearing in ceremony that evening was held behind closed doors and with two of the Order standing guard inside and another four outside of the building, one on each corner. The meal was nothing lavish, but meant only to satisfy the members having travelled from all four corners of the kingdom although Kathleen believed that some had come from further afield going by the way that they were dressed. At the head table were seated five figures, three men and two women. Kathleen leaned closer to the man sitting next to her.

'Who are they?' she asked.

'The elect member of the Order, the Grand Master and his advisors who officiate and welcome new members.'

Kathleen thanked him and a moment later the man sat in the middle of his other colleagues stood and tapped the side of his glass with a spoon, instantly the room went silent.

'Good evening ladies and gentlemen, the order welcome you here once again.' He faltered for a moment while the lady next to him charged his glass with more wine. 'Sadly, it falls upon me to announce the departure of distinguished members, indeed very brave souls taken before their time defending our principals and the laws under which we serve to protect and keep safe all races.' He raised his glass as everybody in the room stood and honoured the passing of Elizabeth, Harold, Reg, Albert and the others. When the room resumed their seats he continued.

'We have however in their place new members who bring to the Order a refreshing new reverence and who have already demonstrated through their courage, the devotion necessary to show loyalty to the Order in fighting our old enemy. Each person is worthy of the title upon which we will bestow upon them here this evening.'

First he called upon Kathleen and announced to the approval of the membership that she was the new librarian. Next William offering him the title of Knight in the Order to which although surprised, he was proud to receive and lastly he turned his attention to Matilda. Standing before the table of the grand elect Matilda saw a face peering through the curtain that was draped from floor to ceiling behind the head table. The smile belonged to Albert.

'Do you Matilda Barron solemnly swear to defend the laws set by the order and defend its secrets with your life?'

'Yes, I do...' she robustly replied.

Like Kathleen and William before her she felt the weight of the long sword land upon each shoulder before gently caressing the top of her head. Holding the blade in his hands the Grand Master then incited Matilda to kiss both sides of the sword. Holding the sword aloft he had a final announcement to make.

'And thus the seal is made. As from this moment forth Matilda you with be known throughout the order as the High Sorcerer.'

'Thank you,' Matilda replied leaning close to whisper. 'I'll take my seat again in a minute, but do you mind if I slip away to the ladies only it was a long journey down and the wine has gone straight through?'

The Grand Master smiled as he gestured that it was acceptable for her to leave the room. 'The amenities are through the rear door and second door on the left.' Matilda was out of the room in a flash to the amusement of some who were sat watching from their tables.

'Where's she going?' asked William.

'The ladies I would expect. Lots of excitement and big surprises always makes Matilda rush to the loo. Albert was halfway through the proposal when Matilda had to rush away.'

William grinned. 'Ah yes, a euphoric flush. I've had similar in my time.'

In the bathroom she was met by Albert who was elated with her new found distinction. 'Well done old girl, I am so very proud of you and a High Sorcerer, that's an honour that very few members get given.'

'I hope that I can serve as bravely as you Albert. I am however a little worried that I might suddenly lose my power of communication with the other side.'

Albert lay an encouraging hand on her shoulder. 'Now that they have been given, they're there to stay. The Order needs you greatly in the war against the Hashyshan.' Matilda could feel the confidence rising.

'Did you know about Kathleen becoming the next librarian and William a knight?'

'William yes, but not Kathleen although the role suits her perfectly with her enquiring mind and analytical reasoning. Elizabeth told me that she proposed Kathleen to the elect members.

'So what happens now?'

'You go about your ordinary lives until you are needed or you yourselves need the Order.'

'How do I make contact?'

'At the front of the address book in my study you'll find a telephone number for an Auntie Beryl, ring it and a voice at the other end will tell you where to meet them.'

Matilda nodded. 'I found the address book after you had died. I always wondered who Auntie Beryl was. And how do they contact me?'

'An envelope will arrive through the post. Top left hand corner you will see a small blue butterfly.'

Matilda held up a finger. 'The spiritual symbol to represent transformation and change in a soul, past, present or the future.'

'That's right.' Agreed Albert. 'The Order see the butterfly as the bringer of good luck although luck doesn't always cross our path.'

She tried to hold Albert's hand, but her limb went right through his. Matilda didn't understand how she could feel him when he touched her, but not her him.

'I would like to have had children Albert, your children. At least two or three.'

Albert started to fade making Matilda rub her eyes. She wondered if it was due to the wine.

'You will one day.' He suddenly looked up and behind. 'I am sorry Matilda, but I am being called back. I will visit again.'

Albert vanished almost instantly calling back that he loved her and that he was proud of her. Matilda felt the sudden urge to use the facilities quickly find a free cubicle.

Applying more lipstick to her cover the cracks she looked back at the reflection in the mirror. 'You're a High Sorcerer now Matilda Barron. Time to step up to the challenge and show the world what you're made of. Time to think about the future.'

Matilda turned sharply when the door to the bathroom opened, she was relieved to see that it was only Kathleen.

'Are you re-joining this party or what?'

'Yes… I'm sorry I was just talking to Albert.'

Kathleen checked the cubicles. 'Well I hope he's gone only I need to empty my bladder urgently.' Matilda laughed with friends like Kathleen and William around she felt incredibly lucky.

Chapter Thirty Seven

Visibly noticeable going around the seating arrangement around the table were the two absent chairs that had previously been occupied by Harold and Reg. Having considered others thoughts and feeling regarding recent events Matilda had pulled them to one side leaving just the six. Also absent was William who had been called away to work on a new case and it was no surprise that Margaret Buckworthy had ignored the call to her invitation.

'I wonder if curiosity alone will have her come.' Kathleen asked as she gave the top of the table a quick polish.

Matilda stopped brushing the tops of the padded chair. 'I'm am sure that by now she's aware of our trip to York. Having to endure an uncomfortable evening facing us wouldn't be in the least bit enjoyable.'

'It would for me.'

'That because of who you are. You could make the boys feel uncomfortable in class just by staring at them.'

'That was fun. I liked to make them squirm not knowing what I was thinking.'

'And what was you thinking?'

'I was wondering which one I would like to kiss first and if any were suitable candidates for marriage.'

'Maybe it's just as well that William wasn't in our class.' Matilda placed the upholstery brush on the side. 'Of course. If she were to make an appearance it might be to gloat that poor Reg and Harold are no longer here.'

Kathleen folded the duster neatly into a triangle. 'She would see that as the price of battle.'

Matilda was quick to answer. 'Not when the enemy doesn't play fair.'

'What nemesis does ever play by the rules?' Kathleen left her response hanging in the air as she walked through to the kitchen to put away the tin of polish and duster. She returned moments later. 'I would probably do the same if I were in their shoes.'

Matilda looked up from under the table where she was crouched low.

'What are you doing?'

'Removing the foot pedal that worked and dimmed the lights. I have made the conscious decision that from now on there'll be no more theatrics. Talking with the other side will be exactly as the light dictates.'

'You are taking this seriously.'

Matilda gave a slight nod. 'I have a responsibility, a duty to the Order and to fulfil my obligations I have to do it way without any theatrics. Albert too would approve.'

Kathleen grinned to herself as she helped untangle the wiring. Matilda had definitely found a new lease of confidence since she had been kidnapped and gone to York, then Oxford. Watching Matilda shuffle backwards awkwardly between the chairs and the legs of the table Kathleen could only admire her friend.

'Yes, you're right. I feel different too. William loaned me one of his history books for some bedtime reading so that I could bone up.'

Matilda smiled wryly as she righted herself onto her knees thinking that Kathleen's bedtime reading normally involved feeling the bones of somebody's ribcage or their muscle tone, more recently belonging to William.

'What are you smiling about?' Kathleen asked.

'Nothing in particular, just you being the librarian.'

Kathleen grinned. 'I know, but maybe a reality check was what I needed. William is happy to have me stay at home reading books rather than skulking around somebody's back garden and especially if we're heading into a serious relationship.'

'I'd be happier too if I knew that you were safe.'

'I'll miss the cut and thrust of the chase, the mystery and the excitement.'

'And the boring bits,' Matilda probed, 'those as well?'

'William would have been there to help fill the gaps.'

'What's he working on this evening?'

'A body was found down near the river. The local police were ready to wrap it up as just another junkie suicide until William saw the photographs on computer taken at the scene. The victim had a tattoo on the right side of his neck...'

'A tattoo of a tiger?' Matilda speculated remembering having seen one similar.

'Yes, that's right. William believes the dead man was a member of the Hashyshan.'

'Hashem...' Matilda muttered. 'Albert told me not to worry about him because he was already dead.'

'Well that's one less bastard to worry about.'

Matilda used a nearby chair to hoist herself upright.

'There'll be others.'

'Yes, but it would seem that the Hashyshan have a vein of dissention flowing through their ranks. My guess would be Abby Smith. I hope Margaret does feel courageous and come along this evening. I want to make her feel uncomfortable.'

Matilda grinned. 'You see, you've been given a nice cushy inside role within the Order and yet you're already thinking of not playing by the rules.'

'Reading William's history book has taught me one thing already. Rules are there to be broken and great warriors past and present bend them to gain the advantage. To gain extra ground on the battlefield you have to cheat a little and make sure that your tactics, however noble knobble the opposition.'

'Is that why you was always so good at the hurdles come sports day?' Matilda asked.

'No, that was genuine natural agility and possessing a decent shaped pair of swift legs.' To prove the point Kathleen raised the hem of her three quarter length skirt. 'They're still in good shape even now.'

Matilda automatically found herself running her palms down her thigh. 'You make it sound like you're turning us into old women.'

Kathleen dropped the pleat of her skirt. 'Well time will soon be marching on and I admit that recent investigations have taken their toll on my body. I'd be the first to admit that I am no spring chicken, but my cluck is still working well and I can cockadoodledo as good as any young hen in the chicken coup at night.'

Matilda was about to ask how when her thoughts were interrupted by the bell chimes from the front door. First in was Emma Scott-Jackson, she immediately hugged and kissed Matilda on the cheek then did the same to Kathleen.

'What's got you clucking like a spring chicken?' asked Matilda.

'I was at home the other day when I suddenly sensed that somebody was watching me. I turned around and although there was no physical presence in the room I felt Ernest was with me again, in spirit. We talked and he told me to come to my senses, bury the hatchet and look to the future. I feel different.'

Matilda and Kathleen smiled. 'And so do we...' they both replied.

Emma bent down to stroke Ermintrude on the back of the head. 'Penny is just parking the car. She'll be here in a minute or so depending upon how many times she needs to check the distance between the kerb and the tyres.' Matilda was pleased to hear Emma talk about Penny so warmly rather than with a forked tongue like a viper spitting venom. Moments later Penny Pringle entered the room. She smiled at Emma and hugged Matilda seeing the large box waiting on the table top.

'Ohhh, this is going to be so exciting this evening. The last time that we did this was...'

'School camp...' Emma said finishing the sentence.

'That's right although Rebecca Turnbull had us all go to bed petrified that night when she introduced her Ouija board and brought back a dead uncle. He gave me the willies that night in the girl's dormitory.'

'I promise that there will be nothing as sinister here tonight.' Replied Matilda. 'Now sit yourselves down and make yourselves comfortable. We've just a couple more to come then we can begin.'

Penny turned to face Kathleen. 'Is that nice police sergeant coming as well tonight?'

'No, unfortunately he is busy working on a new case that only came in today although I dare say that he'll come along to the next meeting.' Satisfied that she hadn't seen the last of William Jenks, Penny Pringle took her seat alongside Emma Scott-Jackson. Like old times they were soon engaged in a deep and senseless conversation. Standing at the side of the room with Kathleen where she had a good view of anybody approaching the front door Matilda watched Emma and Penny as they laughed and talked together.

'It would seem that the wind of change hasn't just blown through our destiny.'

Kathleen leant in close so that what she had to say wasn't overheard. 'No. It's certainly spread itself about in the last week, although I'm a bit guarded about Penny Pringle as I think she has the hots for William.'

Matilda chuckled. 'You have to admit that he is a handsome man, single and possesses a spirit of adventure.'

Kathleen looked across at Penny Pringle who was still talking non-stop. 'Well she can go stoke somebody else's fire. William is mine and I got there first.' Matilda didn't respond instead she went to answer the doorbell leaving Kathleen to glare at Penny and Emma.

Next to arrive was Arnold Peabody surprisingly accompanied by Margaret Buckworthy. She politely kissed Matilda on the cheek, went through to the sitting room leaving Arnold to hang their coats on the pegs by the front door. She nodded her arrival at Kathleen then took her place at the table.

'She called me out the blue,' Arnold whispered to Matilda, 'to ask if I could give her a lift this evening. Naturally I said yes unable to refuse. In the car she told me that she still grieves for poor Derrick, like I do for my Malcolm.'

Matilda wanted to tell Arnold the truth, but she left it hoping that eventually he would find out for himself through his own enlightenment, maybe even a visit from Malcolm as the spirits seemed to be doing the rounds.

'Go on through Arnold and I'll follow in a minute.' With a flick of her head she indicated to Kathleen that she was needed in the kitchen.

Clasping his fingertips together that there might be cake with refreshments later Arnold joined Margaret, Emm and Penny.

'I would like to know what she's got planned.' Matilda said as she filled the kettle in readiness.

Kathleen mused. 'I wonder if she knows that I went to see Arnold that day. If so the Hashyshan would know that we discussed the events at the museum.'

'But, they've let Arnold live which seems odd when they've eliminated, murdered the others.'

'Maybe because they're watching him,' replied Kathleen, 'maybe they want to see to whom he runs to next. Now it's our turn to watch her this evening. Let's see if we can turn the tables around for once and in our favour.'

They took their places either end of the table.

'No Sergeant Jenks this evening?' asked Margaret.

'No, he's busy on a very important police matter,' replied Penny jumping in, much to Matilda's amusement, although as she noticed Kathleen didn't look amused that Penny was taking so much interest in William's routines.

'That's a shame,' replied Margaret turning her focus to Kathleen, 'still I am sure that he'll get told about this evening's outcome later. If he's available.'

Kathleen frowned wondering what Margaret had implied *if he's available.* She was tempted to make her excuses and call William to make sure that he was alright, but she realised that her reaction would be playing right into Margaret's hands. Annoyed she also accepted that the first round had been lost already.

Pulling the square shaped box to her Matilda removed the lid. 'This evening we're going to do things a little different and we're calling upon help via a Ouija Board.' She saw the look of trepidation as it passed across Penny's face. 'And it's up to us who we invite through!'

Margaret spoke up not pleased that the evening wasn't following the normal routine. 'Otherwise called the spirit board or referred to as the devils tool. Why the change Matilda from spiritual messages, hand and cards?'

'The board gives clear messages and doesn't rely upon my interpretation Margaret. Tonight I sense that the truth will out.' Sat opposite her friend Kathleen fisted under the table in triumph. Matilda had definitely found a new confidence and so far the score was fifteen all. This was going to be an interesting evening. Matilda continued. 'No introductions are necessary now as we've known one another for quite some time. Is everybody ready?' she asked. There were responsive nods and grunts as each person reached forward placing a finger on the flat board marker with the pointed end facing away from them.

'Good the connection is made,' said Matilda, 'does anybody have a question to ask?'

'Will William propose marriage?' asked Kathleen eagerly as she looked around the table and lastly at Penny Pringle. Almost immediately the marker started to move held by Kathleen landing on Y then the E and finally the S. Emma Scott-Jackson uttered a low *wow that's amazing.*

'And another...' prompted Matilda.

'I woke the other night when the moon was very bright and Malcolm was sitting on the end of the bed. Was I dreaming or was it real?' The marker moved slowly across the board touching on the N and O. Arnold clutched his chest. 'That's a relief. I wanted to make sure that I wasn't going mad.'

Matilda smiled. 'I assure you Arnold that you are as sane as the rest of us.' She made a point of looking at Margaret. 'And the next one?' she asked.

'Was my Ernest poisoned deliberately?' asked Emma Scott-Jackson. Matilda found herself looking at Margaret knowing that Kathleen would also be burning her eyes deep into Margaret's soul. It hadn't taken long for a direct question to be asked. The marker spelt out Y-E-S.

'Is the killer sitting around this table?' Emma asked next. The marker moved to reply N-O.'

'And what about my Cyril,' asked Penny nodding at Emma, 'was the props on the stage tampered with?'

Y-E-S came the reply as the marker moved back and forth across the planchette. Penny immediately followed up asking the same question as Emma had. This time the marker appeared to stutter until eventually it spelt out Y-E-S.

Matilda had expected them to look at Margaret, but instead they looked at Kathleen.

'I did some digging into each of your backgrounds… that of your husband's and lover's deaths with some surprising results.' She added the last bit knowing that Margaret would react which she did. 'In each case the circumstances surrounding the death was different and yet each ended tragically. What my investigation uncovered had me discuss my findings with Detective Sergeant Jenks. It is one of the reasons why he couldn't make our meeting tonight. I have another question to ask of the board.' Kathleen placed her finger on the marker and had it ready. 'Is there a murderer amongst us?'

The marker moved to the Y, then E, and finally S.

Penny gasped. 'It's definitely not me. I can only flush spiders down the loo pan, but I couldn't squash one.' Emma squeezed Penny's for reassurance. 'And I would vouch for Penny. At school she passed out when we had to dissect a frog in biology. She goes weak at the knees at the sight of blood.'

'And what about you Emma,' asked Margaret, 'before you married poor Ernest you worked as a medical secretary to an eminent pathologist. Seeing numerous body parts in glass jars or walking through a mortuary was second nature to you.'

Emma's eyes narrowed. 'And how precisely would you know that Margaret. My life before I met Ernest was always a closely guarded secret.'

Kathleen fisted under the table once again, thirty – fifteen, as Margaret faltered for a reply. 'I think it must have been mentioned sometime back in a passing conversation.'

Kathleen continued to watch Margaret, watching the expression on her face search for answers. She noticed that she was getting rattled, made to feel uncomfortable.

'*A conversation with whom?*' Emma pursued.

'Oh, I can't remember exactly who now. Women in general tend to talk to so many different women throughout a week. It would be impossible to say exactly who.'

'Is Margaret Buckworthy the murderer?' Emma asked her eyes fixed on Margaret sat opposite. Instantly the pointed marker spelt out Y-E-S. Margaret let go of the board and her marker standing up and knocking her chair over in the process.

'I am not going to sit here and be insulted by you lot or this stupid board game. I came here expecting to get a message from my dearly beloved Derrick, not to be accused.'

Matilda quickly intervened putting right the chair and inviting Margaret to sit back down.

'Please. We should keep our questions to personal preference and not be asking any accusing questions. Now everyone please just calm down otherwise the spirits will become annoyed.'

An uneasy silence descended upon the six people gathered about the table as Matilda continued with Kathleen watching Margaret. The score was definitely rising and set at forty – fifteen. The first game was almost over.

'Spirits do you have any messages to send us?' she asked.

The wooden marker moved again only seemingly much more freely almost as though it was ignoring the fingers which were connected. It replied with Y-E-S.

Matilda offered the invitation to begin. Slowly the marker began to move picking up eager momentum.

E-R-M-I-N-T-R-U-D-E-N-E-E-D-S-T-O-G-O-O-U-T

Matilda looked around and saw that Ermintrude was indeed missing. She stood, rushed through to the back door and let the cat out. Returning moments later she was smiling to herself.

'Well at least we know that this spirit has a sense of humour. They settled back down again as another message came through.

Y-O-U-N-E-E-D -T-O -L-O-O-K -A-G-A-I-N -A-T -T-H-E -S-C-O-U-T- P-H-O-T-O-G-R-A-P-H

'Why...' asked Kathleen.

Y-O-U -W-I-L-L -U-N-D-E-R-S-T-A-N-D -W-H-E-N -Y-O-U -L-O-O-K, came the reply.

'What scout photograph?' Emma asked.

'The one that we found in Albert's garden shed. It's a snapshot, an old one of when the men were young boys and they all belonged to the same troop.'

'Can we see it?' begged Penny.

'Yes, after the session is over. First though I need to ask another question of the board.'

Matilda asked if the spirits had come in unison or if there was just the one. The board replied with a Y-E –S not defining either way.

Without any warning the lights suddenly began to flicker of their own accord. Kathleen looked at Matilda, but she herself had untangled and disconnected the wiring. When the bulb overhead popped Penny screamed out and Emma grabbed her hand. Reaching out to the mantelpiece behind Matilda located a box of matches. Lighting the candle over the fireplace they all heard a solitary click coming from the hallway.

'That was the front door,' said Kathleen who was instantly out of her seat. Matilda wasn't surprised to see that Margaret Buckworthy was missing from the room.

'Where's Margaret?' asked Arnold.

'She's gone,' Kathleen replied, 'just as we expected she would when given the opportunity.'

'What do you mean?' asked Emma.

Kathleen smiled back at Emma.

'First things first, I will make the coffee while Matilda slices the cake. Then she'll fetch the photograph. We have some things to tell about your menfolk and how a group boys from one particular photograph were bravely connected to keeping safe the history of our world.'

Arnold pressed onto his chest. 'Including my Malcolm?'

Matilda placed an encouraging hand on Arnold's shoulder. 'Yes, Malcolm also was instrumental in what is taking place right now.'

'And Margaret?' asked Penny.

'We'll get to her soon,' replied Kathleen as Matilda gathered together the markers, placed the board back in the box and closed the lid.

'Right, coffee and a piece of cake. Then after that we will see who is still around who wants to send us any messages from the other side. In the meantime I will fetch the photograph.'

Chapter Thirty Eight

'There in the photograph, that's you Arnold,' said Penny pointing to where he was sat next to Ernest, 'and there is Cyril and Albert, and my goodness, if I am not mistaken Reg Smith.' Arnold smiled looking at the faces as he scanned along the rows remembering affectionately his days as a scout.

'You're right Penny,' agreed Kathleen as she placed her finger beneath the face of a woman standing at the back on the far left. 'Take another look, only go in closer,' she advised.

Penny stared hard then turned to Emma wearing a look of apprehension. 'She was a young woman back then, but there's no mistaking and that is definitely Margaret.'

'That's right,' said Arnold. 'Margaret was a scout leader. Several of the boys had a crush on her at the time.'

'Including Derrick?' asked Kathleen.

'Not necessarily. At the time he was more interested in collecting seasonal butterflies.'

'He should have stuck with butterflies,' Kathleen added, 'he might still be around today.'

Matilda dished out the cake.

'What do you mean?' Penny asked.

'To fit everything neatly in a nutshell Margaret Buckworthy and Abby Smith, her half-sister are real bad news. They belong to a secret organisation called the Hashyshan. Not quite the full terrorist movement, but they are not to be tampered with or misunderstood.'

'You mean killers?' asked Emma pulling her cake closer to her.

Arnold nodded. 'Almost certainly killers. I was reading through some of Malcolm's old journals the other night when I couldn't get to sleep and I came across several names that he believed to be involved in very suspicious activities, events that left somebody dead.'

Emma mocked. 'It sounds like something that you should find on a Tai menu.'

Matilda put down the cake knife. 'Well trust me, you would not want to order what they serve up. They deal with kidnap and torture, monetary extortion and they kill when they are finished with you.'

Emma turned and looked Matilda's way. 'And Margaret, you believe that she had a hand in organising the deaths of my Ernest, Penny's Cyril, Arnold's Malcom and your Albert?'

Matilda nodded.

Emma who had cut slice of her cake with her fork was pushing it around the plate as she gathered her thoughts. 'The spirit that guided us through the evening with the Ouija board, do you know who came through?'

Matilda puckered her lips as she replied. 'No. The board never reveals which spirit is giving the answers.'

Emma then looked at Kathleen. 'And your boyfriend is he really looking through the files back at the station?'

'Yes. I trust his judgement.'

Emma gave a shake of her head as she let the gravity of the situation fall into the light. 'Abby and Margaret went to the same school as us.' She looked at Penny. 'Those two conniving cows had been plotting all that time to do away with our men. They were as thick as thieves and always stealing things.'

Arnold surprised Matilda and Kathleen when he announced that the Hashyshan were still taking things of importance. 'Well now they're after a really big prize, something that has eluded them for centuries.'

Emma needed to know what.

'A book that contains many secrets. Malcolm wasn't specific, but he hinted that it could be hidden here.'

'In Matilda's house?' asked Penny.

'No...' Arnold laughed, 'somewhere very safe.'

Matilda see Kathleen smile as she lowered her eyes so as not to be detected by Emma and Penny. 'Was there anything else of interest in the journal Arnold?' asked Matilda.

'Nothing that I really understood. It was mainly records of dates, times and co-ordinates, many looked to be a reference from quite a way back. Malcolm was a well-travelled man before we met.'

Kathleen changed places so that she could sit next to Matilda. They both recognised the danger that Arnold had put himself in by finding Malcolm's old journals and reading through the content. It wouldn't take the Hashyshan that long to realise the same. Matilda could already see the dark cloud of destiny descending over Arnold.

'I would like to see the journal if I could at some time Arnold.' Kathleen asked. 'My guess is that William would too.'

Turning the photograph over Emma read the words that were scribbled on the back. '*The Order of Tintagel Knights*', what in heaven's name is that... a branch of the Masons?'

'The good guys,' Arnold responded enthusiastically. 'According to Malcolm. The Order protects our nation's secrets.' Matilda and Kathleen wondered why Arnold had never been introduced to the Order or become a Knight. Maybe Reg had intended to invite Arnold along to a meeting of the order, but his death had thwarted his intentions. Now they would never know.

'Think of them as the warriors of old,' Matilda said supporting Arnold. She was immensely proud that Albert had been a Grand Knight.

'Did you ever find Elizabeth?' Penny asked quite out of the blue. Kathleen could feel Matilda tense sat next to her.

'No, although a couple of neighbours told us that she was travelling. Somewhere exotic around Egypt or the Middle East. Elizabeth possessed a restless spirit and she was always away on some adventure or another.' Kathleen momentarily closed her eyes and sent a telepathic *'sorry'* hoping Elizabeth would understood.

'I wonder if she ever went away with the boys?' asked Penny.

Emma replied saving Kathleen and Matilda the trouble. 'You mean going on their weekend jollies as Ernest called them. A packed tent, groundsheet, compass and an ordinance survey map. I never did believe that he would rough it, eating berries and off the land.'

Matilda saw the danger and can of worms that Emma's insinuation might provoke. She intervened quickly before Penny latched on. 'If we're all done with refreshments perhaps we should see who's still about in the spiritual world?' With Emma and Penny helping clear away the crocks it left Arnold alone with Kathleen.

'There is something else,' he said, 'something in the journal that I think you need to see.'

'Can I call tomorrow and take a look?'

'I have an appointment with the dentist at lunchtime, but I should be back home from around two thirty if that is acceptable. Please feel free to visit.'

'Two thirty is perfect Arnold.'

Chapter Thirty Nine

Elizabeth looked once again just to make sure that she had not misread what had been written by Malcolm Swift:

'I have the distinct feeling that I am being followed, although I cannot rightly say by whom. Twice now I have spotted the same man at a different location where I had an intended rendezvous. I believe that man to be Detective Sergeant Jenks.'

'There had to be a reason Arnold, a plausible explanation or it could merely have been a coincidence why William was there the same time as Malcolm.' said Kathleen. 'It's a pity Malcolm didn't record either location which would have helped.'

'Malcolm wasn't given to flights of fancy and he definitely didn't suffer from a nervous disposition. Would you like coffee?'

'Coffee please Arnold.'

'I made fresh scones earlier and bought double thick cream, can I tempt you with one?'

'Why not. Will your dentistry work hold up?'

'Yes. The dentist only cleaned them today.'

Kathleen took a seat at the table. 'When Emma read out the inscription on the back of the photograph you responded instantly stating that the order were the good guys, do you know the history surrounding King Arthur and his famous knights?'

'Yes, I should think every schoolboy up and down the land knows about the round table and the beautiful Lady Guinevere. You and Matilda are most probably wondering why I wasn't a Knight in the Order.'

'We did think it was odd.'

'There were two reasons. I am not brave, unlike Malcolm and the others. Reg tried to recruit me after Malcolm died, but I was too distraught to be focused. I need somebody to look after me, rather than me look after them. One look at the Hashyshan and I'd more than likely faint.'

'So you knew Reg Smith?'

'Only through Malcolm, but more after he failed to return from his museum visit. Reg tried his best to protect me although I didn't understand why I read Malcolm's journals. Now I understand.'

'You might be in danger Arnold. Is there anybody else that you can stay with?'

Arnold sighed deep and long. 'This is my home and I refuse to be intimidated by a group of merciless thugs. I've installed a house alarm which I will set at night.'

Kathleen wanted to give her opinion on the alarm, but she didn't want to frighten Arnold any more than he was already. 'These scones really are very good Arnold and so is the jam with cream.'

Arnold pushed his half-eaten scone to one side. 'I watch those animal documentaries, you know the ones where the predator stalks his prey. The stealth with which they employ is breath-taking until the moment that they pounce and then it is over in a second. Death is a mercy. Malcolm's moment was when he stood underneath the pterodactyl.'

'Did Malcolm confide in you and tell you about any of his assignments, anything that had lots of meat on the bone?'

'He was always selective and at times secretive about his investigations, but I got the distinct impression that he had uncovered information about a certain group who were extremely active. During dinner or an evening glass of wine, he would say that this work led him to believe that like Hitler this group wanted world domination. There are crackpots everywhere.'

Kathleen wiped away the crumbs from her mouth. 'World domination at any price. It rears its ugly head every so often through some madman.'

'Do you trust your boyfriend William Jenks?' Arnold suddenly asked.

'Yes… with my life, why?'

Arnold nodded and smiled. 'I wondered if he was at those locations to look after Malcolm.'

'I'd like to think that he was Arnold and not through anything sinister. William is courageous and if he could have prevented Malcolm's death he would have.'

It appeared to Kathleen that Arnold's thoughts were jumbled and that he had invited her over to talk and clear his mind before anything happened.

'Matilda is very different lately,' he said, 'more intuitive and much more tuned than ever before with the other side.'

'She feels that she has been given a gift to help us Arnold.'

'And that cat of hers Ermintrude it's always present, always watching. If I didn't know different I'd say that animal could tell what we are thinking sat around the table.'

Kathleen laughed as she nodded in agreement. 'She's as docile as a stuffed teddy bear unless she spots a mouse, then you should see her move.'

Arnold went on. 'And whenever I look at Emma Scott-Jackson she reminds me of the cat.'

Kathleen laughed once again. 'Yes, I suppose she does. Emma can be quite a formidable lady.'

'You know I liked Ernest. He was a gentle man, extremely clever and there was nothing that he didn't know about gardening, his flowers, the shrubs and trees. Did you know that even picked the rose bush that was to be placed behind his headstone, not that he should have died the way that he did, although ironic that it was a flower which killed him. In many ways a fitting tribute to an eminent horticulturalist.' Kathleen wrote down in her notebook that she should check the name of the rose in case it contained a hidden message. Arnold took a breath of air before continuing. 'I was going through some of Malcolm's other effects yesterday when I found something that I thought might interest you.' He reached into his jacket pocket and produced a small red leather book. He handed it over to Kathleen. 'I have no use for such a thing, but you might find it helpful.'

Leafing through the pages she noticed that the text was Latin. She thanked him. 'You don't happen to know where Malcolm got the book by any chance, do you.'

'Malcolm told me that he picked it up in some flea market in Cairo on one of his journalistic jaunts. Looking at it, it looks more like it would have been more at home in the library of some Italian scholar than in Cairo.'

Kathleen stopped flicking though the pages.

'I don't confess to be a Latin scholar, but I did a bit in school. Midway through one chapter there is reference to King Arthur dated from seven to twelve hundred, Historia Brittonum. I don't have the time to have the book translated, but you might. I sense that you are on a quest Miss Lee.'

Kathleen tenderly ran the tips of her fingers over the soft red leather. In a way it would be her first find as the Librarian.

'I promise that I'll will have it translated and it will always be a testament to Malcolm's bravery.'

Arnold smiled. 'That is why I have entrusted it to you. Keep it safe.'

*****

When Kathleen arrived at Matilda's, William's car was already parked outside. Coming face to face with William she needed the answer to a question. 'Was you following Malcolm Swift?'

'Not in the way that you think I was following. Swift was a good journalist, but his nose would get him in trouble. He came to the notice of the police on several occasion digging deeper than his counterparts. He fascinated me privately as well as professionally and I had an inkling that he was onto something big. The last time that I saw Malcolm Swift was at Convent Garden where he met with another journalist. I was there on my day off. I only recognised the woman because I read her column. Why do you ask?'

'Because your name appears in a journal that Arnold found which belonged to Malcolm. He was initially suspicious, but believes now that you were there to be some sort of guardian angel to Malcolm.'

William shook his head. 'If that was the case, I did a bad job and St Peter has already disposed of the key to the gate.'

Kathleen showed them both the red leather book flicking through the pages until she found the one that she had marked. 'It makes reference to King Arthur. What you read is more than just legend.'

William read down the text. 'What is written describes the battle against dark forces. Devils in disguise that come in the night. The slayers of men.'

'The Hashyshan,' said Matilda.

William nodded. 'I believe that is who they mean. Did Arnold say where Malcolm got the book?

'A Cairo flea market.' William flicked through the book putting the pages close to his ear.

'What are you hoping to hear, it secrets?' mocked Kathleen.

He gave her a smile in response. Yes. Books can talk you know and they can give up their secrets. You just have to listen intently without interruption.'

'Poppycock,' said Kathleen taking the book back. She closed her eyes and commenced flicking through the pages. Moments later she wasn't sure if it was the draught caused by the pages or the whisper in her ear canal that was talking to her, but she opened her eyes again looking at Matilda. 'Here you try it.'

Matilda flicked the pages several times and like Kathleen felt the energy of the book as it spoke to her. 'It tells me that a great many secrets are yet to be uncovered and that we three should stay together.'

'Is that what you heard too?' William asked Kathleen.

'More or less, 'she replied.

'I wonder if the Hashyshan knows that this books exists?' asked Matilda.

William was handed the book by Matilda. 'It could have been the reason that they killed Malcolm Swift and grabbed his shoulder bag at the museum believing that the book would be inside. At least it's now with the rightful owner.' He listened one more time before giving it to Kathleen. 'We should hide this book somewhere safe until we find somebody trustworthy to translate it.'

'Where,' asked Kathleen, 'I am open to suggestions?'

'At the bottom of the grandfather clock,' Matilda suggested, 'it hides the secrets throughout time, so why not let time hide them for another day.'

'An excellent idea,' William agreed. 'I'll pop along to the nearest cabinet maker and have a false bottom made to match the original timber of the clock. Nobody ever checks how deep anything is these days and dark places have a way of distorting the truth.'

Kathleen looped her arm through his. 'No wonder they made you a detective sergeant.'

William grinned. 'I once found a suspect hiding at the back of a boiler cupboard behind a false wall. I've never forgotten it.'

'Should we tell the Order about the book?'

'No, not yet.' William answered. 'Never present anything without evidence.'

Kathleen and William both turned to look at Matilda who had gone very silent. 'Are you okay?' asked Kathleen.

Matilda looked from one to the other. 'I felt a sudden dark shadow pass through my soul like it was something evil. It was looking for somebody.'

William immediately left the house to check outside telling Kathleen to have her knife ready. He returned several minutes later confident that there was nobody outside. He had only just walked back into the kitchen when Kathleen gasped and clutched her chest.

'I saw it as well. At first I thought it was Arnold, but now I know that it's Jane Kersholt, the vicar. Those bastard Hashyshan have found St. Jutes.'

William was on the phone in an instant. The Yorkshire police control room sent the nearest patrol to the vicarage and church. Twenty minutes later he received a call back to say that the vicar had been seriously attacked and that an ambulance was on its way to hospital with the vicar in the back.

'You stay and make the necessary arrangements to hide the book,' said Kathleen, 'Matilda and I will travel north again to York.'

Despite his reluctance William agreed. His instinct told him to go with them, but as a knight his first duty was to protect any secrets. Matilda was stood at the sink drinking a glass of water when the glass suddenly slipped from her hand and into the sink basin. 'There was another shadow. I heard Arnold cry out my name although it came to me more as a terrified scream.'

'That settles it,' said Kathleen, 'now you have two reasons to stay in London.'

Chapter Forty

Standing beside the hospital bed both Matilda and Kathleen were distressed to see that Jane Kersholt had medical tubes inserted in both nasal passages and her mouth, plus various different coloured monitors attached to parts of her body.

'Will she pull through?' Matilda asked of the nurse adjusting the heart monitor.

'It's too early to say and she has been badly injured. The surgeon did his best in theatre... now it is up to Jane to prove that the spirit is willing.'

'Where exactly was she stabbed?' asked Kathleen.

'In the back. The good news is that the wound missed the lung by a narrow margin otherwise she would have drowned in her own blood.' Marking up the chart that she had altered the monitor the nurse left the room.

Matilda swiftly held Jane's hand. 'Quickly take her other hand,' she told Kathleen who looked across the bed suspiciously apprehensive.

'You think this'll work. Transference of spiritual energy is not always easy nor as strong when it is affected by traumatic events?'

Matilda nodded. 'As the nurse said it depends on the strength of Jane's will to live.' They closed their eyes and let their minds open up to Jane's subconscious thoughts hoping that they could make a link. 'Concentrate hard,' Matilda urged, 'there is a faint glimmer in there somewhere.'

'I am concentrating,' Kathleen responded, 'it's creasing my brow with deep furrows where I'm concentrating so hard.'

'Sccchh,' Matilda replied. 'Jane is trying to make contact.'

The voice was initially weak, but when Jane cleared her throat it helped. She concentrated hard urging her willpower to help with the link. *'I resisted as long as I could and I told them nothing!'* she said.

Matilda squeezed her hand gently. 'You have nothing to reproach yourself for Jane and you fought valiantly. We're here with you.'

'It was the two sisters who came. They wanted to know why you visited St Jutes.'

Kathleen felt the urge to open her eyes and look across at Matilda, but it was important to keep channel of communication strong. 'Who else Jane, knew that we had visited St Jutes?' she asked.

'Nobody as far as I know. I watched you leave and there was nobody else about. I can only assume that they visited every church in the area, but there has to be inside information. St Jutes is a closely guarded secret.'

'But you were the only vicar in the area assaulted?' Kathleen question was answered by an almost inaudible *Yes.*

Matilda continued to gently stroke Jane's hand. 'I did say that Abby possesses some spiritual intuition. Maybe she felt a connection when she entered the church, it's possible.'

'Did she find the vault with the Book of Secrets?' Kathleen asked.

'No. They searched the vestry, ransacking every cupboard and desk drawer, but found nothing. That is when the larger woman got angry. She stabbed me when I refused to tell them anything.'

'Margaret Buckworthy,' uttered Matilda. 'The mild mannered creature turned killer. I had so misjudged her.'

'And an evil monster,' Kathleen added. 'Jane we found another book, a red leather edition written again in Latin. It was purchased by Malcolm Swift from a flea market in Cairo. William is putting the book somewhere safe as we talk. He is sorry that he couldn't come to see you, but he sends his best for your recovery.'

'The Book of Souls. Yes, I had heard that there was such a book in existence although nobody has ever laid there eyes on it before. It was reputed to have been lost several centuries back maybe longer. It is as valuable as the Book of Secrets.'

'Do you know if the same authors contributed to both books?' asked Matilda.

'Quite possibly. Take the book to Father Nolan at St Luke's in Fyndlene. He is the official translator for the Order. You will find Michael Nolan an old man now although you should not underestimate him. His knowledgeable mind is as sharp as that of when he was a young man.'

'Fyndlene near Cork?' asked Kathleen.

'Yes, the very same.'

'How did you know that?' asked Matilda.

'I have an uncle who lives in Cork.'

Jane jerked and Matilda felt the pressure holding her hand increase.

'My time here is almost done and I have served my lord and the Order, but now it is time for me to take my long sleep.'

Kathleen broke her connection as she ran to get the nurse leaving Matilda alone.

'I will be gone by the time she returns Matilda. Don't worry. I'm not in the least bit scared about dying and my destiny on earth has long been fulfilled. I liked St Jutes and my time there was short lived, but soon another will soon take my place put there by the Order.'

'Now that Kathleen has gone for a minute maybe longer, how did the Hashyshan find you Jane?'

'A long time ago I was one of their kind Matilda, but I saw the evil that had infested the soul. One day I ran away and turned to the Lord instead. I became a hunted woman and it was only a matter of time before the Hashyshan caught up with me. The Order took a leap of faith in taking me *in. I hope that I have repaid their faith and that I can go onward and upward with a clear conscience.'*

'You're a very brave woman Jane and one of the bravest that I have ever known.'

Jane opened her eyes one more time, smiled at Matilda before she closed for the final time. Everything in the room went silent not that Matilda could hear the machine alarms. Leaning forward she kissed the vicar on the forehead.

'They're waiting for you in heaven Jane, go now and be at peace at last.'

The nurse rushed to the monitor, but instead of peaks and troughs there was a single flat line. A call went out for the crash team, but Matilda caught hold of the nurse's arm. 'Jane wanted it this way nurse. She didn't want to be revived.'

'But she's so young, too young to die,' said the nurse who was younger than the dead vicar.

'The good have to die young to become new angels and give the older ones time to go into retirement.' At the end of the bed Kathleen listened and watched. Matilda had changed a lot. She was more philosophical and Kathleen too had found an inner peace. Life had changed since the arrival of William Jenks. They waited until the nurse went back to the nursing station to fetch the ward sister and the doctor who needed to pronounce the patient deceased.

'Did she really want it this way?' asked Kathleen.

'Yes. Jane was ready to accept her fate and felt her time here on earth had gone full circle. She will be rewarded with peace and quiet for all eternity now. I think you should call William and let him know.'

'Okay, will you stay with Jane?'

'Yes although her soul has already gone on ahead. I'll make sure that there is nothing else we can do before we leave to go back home.'

Twenty minutes later Kathleen returned having spoken with William.

336

'Is the book safe?' Matilda asked.

Kathleen responded with a nod. 'He's added the false bottom. When I spoke to him he was at Arnold's house.'

'He's dead isn't he?'

Kathleen nodded. 'I'm sorry to say that he is...'

Matilda and Kathleen watched the porters wheel the metal cabinet from the room draped in a velvet cloth on its journey to the hospital mortuary. Standing in the hospital corridor Matilda told Kathleen that she needed to use the bathroom before they travelled back. Kathleen said that she would meet her back at the car.

Matilda was standing at the sink washing her hands when she felt a presence standing behind her. She turned sharply to find Albert looking at her.

'Goodness Albert, I hope we're not always going to meet in bathrooms!' she declared.

Albert laughed. 'I can't always pick the place or the moment Matilda. When I get permission to come back somebody must hit the switch and here I appear. In a way you have control over where.'

'Did you know that the Hashyshan would find Jane?'

'We cannot always predict current events Matilda and neither can we intervene. Fate overrides even our powers.'

'Albert, why me exactly. There must have been others in the Order more suitably qualified for the role of High Sorcerer?'

'Do you know where the name Matilda originates?' he asked.

'No.'

'Matilda is synonymous around the world although I bet you didn't know that William the Conqueror as married to a Matilda. She was the daughter of Robert II of France. Matilda of Flanders as she was known was not only a loyal queen, but she gave birth to ten of Williams children.

'Derived from the Old High German the name means might, strength and 'hild' which translated means mighty in battle. Abby Smith recognised these qualities in you when she held you captive and interrogated you.'

'Why did she let me go rather than kill me?'

'Because Abby or Abigail as she was christened is an old Hebrew name and her family ancestry can be traced back a long way. She seeks the secrets contained within the book believing that her ancestral scholars had a hand in writing some of them. As the High Sorceress she needs to keep you alive Matilda until she is certain that you are no longer of any value to her quest.'

'That's reassuring.' Said Matilda. 'So back to William and his ten children, which I must remember to tell Kathleen and William about, what else is significant about Matilda?'

'Williams's half-brother was Odo, the Bishop of Bayeux.'

Matilda recognised the connection. 'The Bayeux Tapestry.'

'That's right,' Albert replied, 'and records made at the time show that Matilda might have had a hand in creating the embroidered tapestry.'

Matilda exhaled the air from her lungs. 'Events sewn on cloth to depict the Norman Conquest through the Battle of Hastings.'

'It's slightly more than that Matilda only sewn into the weave and armoury is reputed to be a binary code, hidden messages.'

Matilda sighed. 'Is nothing ever simple Albert. Don't tell me translated we'll find some in the Book of Secrets.'

Albert smiled. 'You're catching on fast Matilda, but you don't have to worry about the tapestry. Securely ensconced in France in the Musee de la Tapisserie de Bayeux in Bayeux, Normandy, nearby members of our Order ensure that it remains safe.'

'It was a pity that poor Jane Kersholt didn't have more protection.'

'Jane is in a safe place now and she's happy.'

Matilda was still curious. 'So why me Albert, as I said I am just Matilda and nobody special?'

'Because you have the same blood line as your ancestor.'

Matilda stood in the hospital bathroom open mouthed.

'Get out of here Albert. You know that I have no blue blood running through my veins and the last time that I donated blood they would have found something strange.'

'A DNA match was taken when you gave your last pint. The nurse at the blood bank is in the Order.'

Matilda was flabbergasted. 'So you're saying that I'm of royal descent?'

Albert smiled. 'Quite possibly.'

Matilda checked herself in the mirror. 'Did the original Matilda, you know the one who married William the Conqueror, did she have a pair of knockers like mine?'

Albert raised his palms in uncertainty. 'How would I know although she did have ten kids.'

Matilda remembered when Albert had asked her out on a date as teenagers. She wondered if her bust had influenced his decision. 'Okay, so I was picked because of my blood line. I'll have to tell William and Kathleen. Maybe I'll ask her to courtesy now.'

Matilda paused gathering together another thought as Albert knew she would.

'And William, why was he made a knight. Don't tell me he has a blood line going back to the tenth century as well.' Albert was non-committal although he did say that everybody alive had a blood line somewhere that could be traced back many generations.

Matilda passed to another thing troubling her. 'In your study Albert I found a rather unusual book entitled *'Idiotic Expressions in Mirrors'*, it's full of stupid saying's and some that date back several hundred years. Don't tell me that has a hidden code as well?'

Albert smiled broadly.

'Indeed, take *Barking up the Wrong Tree* as an example. What the expression actually refers to is *Ark in the Wrong Tree*. Certain letters taken from the expression make a message. In this case what the author means is that the ark is in the wrong place and the Hashyshan are close. It needs to be moved as soon as possible to a safer location.'

'Not the actual Ark?'

'No, but it is a boat. An Arabic boat and upon which the timber deck is inscribed with important writings.'

'How did the Order find all these secrets Albert?'

'Ordinary people who recognised their significance. Centuries back they realised that if they fell into the wrong hands, others perhaps many would suffer as a consequence. It has taken the Order centuries to find them, record them and keep them safe.'

Matilda looked surprised. 'I just hope that Kathleen knows what she has taken on. She's going to be exceptionally busy and she was only telling William the other day that she wants a family when they're married.'

Albert yawned. Matilda recognised that he was getting tired and that his visit was coming to an end. She saw her late husband wink.

'Well she had better a move on and quick, only there's a big surprise in store the next time she visits the surgery for a blood test.'

With that Albert began to fade. He just had time to tell Matilda that he loved her.

Settling herself into the passenger seat she found Kathleen drumming on the steering wheel. 'You've been a long time, did you get your knickers in a twist?

Matilda couldn't stop herself from laughing. 'You had better switch off the engine for a minute only I have a message to give you about William.'

Other Books by Jeffrey Brett

A Moment in Time
ISBN – 979 - 8642194461
Barking Up the Wrong Tree
ISBN – 978 - 1073495290
Beyond the First Page
ISBN – 978 - 1980681991
Leave No Loose Ends
ISBN – 978 – 1549552984
Looking for Rosie
ISBN – 978 - 1980369400
The Little Red Café
ISBN – 978 - 1980912583
Rabbits Beside the Track
ISBN – 979 - 8635555187
The Road is Never Long Enough
ISBN – 978 - 1794541948
The Moon, Balloon and Stars
ISBN – 979 – 8634519852
Shadow of Blame
ISBN – 979 – 8672633008
The Magic of the Little Red Café
ISBN – 979 - 8576921348

©

About the Author Jeffrey Brett

I was born in London during the middle of the last century and I have been writing fictional stories for many happy and enjoyable years. My genre follows no particular pattern and I produce short stories, romance, psychological thrillers and hopefully humorous books.

After working for so many year in the public service sector I have finally found the time to enjoy my writing and publish my books. I have a very good friend in fellow award winning writer and author Kathleen Harryman. More recently Kathleen and through her expertise has helped design this book cover, plus others. I am eternally grateful to Kathleen for her encouragement and inspiring images. She can be found on her website – kathleenharryman.com

I wish you many hours of happy reading and if you have any comments regarding any of my books please email me and let me know.

magic79.jb@outlook.com

www.Jbartinmotion.co.uk

Printed in Great Britain
by Amazon

56343099R00197